MISSING

RUBY SPEECHLEY

Boldwood

First published in Great Britain in 2023 by Boldwood Books Ltd.

Copyright © Ruby Speechley, 2023

Cover Design by 12 Orchards Ltd

Cover Photography: Shutterstock

A CIP catalogue record for this book is available from the British Library.

Paperback ISBN 978-1-83751-388-8

Large Print ISBN 978-1-83751-389-5

Hardback ISBN 978-1-83751-387-1

Ebook ISBN 978-1-83751-390-1

Kindle ISBN 978-1-83751-391-8

Audio CD ISBN 978-1-83751-382-6

MP3 CD ISBN 978-1-83751-383-3

Digital audio download ISBN 978-1-83751-386-4

Boldwood Books Ltd
23 Bowerdean Street
London SW6 3TN
www.boldwoodbooks.com

In Memory of our dear friend, Lloyd Ridgwell,
who discovered his love of reading through my books.
13/5/1936 – 30/10/2022

PROLOGUE

I'm finally drifting off. Traces of thudding music and raucous laugher are still coming through the wall. I don't care any more. I'm sinking deep, on the cusp of sleep.

A faint rattling. Click. Creak. Bedroom door opening? Can't be. It's locked. Must be dreaming. A bad, bad dream. Clicking again. Louder. The rustle of someone shuffling forward. The stench of beer. Cigarettes. A shot of fear zips through me. I raise my head an inch, eyes widening. A dark hooded figure is standing at the end of my bed. Someone wearing a distorted rubber clown mask stares back at me.

I sit bolt upright and scream.

1

FOUR YEARS LATER

I need to tell someone what happened that night. What I think happened. Because even after all this time, it's weighing in my stomach like a bag of stones.

I park my old VW in the middle block, on the edge of a row of cars for a quick getaway. I like to think of it as my own safe space. I switch off the engine and the car shudders to a halt.

What if I imagined it? I read somewhere that the brain can invent memories of trauma. But it feels like I was there only yesterday. I've tried so hard to move on. To become a better person. To bury the shame that is constantly eating at my insides.

Hayley parks opposite me outside the pre-school. She climbs down from her Range Rover Vogue in a pair of bright orange strappy heels. As usual she's glued to her phone, her talons tap-tapping away at the screen. She doesn't seem to notice me as she glides past, but then she hardly ever does. I'm not qualified to join her tight group because I'm not high maintenance enough. On my days off, I wear faded dungarees, cheesecloth shirts and messy scooped up hair.

I glance at my mobile on the passenger seat. Molly, my oldest friend, is the only one I could talk to about that night, the nightmares I'm still having. Problem is, I haven't talked much with her about personal stuff since that holiday because I'm embarrassed and ashamed. Not to mention she lives too far away to pop over at such short notice. And that's my fault for running away.

She was so mad I was late to the ferry; things haven't been the same since. If I confide in her, I think she'll be disappointed in me. But this time, I don't think it was my fault. Trouble is, everyone remembers me from before. Which means no one, absolutely no one, will believe me.

Lauren waves to Hayley from the other side of the car park, pushing her double buggy towards where the daily queue is forming around the front of the village hall. Lauren is one of the many mums who arrive at pick-up time wearing fashionable running gear, ponytail pulled so high up on her head, it gives her face a lift, not that she needs it. I can think of more fun ways of building up a sweat than pounding pavements. From what I've heard, they reward themselves after their run with an enormous glass of Chablis, so what's the point?

I rest my head on the steering wheel and wait for the last few minutes to tick away to 3 p.m. Hayley trots over to catch up with Lauren but instead of joining the queue, they stand huddled together. Hayley shows her something on her phone. I imagine it's a photo of Jamie Dornan or some other Hollywood hunk. Except they're not smiling, and then they crane their necks round to frown at me.

My pulse spikes and I sit up, puzzled. What have I done? It cannot be good. They're still not smiling. At least if they were laughing by now, I'd know the joke was on me. Could it be Tyler again? Is Hayley showing photos of where Tyler sunk his milk teeth into Charmaine's arm? I thought his biting spree was over. Tyler and I talked about it so many times, how unkind it was, and he seemed to understand that hurting other children, girls in particular, was wrong. Mrs Keenan had a word with him, too. She tried to find out the source of his anger. I was mortified. They must have thought something bad was going on at home, that he was playing out a behaviour he'd seen, but I've no idea why he was doing it. I heard all the whispers in the queue: no discipline at home, needs a father figure to keep him in line, who is the father anyway? Does he even see his son? Poor kid. Then one of the other boys bit him back, left a nasty red mark on his chubby little finger, and after that he stopped.

I sigh and turn away. It's 3 p.m. I push the car door open and sit there for another minute in the autumn sunshine, smoothing down a loose tendril of hair.

Maybe I could tell Katie about that night. Since we moved into the flat next to hers, she's always been kind to me, but can I trust her? What if she laughs or thinks I'm making it up? Perhaps Molly's more likely to understand.

Hayley and Lauren hurry to join the back of the queue which has started to move. Some more latecomers arrive. I meander over and stand behind them. They give me a cursory smile but no one speaks to me, and I'm not good at small talk. I try to think of something casual to say, but my stomach knots up at the thought of speaking first in case they ignore me or laugh at me. It doesn't help that whatever Hayley has decided I've done wrong is already spreading like Chinese whispers down the line. Front-of-the-queue Annie rushes past, gripping Dean's hand and his *Paw Patrol* lunch bag so tightly, he's grimacing. She's clearly trying not to look at me as she hurries him back to her car. I narrow my eyes at the parents that follow, attempting to read their faces. They also seem to be avoiding my eye too, but they can't stop themselves snatching a glance. It can't be Tyler's behaviour again. It's probably just me imagining it. When we moved here two and a half years ago, I thought having a baby would be the perfect ice breaker. But I was wrong. Other mothers do speak to me, but I can never think what to say to keep the conversation going, let alone start one.

By the time I reach the front of the queue, there aren't many parents behind me.

'Tyler's been such a good boy today,' says Mrs Cooper, the pre-school deputy supervisor. Her hand rests on Tyler's shoulder; she smiles down at him then up at me.

'Really?' I try not to sound too surprised.

'So helpful and kind, aren't you, Tyler?' Mrs Cooper pats his arm.

His chin sticks up as he nods at her, a wide grin on his face.

'I'm so pleased. Well done, Tyler,' I say.

I have to press my fingers to my lips to stop myself from tearing up. The last few weeks have been a total nightmare.

Tyler opens his arms and runs at me and hugs my legs. I hug him back and kiss the top of his chestnut mop. Funny how dark it's gone. He was white-blond when he was born.

Back at the car, I'm about to open the door for Tyler when I spot Louise hurrying towards me.

'Hi Ellie, have you got a sec?' she calls in her soft buttery voice. She's pushing Callum in his buggy with one hand and holding Jordan's hand in her other. Has Tyler 'borrowed' Jordan's favourite toy again? They were best friends at the beginning of term, if there is such a thing for three-year-olds. Now I'm not sure they are any more.

I beam at Louise. She is one of the kindest souls I've ever met. Just being in her company makes me want to be a better person. She is naturally pretty and completely, refreshingly unaware of it too. Always focusing on helping others. She can't see badness in anyone. She was one of the only people who understood that Tyler is not an aggressive child but was going through a tough time.

'Could we have a quick chat?' She frowns momentarily. Her ditsy print tea dress swishes to a halt.

I nod, my smile well and truly fixed in place, as I wonder what's coming. She gently takes Jordan's hands and curls them around the handle of the pushchair, then dips her hand into her pocket and plucks out her mobile. 'There's something I think you should see.' Her bright inviting demeanour clouds over again into a dark troubling frown. For a moment she doesn't speak, as though she's trying not to cry.

It can't be Tyler, he's been a good boy. Have I upset her? She's the closest thing I have to a friend around here, apart from Katie. I hope I've not bloody messed that up.

'This came up on Facebook.' She taps her phone and scrolls up. 'I'm guessing you haven't seen it.'

Tyler is wriggling in front of me and I'm desperate to get him in the car. I cannot face seeing bitchy comments about my parenting skills. It's part of the reason I came off social media, but now I'm curious; it must be bad if Louise feels the need to show me, because she is not a gossip.

'Is this what they've all been whispering about?' I fold Tyler into my arms, swallow hard and nod at where they were all standing in the queue, shooting venomous glances at me.

'I'm sorry. It was only posted last night. I know you're not on Facebook... but I think this is something you have to see.'

'I'd rather not, actually, but thanks.' I turn away and clench my teeth as I open the car door. Tyler scrambles inside. I really don't want to know. I lean in after him and have the usual tussle trying to get him to sit still for ten seconds so I can strap him in.

'It's... different this time,' Louise says a bit louder.

When I duck out again, Louise and I frown at each other. She seems to be standing further away from me than a moment ago.

I tut at Tyler stomping up and down on the back seat. 'How'd you mean?'

'It's... it's from the police.' Louise holds her screen up at arm's length, as though suddenly not sure how I'll react.

I squint at the image. Not because it's tiny and I can't make it out, but because it's big and fills the whole screen. My brain can't work out what I'm seeing, what it means. It doesn't make any sense. A pain pinches my forehead.

'I don't understand. Why are you showing me a photo of my own son?' I try to swallow but my mouth is dry.

Louise half turns the mobile back to herself and dabs the screen down a touch. She holds it up to me again.

Now I can see; it really is a police poster of Tyler's face. My heart thuds in my chest. Above his cheeky, gappy grin in bold capital letters, it reads:

MISSING

2

I gasp and cover my mouth with my hand, searching Louise's face for an explanation, but she's staring at me blankly. At the bottom of the post is a telephone number, inviting people to call and report any sightings. It's already had over four hundred likes and ninety-two shares. Nausea creeps up my throat and I swallow it back down, trying not to give in to the urge to throw up.

'I don't understand. Who would do this to me?'

Louise slowly shakes her head, peering at me from the corner of her eyes. My God, she's a little bit unsure of me. Does she think I've abducted Tyler?

'Could you screenshot it and text it to me please? I need to find out who's doing this, who has given the police false information. I have to let them know Tyler is safe and sound.'

Louise clicks the sides of her phone and a moment later mine beeps in my pocket. I check it and thank her.

Tyler is pressing his face to the car window, tongue sticking to the glass. His fringe is uneven where I've tried to trim it. When I look back at Louise, she seems to be examining my light auburn hair. She looks away when she sees me notice this; I can guess she's thinking how different we look for a mother and son.

'You know this is malicious, don't you? Someone is out to slander me.' My voice rises. Christ, if Louise doesn't believe me, no one will. I take a breath to calm down. It's not her fault. 'I'm sorry, it's just so...'

'Evil?' She reaches out and touches my arm.

'Yeah, it is. Thank you.'

She nods.

'I'm coming to the committee meeting tonight, if you still want me to?'

'Yes of course, I'll see you there.' She smiles but it seems forced. 'Are you going to be okay?'

'I'll be fine. Thanks for showing this to me. I know how bad it looks, but believe me, it's a sick hoax. Tyler is my son.'

She smiles again and it's so brief I wonder if I imagined it. She strolls away and I'm left not knowing for sure if she's my friend or not. Perhaps I imagined she was my friend because it made me feel better. What if she only talks to me so she can gossip to the other mums about me? If she really does doubt me, how am I going to convince everyone else I'm telling the truth?

I drive home in a daze, going over and over Louise showing me the chilling poster. The words 'Missing' and 'Can you help?' underneath the photo of my son. It's a direct attack on me as Tyler's mum. Someone who knows he's okay but wants it to look like I've taken him. I don't know who could hate me this much.

The light changes to red and it only registers in my mind at the last moment. I slam my foot down hard on the brake and the car screeches to a halt just over the line. Our bags on the passenger seat shoot onto the floor. A man at the crossing carrying his shopping glares at me. In the rear-view mirror, I see Tyler's mouth open in surprise, his head forced forward. I look away, not wanting to catch his eye, not wanting him to see the shame on my face.

I drive on, making sure I concentrate and as I reach the estate, I pull up at the Co-op. I'll pop in for two pints of milk and a packet of choco-late digestives, Tyler's favourite. As I enter, I glance up at the security camera almost expecting someone to be looking back at me, waving their finger. *We know what you're up to*, they'd say, *trying to make it up to your son for being such a bad mother*. In front of me is an old lady filling her shopping trolley with value butter, white bread, a handful of baby potatoes and a small tin of corned beef. Will that be me in fifty years' time? Still coming in here, only being able to afford the bare minimum. I hope not. Processing orders for a window and door company doesn't pay that much, but it means I can work from home and be around for Tyler. If I do well in the next few months, I could be in the running for assistant manager and that will bump me up the pay scale.

When we get home, I park out the front of our block of flats. There's screwed up litter strewn across the grass, remnants from somebody's takeaway, from where the binmen have emptied the communal bins, which always seem to be overflowing no matter what day of the week.

Most people are still at work at this time, so there's that eerie daytime stillness. Two other cars are parked in their allocated bays and that taxi's still there, its engine running, half parked up on the pavement a little way down the road. It's been there since early this morning. No one seems to get in or out. Maybe I should go and tap on the window, ask him what he's hanging around for. He could be checking who's coming and going. There was that spate of break-ins a few months back. I make a note of the number plate to pass on to the neighbourhood watch.

'We're home, Tyler. Are you okay?'

He nods and holds up his favourite rabbit. I grab our bags and jump out.

A distinct rustle in the bushes near the entrance spooks me. I pull Tyler closer. I want to believe it's a bird or me imagining things, but I can't help feeling uneasy.

I sling our bags over my shoulder and hold Tyler's tiny hand. I unlock the main entrance door, have a quick look around me and step inside, glad to hear it click behind us. I peer back through the glass panel in the door. The taxi is still chugging out a load of exhaust, but I can't see anyone walking towards it, although that doesn't mean he's not picking someone up. Still, a man hanging around unnerves me.

I grab my post from the little box and secure it shut. As I head up to our flat at the top of the stairs, a piece of paper from the bottom of the pile flutters to the ground.

A picture of Tyler's face is gazing up at me from the bottom step. It's a flyer exactly the same as the missing poster on Facebook.

What the hell? A chill darts through me. Whoever has told the police, posted this here too. They know where I live.

'Is that me?' Tyler points as I unlock our front door. It's not until I've dumped our bags on a chair and the envelopes on the table that I look at the flyer properly. The police logo is slightly pixelated. Maybe it's been copied from a website? I try the emergency number at the bottom, but it goes straight to answer phone, the inbox appearing to be full.

I think it's fake. Someone's pretending this is an official police poster. A little of the tension across my shoulders and neck releases. But who would go to so much trouble?

I drag out my laptop from under the sofa and search online. Not much comes up for Tyler's name except an article in a national paper from over a year ago when I was interviewed by a journalist about women giving up drinking. Tyler was named in the caption for a photo of us. I gave permission for it to be taken and they used it in the print copy as well as on their website.

What was I thinking? I've opened him up to someone targeting us. Maybe it's not a stranger but someone I know; isn't that what the statistics say? Could it be whoever was sending me nasty messages on Facebook, before I came off it?

I look up my ex, Darren's number on my mobile and press call. It could be him trying to mess with my head. Get me back for all the hassle I caused him and Simone. The dialling tone drones on then clicks off. No answer phone kicks in. He's never wanted anything to do with Tyler, and won't even acknowledge he's his father – not for lack of trying on my part – and I hate him for it. I call again two more times, but he doesn't pick up. I'm tempted to try once more, but I promised him and myself a long time ago, only three attempts at a time.

Tyler is oblivious, racing around the flat wearing his plastic policeman's helmet making nee-naw, nee-naw siren noises. I close my laptop and call after him to go and wash his hands. I pour him a drink of orange squash and chop up a banana into his favourite *Paw Patrol* dish.

The sound of a car door slamming hard makes me jolt, and a splash of juice spills over the edge of the beaker in my hand. I look out the window. The taxi's back passenger door is open, the driver standing talking to whoever it is inside. I crane my neck to see who it is. The driver points up and I'm certain it's at my flat.

I draw in a breath, duck behind the curtain, my heart thudding so fast I press my hand to my chest to calm it down.

'Got you!' Tyler cries, grabbing my arm with his hot little hand, making me jump. He giggles. 'You are under the rest.'

I laugh at his innocent mistake, his happy flushed face beaming at me.

What on earth am I doing hiding behind a curtain in my own flat? I feel so silly. But why were they pointing at my window? I pull the curtain aside and look again. Is it someone I know? Whoever it is, they're wearing a hoodie and sunglasses so it's impossible to tell.

3

Tyler follows me along the landing as I head next door. I'm hoping Katie and Joseph are in. I let Tyler knock three times, evenly spaced out, our secret code so they know who it is. The familiar sound of Katie's bare feet striding up the laminate hallway comes quickly. She opens the door and the warm inviting aroma of chicken cooking fills the air.

Katie is wearing smart pink velour loungewear, her poker straight blonde hair tied back in a ponytail. Her son, Joseph, runs up behind her.

'How did it go this morning?' I ask.

'Really good thanks, come in, come in.' She stands aside. 'Not been back that long, just changed out of my suit.'

Tyler and Joseph run off to the living room together. I follow Katie and we sit at the table in the kitchen diner area.

'I should hear if I've made the next round in a couple of days. They seemed impressed with my previous experience. Anyway, can I get you a drink?'

'We're fine thanks. I wasn't sure if it's still okay about tonight?'

'You've decided to go, have you?' She laughs. 'You must be feeling brave.'

'I kinda promised and... well... something weird happened today and I feel like it could be the best chance I'll get to explain myself.'

'What do you mean weird? What did you do?'

'Nothing. That's the thing.' Tears prick my eyes, and I swallow hard. I tell her about the post on Facebook and the same poster in with my letters. 'You didn't get one, did you?'

'I've not checked.' We both glance over at the pile of unopened letters on the kitchen counter. There's at least three days' worth there. 'You can have a look if you like. You know how much I hate opening bills.'

'I'll have a flick through if that's okay?' I sift through the top few and sure enough halfway down is a copy of the flyer. My stomach flips seeing it again. I hand it to her, and she raises her eyebrows.

'God, I can't believe this,' she says as she glances over it.

'Whoever did it has lifted this photo from my old Facebook page.' Hot tears push at my eyes again. 'It's someone who knows me.'

'You came off there ages ago, didn't you?'

I nod. 'Which means they must have had that photo for a while.'

'One of your so-called mum friends?' Her head tips to the side.

I shrug. 'I'm not pointing the finger, but Hayley Marsh is certainly capable.'

'That's Tyler on there, Mummy,' Joseph says.

Katie nods and glances at me.

'Can I be on it too please?' he asks.

'Not really, darling, sorry. Whoever used Tyler's photo didn't ask his mummy's permission and that's very naughty.'

Joseph pulls a sad face then runs back to Tyler who is playing with a light-up toy fire engine.

'All our neighbours must have got one,' she says, flicking the flyer over in her hand.

'I wonder if it's just this block. Could you possibly have Tyler while I go and check round?'

'Go ahead. Maybe someone saw who delivered them. It's not likely to be your regular postman.'

'That's what I was thinking.'

I reach over to Tyler and kiss the top of his thick head of hair and let him know I'm just popping out but will be back in a few minutes. Then I close the front door, run down the stairs and check our flat's post box area. Everyone's pigeonhole is locked as expected. I try the residents I know might be at home at three in the afternoon – I know a few of them to say good morning to and Katie and I know a couple of other single mums by name – but no one answers.

I check my phone. No return call from Darren. His girlfriend Simone doesn't like him having any contact with me, which I suppose is fair enough after my behaviour. Maybe he has to wait until she's not around before he calls me back.

I go back downstairs and outside to try a few more doors. It's gusty now and there seems to be more rubbish blowing around than ever. This place used to be kept so tidy and pretty. When I first arrived for a viewing, the outside was spotless and the two-bedroomed flat smelt brand new. The new landlord was doing a refurb. All the skirting boards were glossy white and there was a low-level smell of fresh plaster and paint. I picked a shade of sage green for the walls and a gorgeous, bleached pine effect laminate for the flooring. It reminded me of going to the seaside when I was a child. Moving here from Bristol was the fresh start I needed. And I thought if I was nearer to Darren, he'd see sense. But then he moved to Bedfordshire – to get away from me, Simone said. She would say that.

I cross the narrow road and note that the taxi has gone. I try a couple of doors but there's no answer, so I knock on a ground floor flat belonging to a retired couple, Jan and David. Jan answers and I explain about the poster and show her the folded copy from my pocket.

'Yes, we did get one of those. I was ever so worried thinking Tyler had gone missing. I'm so glad he's with you and is okay. Why has someone sent this out if there's nothing wrong? Sorry, you know I'm a bit slow sometimes.' She bunches the top of her cardigan closed.

'You're not slow, Jan. It's a puzzle to me too. There's no reason for it except to be malicious.'

'Goodness, someone's gone to a lot of effort to upset you.' She looks over her shoulder at her husband who is standing there. 'I don't suppose you saw who posted it, did you?' she asks him.

'I caught a glimpse of someone,' David says. He puts a hand on her shoulder as he talks to me. 'I was walking Henry along the footpath behind the shops, towards the big field, and a man in one of those hoodies was going in and out of people's front gardens. Had big sunglasses on and a bag across his body. I saw him reach in the bag and pull out a piece of paper, I think it must have been a flyer. Didn't think anything of it at the time. Common occurrence round here with all the junk mail we get through the door.'

'And that was today?'

'Oh, yes. And he was still at it until about forty minutes ago. He got in a taxi just out here and off he went.'

'God, I saw that, but I didn't see his face. The taxi was there for a while, wasn't it? At least from before I left for the school run, and it was still there when I got back.'

'Yes, waiting for him. He came from the direction of the next estate, the one that's just been finished. But as I say, he was wearing big sunglasses; I couldn't see his face properly.'

'How do you know it wasn't a woman?' Jan asks.

He shrugs. 'Looked like an athletic man to me.'

'It could be anyone.' I shake my head. 'Whoever it was has dropped flyers everywhere around here, possibly in quite a wide area, trying to make it look like Tyler is a lost child.'

'Looks like it. Who do you think is doing this, love?' David asks.

'I honestly don't know.'

I thank them and head back up the path to the road, trying to think why someone would target us. Is someone trying to have Tyler taken from me? But why?

And how long can I keep him safe?

4

Back up in Katie's flat, she makes me a black coffee and we sit at the kitchen table while I tell her what Jan and David said.

'Everyone around here must have a copy,' I sigh, smoothing my palm across the flyer.

'Do you think you should contact the police and let them know Tyler is safe and well?' Katie says, glancing up from where she's peeling potatoes.

'There's no point, this isn't a genuine appeal, so I doubt it's even on their radar. I'm his mum and legal guardian. He's safe with me.'

'But some people don't know that; you might need to prove it.'

'True.' I glance at my watch. It's almost 4.30 p.m. 'Look at the time. Maybe I'll call in at the police station after the pre-school meeting. See what they suggest I do about this. But I'll see how the meeting goes first.'

'Hope it's all right. And don't worry about Tyler, I'll feed him.'

'Oh, sorry, I meant to do that before I brought him round to you.'

'It's fine, you've got a lot going on. Perhaps you should take his birth certificate with you, you never know.'

'Seriously?' I groan. 'You're right though.' I sigh. 'If the other mums really believe I've kidnapped him, I may need proof he's my son.'

Before I head off, I say a quick goodbye to Tyler and try to ignore the rumble in my stomach at the delicious smell of roasting chicken. I'm salivating at the thought of eating the crispy skin, my favourite bit. I really need to be more organised so I can cook healthier meals like Katie does. She makes it seem so effortless.

I call into our flat and pick up Tyler's birth certificate, passport and red NHS medical book and slip them into my handbag, just in case I need to defend myself. Any one of these prove he's my son. The NHS book shows his newborn weight, development and even my breast-feeding pattern for goodness' sake; who could deny I'm his mother after seeing that?

* * *

The main pre-school room is filling up. Silence hits the room when I walk in and everyone looks round at me. Louise is sitting at the front but doesn't come and talk to me, maybe because the meeting is about to start. I feel my face heating up, the nerves kicking in, but I will not let their gossiping drive me away. I decide to sit at the back so I can make a quick getaway if it gets too much.

The room is about half the size of a school hall and lined with trol-leys of toys such as bricks and dolls. There's a child-height clothes rack of all the dressing up outfits and a box beneath full of wigs and hats. Plastic children's chairs have been laid out in rows as well as a table at the front with four chairs – I guess they are for the supervisor, her deputy, the treasurer and head of fundraising. On one side of the room is a tray of plastic wine glasses and a couple of open bottles. Small groups of parents stand huddled together, each person holding a glass. I've not touched a drop for four years. Another thing they find odd about me. One of the dads stares at me and I think I detect an element of sympathy in his eyes, but when I smile back, he turns away.

Mrs Howe and Mrs Cooper, the woman who told me Tyler had been good today, sit at the table and everyone else gravitates to their seats, clutching their precious drinks.

'Are you seriously letting her stay?' a woman's voice pipes up. I can't see who said it. A few heads swivel in my direction and several 'yeah's follow. A murmur of further agreement circulates the room.

'We're not here as judge and jury,' Mrs Howe says firmly.

I give a tiny nod of thanks.

'The police don't put these missing posts up lightly,' someone else says.

I wish I'd sat in the front now, so I could turn and see who these people are who want to speak against me so quickly.

'How do we know she's not kidnapped that poor boy?' one of the dads says, standing up and shamelessly pointing at me. It's the dad I thought might be on my side.

'That boy is my son,' I reply without hesitation. A flush of anger burns my cheeks. I shift to the edge of my seat, trying not to lose control and shout back.

'All right then,' the man says and turns back to the room as though they're all gathered here just for him, 'but what if she's taken him away from the dad and is stopping him seeing his son?' He shoots a poisonous look over his shoulder at me.

'Just because your ex tried to do that to you, Carl, doesn't mean that's what's going on here,' another woman says.

Louise swivels round and scrunches her face up in sympathy at me.

'Who is the dad anyway?' a woman shouts out, and a few people snigger.

The woman sitting on the other side of Mrs Howe stands up. I've not seen her before. She has short fair hair and glasses, which she pushes up the bridge of her nose, and she reminds me of a strict teacher in my primary school who made sure we all stuck to the rules.

I sink back in my chair. It feels like I'm standing outside the head mistress's office about to be told I'm suspended for a week.

She scans the room to make sure everyone is listening before she begins.

'If you'd looked more closely at the poster and tried calling the number, you'd have found that it doesn't go to the police station, it goes to some dodgy answer phone. In other words, it's fake.'

Everyone looks round at each other. I could hug this woman right now.

Mrs Howe stands up. 'Thank you for clarifying that for us, Ms Lea. We all need to be more careful about what we believe online. It won't be many years before your children will want to have mobiles and other devices of their own, and as parents we need to stay informed and educated about the dangers online, which unfortunately are growing and changing all the time. Fake information is everywhere. Please be mindful of what you read and believe. Can I also point out that we've already done a full DB check on Ellie, like we have for every one of you in this room. I can assure you that if there was a criminal amongst us, we'd certainly find out about it.' She holds the room's gaze with her stern look, making sure her message has sunk in.

I don't breathe for several seconds, trying not to cry. I'm so grateful to them for backing me up. I nod my thanks to Ms Lea. Louise checks over her shoulder to see if I'm okay. I wish I'd arrived earlier, so we'd have had time for a quick chat first. I know she hates conflict, so I wouldn't expect her to take sides, but just being seen talking to her would have shown that not everyone is against me. I thought I didn't have any friends here, but it seems I do have people willing to fight my corner.

'Right, everyone ready to continue?' Mrs Howe says, clapping her hands three times as though we're a bunch of five-year-olds. I smile to myself.

Mrs Cooper then reads out absence apologies for two people I've never heard of and runs through the points that have been actioned from the previous meeting, a month ago.

'It's less than three months until Christmas so we need to book the village hall for our annual fair as soon as possible. It's our biggest fundraiser of the year therefore we always like to plan early. What do we all think about suitable dates?'

I shut my eyes for a few seconds, letting all the chatter fade away. The tension I'd been holding in my body releases. But then I remember why I came off social media. Is that person behind this poster too?

My eyes snap open. This isn't over.

5

The meeting ends on time, but I hang around, waiting until most people have finished speaking to Mrs Howe, Mrs Cooper and Ms Lea, so I can thank them for supporting me. I look at all the children's artwork decorating the walls, and spot a picture painted by Tyler. 'Mummy and me' it says – two red stick people in thick brush strokes and a black cloud in the sky.

'Thank you all for showing me your support today,' I say, once the room has finally thinned out, shaking their hands one by one.

'Not at all,' Mrs Howe says, patting my arm. 'You didn't deserve the backlash you received from such a cruel post. You think these social media companies would be more responsible and take posts like that down immediately, wouldn't you?'

'People share them without thinking,' says Ms Lea. 'They assume it's real, but it doesn't take much digging to work out it's not.'

'Yes, so many people blindly share posts like that assuming they're genuine,' Mrs Cooper adds. 'You can't always believe what you read. Everyone really needs to do more fact checking.' She lowers her voice. 'Fake posts and information are becoming more and more of an issue with the primary school my husband works at, and now it seems it's seeping into pre-school life too.'

'I was surprised so many parents were fooled by it. I thought it was common knowledge that not all those police appeals are genuine, especially after the Arthur Moore case.' Mrs Howe holds her notes tightly to her chest. Just the mention of the poor little boy who was killed by his father is enough to send chills through you.

'I'm not even on Facebook any more,' I say. 'I came off it because someone was sending me inappropriate messages.'

'You might want to download it again just to look through some of these comments. You're named several times and some even say where you live. We're a small village, it wouldn't take much for someone to track you down.'

'I've heard that people sometimes do that, create a fake police post to glean information about a person. Could someone be trying to find out where you live?' Mrs Cooper asks.

'Possibly.' My heart drops wondering who would go to such lengths.

'Do you know who would target you so publicly?' Ms Lea asks.

'I can think of a couple of people. One is Tyler's father, Darren.' But does he need to find out my address? I thought he knew it. Why not just ask me? Maybe it's payback for me hassling his girlfriend when they first got together. I don't know what other reason there could be. 'He left us before Tyler was born; he said he wasn't ready to have children. It's hard to accept that he doesn't want anything to do with him.'

'That must be really tough for you, I'm so sorry.' Mrs Cooper unhooks her handbag from the back of her chair.

'I hope he's paying child maintenance though,' Ms Lea says, lowering her voice.

'He's not actually. He's always refused. I've been trying to get in touch with him because I'm really going to need him to start paying it, what with the cost of living increasing every week.'

'Do you think it's enough reason for him to lash out at you?'

'Possibly. He's a reasonable man otherwise.'

'My ex did everything he possibly could to avoid paying maintenance for the twins. And now he has a baby with his new partner, which makes their child his priority in the CMS's eyes.' Ms Lea sniffs, pushing her glasses up her nose.

'That's so unfair, I'm sorry.'

'Thanks. Sometimes I wonder if he had another child just to spite me.'

'It's always the children who suffer, isn't it?'

We all look round to see who spoke. Hayley is standing a breath away from my shoulder. A prickle of sweat breaks out under my arms. How long has she been standing there listening to our private conversation? I don't want her to know anything about my personal business. None of us answers her.

'If you find out who's done this to you, do please let us know, if you don't mind,' Mrs Howe says. 'It could help us be more alert to future cases.'

'I will.' I check my watch. 'Goodness, my babysitter will wonder where I am. See you tomorrow, thanks again.'

'Bye Ellie.' Hayley sounds genuine for once and her hand shoots out as though she wants to stop me, but her eyes dart around at everyone, probably worried they think she was eavesdropping on purpose.

I head straight for the door.

* * *

I bound up the stairs to the first floor and knock on Katie's door. There's no answer. I knock again and dig around in my bag for my phone. When I switch it on, a message pops up.

GONE TO CHEMIST. BACK IN FIVE.

Katie sent that well over an hour ago. It's gone six o'clock. It doesn't take that long to go to the small chemist on the estate and come home again. I try to message her back, but my phone says it's not been delivered. I plod downstairs and stand outside the main door wondering what to do. It's quiet except for the occasional car driving past. A cold breeze picks up, swirling fallen leaves around and sweeping them into the gutter. I try to ignore the fluttering in my stomach. Knowing Katie, she's probably got chatting to one of the mums and forgotten the time.

It'll be pitch black in about half an hour and Katie is out there some-where with two small children. With my son. I picture them walking along the narrow pavement holding hands, her trying to keep them away from the edge of the main road. Or worse, that something's happened to one of them. What if Tyler's got lost or been snatched? I mustn't think like that. She'd call me straight away if anything was wrong, unless there's a reason why she can't. The knot in my stomach tightens.

Another five minutes ticks by, then another. I try to call Katie's mobile, but it goes straight to answer phone. Panic grips me around the throat. I scream in my head: Where are they?

6

It's not until another ten minutes have passed that I see Katie hurrying around the corner. The children are quiet, not the usual chatter between them. I lurch forward to greet them and hug Tyler to me tightly.

'Where were you?' I snap at Katie. 'Is everything okay?'

Her head jerks back as though I've struck her.

'Five minutes, your note said. Why didn't you text again or call?' The words spring out of my mouth, spiky and accusatory before I can stop them. As though I doubt her ability to look after my child. 'I'm sorry, I didn't mean to snap, it's just I was imagining all sorts, you know me.'

'I'm so sorry, Ellie, I really am. I didn't know you'd be back already. I got chatting to someone and time flew away.' A silly grin spreads across her face. She tries to hide it behind her hand, but her cheeks and neck flush, giving her away.

'It's okay. Who was it then?' I smile with relief that it wasn't something serious holding her up.

'Just a guy. We've seen each other around a few times. Today we said hello to each other at the corner shop. He was visiting his aunty in one of the flats nearby; he seems really sweet. Not handsome in the traditional sense but he has a kind face. I've decided I'm not going for looks this time, I want someone who has a genuine heart, who cares for animals and offers to help old ladies with their shopping.' We both laugh and the relief that we're okay again floods through me. Katie's track record of dating vain beautiful men and the disastrous consequences could be the subject of a documentary.

'Good for you, girl. You deserve to meet someone new after all the shit Dave threw at you.'

'Thanks, you're right. It's time I moved on.'

'You really like him, don't you?'

'I think maybe I do.' She tips her head and grins.

I open the main door to the flats, still holding Tyler's hand tight and we all trudge upstairs. I realise I've not eaten yet.

'I thought you were going to the police station and would be there for a while, so I suppose I assumed I didn't need to rush. I am really sorry.' Katie unlocks her door.

'It's fine. Sorry I snapped. I was worried something was wrong, after what's happened. There's no need for me to speak to the police. The pre-school agree it's a false poster, possibly someone phishing for information about me. I'll still report it to Facebook. They need to take it down. Apparently there's information about my location in some of the replies.' My mouth has gone dry saying it out loud. I've tried so hard to protect our privacy since I came off social media and now someone is freely sharing my personal information online. How am I supposed to feel safe in my own home?

'Bloody hell.'

'Some of the parents tried to gang up on me.'

'I thought they might.'

'Mrs Howe was a real hero, swooping to my rescue.'

'I bet that Hayley was involved.'

I nod. 'She's the ringleader. The pre-school staff were brilliant, stuck up for me and assured everyone I'd been through all the child protection checks et cetera and we should all be more careful with what we believe online.'

'That's a relief.'

'Problem is, I still don't know who was behind all this.'

'You don't think it was Hayley?'

'I don't think so. I thought maybe it could be Darren being spiteful, or the same person who was sending me messages on Facebook before, whoever that was. I never got to the bottom of it.'

She frowns. 'Could be. Can't Facebook tell you?'

'I need to find out.' I take my front door key out.

'Did you hear back from Darren?' Katie asks.

'Nothing. I'm going to try him again when I've got Tyler to bed. I need to meet up with him if I can. I think a face-to-face meeting is the only way to really know if it's him behind the fake poster.'

Katie's phone buzzes and she tries to ignore it, but when it buzzes again, she glances at the screen. Her face brightens.

'Is that the new man?'

She smiles widely.

'He's keen. I'll leave you to it.' Chatting with her has really helped calm my anxiety.

'You don't have to rush off.' But her hand is on her phone; I can tell she's dying to text him back.

'I do. I need to get this boy to bed.' I swing Tyler up into my arms and give him a big kiss. 'Say thank you to Katie and bye-bye to Joseph.'

'Thank you. Bye-bye.'

'Thanks so much for babysitting.'

'Anytime,' she says as she unlocks her door and goes in. The landing is empty and echoey. The main door slams shut. I shiver as a gust of cold air rises. People come and go all the time, so why does it feel like it has something to do with me?

'What's that, Mummy?' Tyler is pointing to our doormat.

A single red rose has been left there. Except its head has been stamped on and crushed so hard, it's left a crimson stain.

7

I unlock our front door and usher Tyler in while I attempt to pick up the remnants of the rose without pricking my fingers. I find a tissue in my pocket and use that to hold it. Inside, I drop it straight into the kitchen swing bin.

After I've got Tyler to bed and read him a story, I go down to the living room, close the door and call Darren. Would he really have put the fake poster up on Facebook? Again, there is no answer.

I don't know what to do. He won't tell me where he lives now. I know it's in Sandy, so not far from Huntingdon. He says he won't tell me because his girlfriend, Simone, doesn't want me turning up with Tyler.

Not long later, when I'm in my pyjamas, curled up in front of *Emmerdale* with a hot chocolate, my phone rings. I don't recognise the number. I leave it a couple of seconds before wondering if it could be Darren working late, so I answer.

'It's me,' he says in a hushed tone.

I wonder what Simone will have to say about that if she finds out.

'Oh, hello. Why haven't you been answering me?'

'I couldn't. And I'd prefer to keep this between us.' He coughs, something he always does when he's nervous.

I take a deep breath.

'I need to see you. To talk in person. I can't do this over the phone.'

'What is it about?'

'I'd rather tell you when I meet you.' If I accuse him now, he'll probably slam the phone down then I'll be back to where I was.

'All right. Can you meet me at the Horse and Dog tomorrow at 1 p.m.?'

'Yeah, I should be able to.'

'Should? Can't be that important.'

'It is. I'll be there, I promise.' Tyler will be at pre-school until 3 p.m., so I'll have time in my lunch break.

'Good. See you then. Got to go.'

I switch the end call button. I need to know if he's behind this poster campaign, work out why he's doing it.

* * *

At 12.30 p.m. the next day, I head off to the pub on foot. It's a warm autumnal day so I don't bother with a jacket. A gentle breeze lifts my curls as I stride down the pavement. I'm wearing a deep red shift dress with capped sleeves, an outfit I know Darren loves me in. I'm also wearing smart trainers but when I arrive I go straight to the ladies toilets so I can change to my black patent stilettos. Then I order our drinks and sit at our usual table. The barman brings over a gin and tonic in a bowl glass for Darren and a lemonade for me, each with a slice of lime. It's what he always used to drink.

Darren is a few minutes early. He's unshaven and wearing a pinstriped suit which looks like it missed a trip to the dry cleaners. His hair is unruly, not sleek like he kept it when he was with me. But he still looks handsome. He regards me in that admiring way he has, a smile drawing across his lips, lighting up his warm brown eyes. I stand up and kiss him on both cheeks, which he reciprocates but then steps away, seeming to remember himself – we're not together any more. And the softness of his greeting is gone.

'Good to see you,' I say quietly, not expecting a similar reply.

'You too.' He's looking at the floor.

'She doesn't know you're here then?' It's a cheeky question but I want to know if she's likely to turn up and start throwing accusations at me – or a drink. The shake of his head is so slight, I wonder if I imagined it.

'Let's keep it that way for now, if you don't mind.' He scans the room then picks up his glass. 'Gin and tonic? I don't really drink it any more, but thanks anyway.' He glugs back a large mouthful and wipes across his mouth with his strong manly hand. Inside, I ache at a sudden longing for his gentle touch, wishing he was still mine to love. The urge to kiss him crashes over me. He wants me to keep his secret. I'm still important to him. The tiny elation lifts me. Anything could happen at our secret meeting. But no, he's moved on and I must too. I grip the arms of the chair and think about why I'm here, what I need to find out. There's no point giving him any warning for what I'm going to show him, so I take out my phone while he's knocking back more gin.

'Do you know anything about this?' I hold up the screenshot of the Facebook poster, Tyler smiling on the screen. His glass rattles onto the table and he snatches the phone from me, his eyes wide.

'Tyler's missing?' He frowns, not quite understanding what I mean.

'No, thankfully this is fake, but someone has deliberately put it together, pretending to be the police and then posting it on Facebook.'

'Whoever it is has gone to a lot of trouble.'

'It's been liked and shared hundreds of times. So I'm asking you, if you have any clue who would do this, please tell me.' I catch his eye and hold him there. All sorts of vibes and mixed feelings pass between us. Normally I can read his reactions but there's nothing there I can clearly decipher.

'I'm sorry but why do you think I would know?' He hands the phone back to me.

'I just thought...' Clumsy. I shake my head, realising how it sounds.

'What... you think I have something to do with this?' He points to himself, incredulous.

'No, of course not.' But my tone gives me away.

'I cannot believe you think I'd do something so cruel. Make out your child is missing when he's not?'

Your child. It crushes me that he still calls him that.

'Are you trying to get a rise out of me, because seriously, Elle, it's not funny.'

'I thought maybe you wanted to... hurt me.'

'You believe I'd use your child as a way of getting at you? Come on, Ellie. You know I wouldn't do that.' He chucks the last of his drink down his throat and places the glass down. 'I still care about you, even after everything. I'm not a vindictive person.'

'I know, I just thought... You've been so angry with me since...' I look down at my lap. Now I feel stupid for even thinking it could be him.

'You kept calling my girlfriend, of course I was angry.'

'I didn't mean to upset anyone. I just wanted to talk to her.' My voice has shrunk. I wish I could disappear. I needed to explain my side of the story to her, that I truly believed Tyler was Darren's baby and that he was in denial because he wasn't ready to become a dad. I thought she'd understand how important it was for our child to have both parents bringing him up, even though we weren't together.

'I found it hard to accept it was over between us, that you'd met someone else, especially as I was pregnant.'

'I've tried to tell you Tyler isn't mine. We've been through this a thousand times.'

'Please don't say that!' I grab his wrist, but he pulls away from me.

'I'm sorry.' He stands up.

'Why can't you accept that Tyler is your son?'

'Because I know he's not.' He holds me in his pitying gaze. Any good memories he had earlier of our time together are blown away into tiny pieces.

8

'I want you to have a DNA test,' I blurt out before Darren has a chance to walk away. He's already turned to go, but he twists back, grimacing.

'No way. I don't have to prove myself to you. I know the truth. I'm sorry Ellie, but you need to accept that we're not together any more, that Tyler is not my son.'

'If you don't agree to take one, I'll contact Simone again.' He's left me no choice. I don't want to threaten him, but Tyler having a relationship with his dad is more important to me. And I can't deny I need the money too. He's got away with paying nothing for too long.

'Do that and I'll never speak to you again.' He's stoney-faced, almost as if we're strangers.

'Look, cards on the table, I need the maintenance money. The bills are going up every month and it's killing me.'

'You know you could get a better job if you wanted to. We've talked about this. You're capable of so much more than processing orders.'

'I like the flexible working; it fits my life so well. But I know I need to push myself and I am going to try to get promoted to assistant manager.' He always encouraged me to go for a management post when we were together.

'Great.' He holds his hands up. 'Failing that, you could contact Tyler's real dad?' He heads for the door.

His words sting, but I swallow hard. 'You are his real dad.'

Darren shakes his head then walks out, leaving me sitting on my own. I finish my drink, trying to avoid eye contact with everyone in the pub, I wipe away my tears and go home.

* * *

As soon as Tyler is tucked up in bed, I sit in the living room and call Molly to see if she's around for a chat. She was never keen on Darren because he wasn't committed to me in the way she felt he should be. Spending his spare cash on his BMW and going out, rather than saving up to buy a house together. To be fair to him, he said he wasn't ready to settle down. Her mobile is switched off, so I dial her house number. Her boyfriend Ian picks up.

'Hey you, how's it going?' He sounds like he's won a prize.

'Good thanks. Is Molls around?'

'Nah, she's out with some work mates, won't be back till late.'

'Okay, I'll try her again on her mobile.'

'Her phone will be off knowing that lot.'

'Could you tell her I called?'

'Yeah, course. What you been up to anyway?'

I sigh deeply. 'Working mostly.' I considered him a good friend once, so I'd feel bad hanging up on him.

'Still at the glazing company?'

'Yeah.' I only speak to him now because he's with Molly. He spoilt our friendship by telling me one drunken night that he'd had a crush on me for years. Things between us weren't the same after that. It was awkward and embarrassing thinking of him looking at me in that way, so I stopped contacting him. Not long after I rejected him – as gently as I could – he started dating Molly. I still wonder whether it was out of spite, a way of still having me in his life, because when they invited me to their parties or barbeques, he'd spend half the night trying to chat to me. I didn't say anything in case he thought I was jealous, and Molly deserved better than being a consolation prize.

'Can I help with anything?' It sounds like he's chugging back a long glug of drink, probably beer. Some things don't change.

'Not really. Just needed a chat. If you could ask her to ring me when she's free please?' I'm about to end the call but he keeps talking.

'Go on, you can tell me what's wrong.'

'Nothing's wrong. We just haven't spoken for a while.'

'I thought you spoke the other day? Not your a-hole of an ex again is it?'

'No.' My tone is defensive. He's the last person I want to discuss my personal life with. He used to private message me on Facebook, say things he shouldn't say to the best friend of his new girlfriend. I tried to laugh it off, make out he was joking, but his messages became more explicit, serious, then nasty when I didn't respond the way he expected me to. It was one of the reasons why I had to come off social media and distance myself from him. I couldn't tell Molls, I was worried she'd blame me, think I'd encouraged him. She knew what a tease I'd enjoyed being with blokes when I was in my early twenties, playing with their feelings.

'You used to confide in me, Ellie. I hope you don't think I'm completely useless?'

'I don't really want to talk about him, but thanks.'

'That girlfriend of his isn't a patch on you.'

'Really.' I want to put the phone down.

'Yeah, he's an idiot for letting you go, believe me, everyone says so.'

'Not what he thinks.' I put my feet up on the sofa.

'You're the one who got away.' He sounds like a dramatic TV voice-over. It's so close to my ear, I have to move the receiver away.

'Ian,' I snap.

'You are. For lots of us poor blokes.'

'Tell Darren that.' I laugh half-heartedly.

'Ah, so it is the a-hole.' He laughs too. 'Still baffles me why you chose to be with him.'

'Sometimes I wish I hadn't.' I speak without thinking, Part of me still can't help leaping at the chance to talk about Darren. 'He's perfectly happy to turn his back on me and our son.'

'What a total loser. Do you want me to sort him out for you? Tell me where he lives, and I'll do it.'

'No, honestly, it's fine.' I clench my teeth.

'Doesn't sound fine to me. Sounds like the bastard has upset you.'

The silence that follows worries me. He might think it's significant, that I do need his help, but I do not want him involved.

'He's still not supporting his kid?'

'I want him to do a DNA test. It's the only fair way to prove Tyler's his.'

'What is wrong with him?'

I bite my lip. I've said too much to the wrong person.

'I don't get you, Elle.'

Another silence I can't fill.

'What is it about Darren that's so special?'

Oh God, here we go. 'Stop right there.'

'What does he have that I haven't?'

'I'm not going through this again.' I'm astounded he's asking this. Instead he should be asking himself why he thought it was okay to send me dirty messages while dating my best friend.

'Ian, please stop.'

'Why didn't you want me?'

'You know we can't choose who we have feelings for, which is why you're bang out of order putting this on me.'

'But why was I never good enough for you?' His voice rises.

There's nothing left to say.

'I could have given you a kid, one that I wanted too. We could have got married and had more kids.'

I stay silent, knowing that whatever I say won't be good enough.

'Why wouldn't you let me love you?'

'I never felt that way about you. End of, Ian.'

'Oh, that's it, dump me all over again.'

'How can I dump you? We never went out. You're with Molly.' I press end call and cover my mouth with my hand.

I sit up and text Molly, asking her to call me tomorrow. I keep the message light so as not to worry her, but there's something I need to speak to her about. Something I should have told her years ago.

9

I can't breathe, I can't move. My hands are tied together above my head. The clown is holding a carving knife to my throat. His rancid saliva drips onto my face, the smell of rubber thick in my nostrils. Except he's not wearing a mask. The black diamond shapes around the eyes, red gash of a mouth and rotten yellow razor-sharp teeth, are part of his real skin. And out of the corner of my eye I see a snake sliding towards me and in the next moment I'm screaming as the bed tips off a cliff, and I'm clinging on as he sinks away from me, down into the crashing waves.

I wake up in a sweat, my heart thudding. It feels so real, I can still smell his breath. It's the same nightmare I always have. It seems the more I try and block out that night at the Airbnb, the more frequently I have them.

After I've dropped Tyler off at pre-school, I bump into Louise in the car park.

'How are you doing?' she asks.

'I'm okay, thanks.' Although the nightmare is still lingering in my head.

'Good, good. I wanted you to know that I complained about the Facebook post being fake and it's been taken down.'

'Are you sure it's gone?' I fiddle with my keys as we stroll back to our cars.

'Yes, I've been keeping an eye on it.'

I let out a breath of relief. 'Thanks, Louise.'

'Most probably from a fake account. Bit creepy because whoever it was had no followers.'

'So they could easily start a new account anytime and do it again?'

'I don't know if Facebook would know if they re-posted it on a new account.'

'I've heard about criminals using multiple accounts to hide behind.'

'Haven't you got any closer to finding out who did this?'

'The person I thought it could be is denying it. I don't know how to find out.'

Louise shrugs sadly. We say goodbye and I sit in my car, wondering if Ian could have made the fake poster. But why would he? What would he gain out of making me look like a bad mother? Why go to all the trouble of posting flyers? He knows where I live, so it's possible. It scares me how nasty he can become in a split second. I didn't realise quite how much he hates Darren and how bitter he still is about me rejecting him. And now I'm worried about Molly being with someone like that. It makes me wonder if he's been nasty to her and what he might be capable of.

I drive home and make a pot of coffee before sitting down to a pile of orders to process. I find it hard to concentrate and find myself checking my text messages. Still nothing from Molly. I'm not sure she's the best person to confide in any more. If she has an inkling how Ian feels about me or Darren, will our friendship survive? It's already shaky. I wonder if I should have confided in her about that night four years ago, as soon as I arrived in Jersey. Told her what I think happened. But I was confused and she was mad at me for being so late. A few weeks later she blamed Darren for leaving me and shacking up with Simone all the way over in Bedford. But maybe she blames me too, for moving nearer to him, because she doesn't reply to my messages straight away any more. It's as though I'm no longer an important part of her life.

My mobile pings with a new message. But it's not from Molly, it's from Simone. I hesitate before I open it.

We need to talk. Meet me in Corner Café in Huntingdon in an hour.

Great. She's found out about me and Darren meeting up. I could ignore her, but there's no point. She'll only come after me. She knows what I want. I could use this to my advantage.

I finish the order I'm doing and head into town. The café isn't that busy when I get there so I buy a coffee. I'm twenty minutes early and when I finish my cup she's still not arrived. I nip to the loo. There are only two cubicles beyond the sink and hand drying area. I'm the only person there although as soon as I lock my door the squeak of the main door opens and closes. Whoever it is turns on a tap, pulls out a paper towel and then it's dead quiet again so I guess they left.

When I step out, a flash of red comes out of nowhere, thumping the side of my face, sending me crashing into the wall.

I hold my throbbing jaw. 'What was that for?' I yell.

Simone is standing with her hands on her hips in front of me. She's in a red suit, pencil skirt tight, heels maximum height, bare legs. Sexy cow.

'Toilets are dirty places, aren't they?' she says in her West London accent. 'Never know what scum you'll find in them.'

I eye up the main door and spot a bolt pulled across it. Why didn't I hear her locking it?

'That's for seeing my Darren behind my back, as if you need to ask.' She smooths her palms together; a job well done.

'He was the one who told me not to tell you he came to see me!' I raise my hands in protest.

'But you're the one who asked to meet him, aren't you? He's a gentleman, didn't want to upset you. Knows you're a bit off your nut. Turning into the green-eyed monster when it comes to anything to do with me. I know your game, thinking you can click your fingers and get him to come running.' She points her finger in my face, so close to my eyes, I feel sweat prickle under my arms.

'That's not the reason.' I step back before she jabs my eyeball. 'All I want is for him to do a DNA test.'

'And you know he won't because he's got no reason to.' She bangs her fist against the hand dryer, setting it off. 'He told me you two weren't all that close the weeks before you fell pregnant.'

'That's not true! I'd forgotten to take a couple of pills when I had a stomach bug, and I can't bear using condoms. I thought we were careful, but clearly not enough. Look, I just need you to persuade him to take it.' I'm almost yelling, trying to be heard over the sound of the dryer. 'If you're both so sure it'll be negative, then why not do it? What are you so scared of?'

'I'm not scared of you,' she almost spits at me.

'But a tiny part of you isn't sure it would be negative. Am I right?'

Her face drops. She turns away.

'I'll be able to rule him out and in return, I promise I'll leave you both alone.'

'Will you?'

'Yeah.' I nod to convince myself.

'So you've got a whole list of other possible fathers, have you?'

'No, I believe Darren is Tyler's father, but he's certain he isn't. All I'm saying is if he wants proof, then he should do it. Don't you think that's fair?'

'Fair?' She laughs. 'We're getting married next year. Do you think him paying out for a kid he has nothing to do with is fair?'

'So prove me wrong.'

Simone paces up and down. I try to work out what she's thinking.

'But if Tyler is his son, he can start spending time with him, get to know him, and you can too.'

Simone shakes her head. 'We want to have our own children, thanks. We don't need yours.'

My mouth opens and I frown at the thought of Darren wanting a child with her. Why not me? I straighten my face before she notices my reaction.

'And we certainly don't want to be paying maintenance to you.'

'Do you really want to marry a man if he's lying to you?'

Simone hesitates for a moment. 'I know my Darren and he's not lying to me. He knows Tyler isn't his.'

'How is he so certain?'

She side-eyes me. 'That's his business.'

'Fine, if he's right and the test is negative, you both get to walk away. I think I've been lenient so far. But if it's not, I could take Darren to court any time I want, and he'll end up having to give me back-pay from the second Tyler was born.' I turn away and swallow hard. She doesn't seem to know I'm making this up as I go along. 'Could be quite a tidy sum. I think you might have to postpone your wedding.'

'You bitch.' Simone shoves me into the wall again and holds me round the neck, her long pointed nails digging into the skin behind my ear. I cry out in pain. Someone knocks on the door. 'Wait your turn,' she shouts over her shoulder. I kick her ankle with the toe of my boot, and she lets go, screaming. Two seconds later the main door is bust open by the owner.

'What the hell's going on in here? Get out before I call the police.'

I bow my head and hurry out. I'll never be able to come here again.

Outside, I blink in the bright sunshine even though there's no warmth in it. I sidle along the pavement, head down in case anyone I know saw me being chucked out. I don't bother to see which way Simone went. That was probably my last chance to persuade them that Darren should take the test. And my last chance to get him to pay maintenance.

As soon as I get home and close the door behind me, the tears come. I hold onto the kitchen counter. How have I managed to make such a mess of my life? I switch the kettle on and take a mug out of the cupboard. My eye lingers on a tall glass. For the first time in four years I could quite easily pour myself a drink of wine. Thank goodness I don't have any in the flat.

10

The next day when I pick Tyler up from pre-school, Louise comes running up to me, waving her phone in the air.

'You didn't send this, did you?' She shows me her screen which is on Facebook Messenger. There's a thread from me full of insults and swear words I'd never normally use.

'I wouldn't do that,' I tell her. She passes me her phone so I can look more closely. I click on the profile, which has the same photo I used when I had a Facebook account. There are even photos of me with Tyler in an album. I have scores of friends apparently, many of whom I don't recognise, but some I do. I hand her phone back, my head in a muddle.

'I may not be the only one who's received a message from this account,' Louise says, scrolling through her feed. She shows me a post from Hayley in the pre-school group page.

Anyone else get a nasty message from Ellie Hunter?

She's tagged 'me' in the post. Several other mums from pre-school have replied saying they have, and one is demanding an apology, or I should be chucked off the committee.

'How do I prove I didn't do this? I haven't had an account for months.'

'If you think someone has stolen your identity, you need to report it to Facebook and the police.'

'How do I report it if I don't have an active account?' Panic rises in my chest. How can I carry on living here with someone out to ruin my reputation?

'Do it through mine. If you're free now, why don't we pop back to my house and we'll go through it together.'

'Are you sure you don't mind?'

'Of course not. Shall I see you there in about five minutes?'

I watch Louise trot back to her car and wonder what I've done to deserve her kindness.

* * *

I've only ever admired Louise's house from outside, with its beautiful front garden full of trees and shrubs and flowers. I park on the road, feeling too self-conscious to park on her immaculate driveway, behind her husband's silver Porsche. Louise pulls up as I'm getting out and I follow her in, holding Tyler's hand.

'I'll have a latte if you're making one,' she says to her husband, kissing him on the cheek as she comes in the door. My pulse quickens. He's a few years older than her, tall and athletic with dark spiky hair, which is white in places. Something about him is familiar.

'Steve, this is Ellie and Tyler,' Louise says.

'Hi.' Steve smiles at me, holding my gaze for a second then he high fives Tyler. Now I remember. We've met once before but he doesn't mention it, so I don't either. 'Coffee?' He begins to reel off all the different fancy ones, the type most people have to go to a café for, counting them out on his fingers.

'Americano please. Black.'

'Just how I like it too. And what can I get you?' he asks Tyler. Tyler grins at Jordan, who whispers in his ear.

'Tango,' he says.

Louise and Steve laugh and I join in, though I don't know what the joke is.

'We have orange squash, is that okay?' Steve says, glancing at Tyler but directing the question at me with a concerned look on his face.

'We don't have fizzy drinks in this house,' Louise explains. 'Bad for our teeth aren't they, Jordan?'

Jordan bows his head, folds his arms and shoves into Tyler with his elbow.

'Jordan!' Louise's face crumples.

'That's not very nice. Now say sorry.' Steve crouches in front of him, waiting for him to apologise, then Steve glances up at me with his startling green eyes.

'So-rry.' Jordan stamps his foot.

'Thank you.' Steve stands up and ruffles his hair.

'We're so sorry, Ellie.' Louise takes the cup of coffee Steve has finished making and hands it to me as if it's a peace offering. Part of me wants to burst out laughing, break the serious atmosphere, but I don't want to be disrespectful.

'Shall we go and open my laptop?'

Louise leaves the kitchen and I follow, glancing back to smile a thank you at Steve, only for him to wink back at me. I frown for a second. Perhaps he winks at everyone.

Louise is in the living room unplugging her laptop from the charger. She sits on their cream sofa, and I sit next to her with my hot black coffee, wondering if I can drink it without letting any dark drops run down the side. I should have warned her how clumsy I am. She opens Facebook and goes to the admin section, where she writes my complaint for me. She reads it back and I approve it. Then she composes a message on my behalf, which she posts in the school group, saying my account has been cloned and any nasty comments or messages are not from me.

'Could I use your loo?' I ask, my head swimming. All this backstabbing is overwhelming. I need a few moments to calm down, breathe deeply.

'Course, it's next to the kitchen.' She barely looks up from the screen.

The downstairs toilet is filled with a floral smell which is not unpleasant but maybe a bit over the top for me. The walls are painted white with subtle flecks of silver and the taps are coloured gold.

When I come out, Steve is just leaving the kitchen, and we almost collide.

'You two busy doing something for pre-school?'

'Facebook actually. Well, I don't use it any more, but someone's cloned my account.'

'Lou told me about the poster. A shitty thing for someone to do.' He's suddenly distracted, looking towards the window. 'Did you order a taxi?' He hurries over. 'There's a guy waiting out here. I just spotted him peering in.'

'No.' I rush into the kitchen and come to a stop next to him, putting my hand out to slow myself down before I hit the sink, but I touch Steve's arm by accident. He glances at my hand but we both look straight at the window again, at the taxi driving off.

'He was in a hurry – ran off as soon as he saw I clocked him.' Steve twists round to face me and I try not to look too deeply into his eyes. 'Must have got the wrong house.'

Could this be anything to do with me? The nagging image of that taxi hanging around outside my flat is hard to ignore. It brings up memories of the last time I was in one, when I was completely out of it. I have to work hard to push intrusive thoughts away before they become fully formed in my head and overwhelm me. I have to remember – I've stopped drinking now, so it can't happen again.

11

I buckle Tyler into his car seat and climb in the driver's side. My phone beeps but I leave it in my bag. I'm guessing it's another low balance alert from my bank. If Darren doesn't start paying me maintenance, I don't know how we're going to survive on my current wage. Everything keeps going up, especially food and energy bills.

I drive the usual route home, only a few streets away. As I'm turning into my road, my stomach drops when I see a taxi lingering ahead, parked on the pavement. I could drive away, go round the block, but I will not be intimidated. Whoever it is and whatever they want, I can handle it. I admit I'm tempted to pull up beside it to see who the driver is, but I can't put Tyler in danger. And who's to say it's anything to do with me anyway.

I park in my space, keeping my eye on the taxi. It doesn't move. Maybe it belongs to one of the neighbours. It could be their job. But the unease churning in my stomach tells me different.

I take out my phone. There's a message from Simone. I don't want to look but I know I'll be worrying about it if I don't.

I'll get Darren to do the DNA test if you promise that's the end of it.

It's the best news I've had all day. At last Darren will have to take responsibility for his son. The extra bit of money from him every month will make such a difference. I watch Tyler in the rear-view mirror playing with his favourite toy plane. The only thing Darren has ever bought him.

Wanting to get away from the taxi driver, I make a game of hurrying Tyler inside the main entrance and up the stairs. Tyler is giggling and flushed in the face by the time we reach our door.

'Yuk, what's that?' He points at a small red lump on the mat. I can't work out what it is either. It's not until I'm closer that I notice a bare tail attached to the skinned body of a mouse.

I let out a small scream and immediately cover my mouth with my hand, not wanting to alarm Tyler.

'Oh no! Don't worry darling, a cat must have been let in the entrance door and dumped it here on its way home.' A couple of the neighbours have recently installed cat flaps in their front doors.

I unlock the door and usher Tyler inside, before finding an old plastic bag to pick up the mouse in. I leave it there, the handles tied together. I'll deal with it in the morning. I don't want to go down to the outside bin now and leave Tyler on his own.

* * *

That night, after Tyler has gone to bed, I'm grateful for some quiet time. I sit in front of the TV but my phone rings, disturbing the calm. I wish I'd switched it off. I pick it up and see it's Darren. I touch the green button to answer.

'Ellie, I thought we had an agreement.' Darren sighs. I'm too tired for this. 'You promised to leave Simone alone.'

'I did, yes.'

'So why are you hassling her again?'

I let out a sigh. Why does he always assume it's me that's done something wrong? 'I'm not. She was the one who asked to meet then jumped out and attacked me.'

'Right, well, please stop winding her up.' I don't answer. He used to stick up for me when we were together, and now I'm the enemy.

'By the way, you should know, we're getting married.' He waits for my reaction. What does he expect me to say?

'So I heard,' I say after a long drawn-out moment. Is he hoping I'll beg him not to do it? He's not been big on commitment in the past.

'Aren't you pleased for me?' He sounds disappointed.

'No. Why should I be? I bet you'll want loads of kids with her.' I clench my teeth before I let the rising bitterness get the better of me.

'... and so I've decided to do the test.'

I don't want to let on that Simone's already told me, that I know it's her who's persuaded him, so I just say, 'About time.'

'I want to put an end to all this bickering.'

'Okay, but I want to be there. Make sure it's done properly.'

He doesn't answer straight away. 'I suppose so.'

'Good. Thank you.'

'Thank Simone. She's the one who told me that the Child Maintenance Service could order me to take a test and charge me over £200. So I'll do it, as long as you promise to leave us alone when you get the result.'

'If you're not the dad, then yeah, of course, otherwise they'll work out how much you should pay me.'

'That's fine. I'll order a test kit and will be in touch.'

'Okay, thank you.'

I put the phone down, deflated by his coldness, his desire to get me out of his life for good, the finality of it. I had such dreams for our lives together. Lots of children and a three-bedroomed house with a double garage so he could potter about fixing cars while I fed our babies and baked cakes. But as soon as I found out I was pregnant he became distant. He had warned me he didn't want kids yet, that he wanted to have fun before he settled down. I thought he loved me enough to change his mind. Stupid, thinking he would. I'm certain he is Tyler's dad but now I'm scared. What if he's not?

No, I can't let myself think about that, because it's not possible.

* * *

I wake the next day dripping in sweat. I can barely open my eyes I'm so exhausted. It takes me ages to drop off to sleep at night, knowing I'm probably going to have the clown nightmare again. But what does it mean? The clown's face is so vivid, it's terrifying. I won't be able to get it out of my head all day.

After dropping Tyler off at pre-school, I message Katie asking her if she's still okay to babysit Tyler for a couple of hours this evening while I go to the next committee meeting. I wave at Louise as she drives past, but she can't have seen me because she doesn't wave back. Perhaps not everyone has seen the message she posted on my behalf, because there were some funny looks from the other mums as I dropped Tyler off.

Katie replies straight away saying it's fine and can I babysit Joseph tomorrow night because she's going on her first proper date with her new man. I send loads of heart emojis and say of course it's all right.

I drive towards town to do a few chores before I settle down to work. It's not so busy at this time of the morning. I'm hoping to go to the bank, post office and supermarket and be home within the hour. Unless I stop for coffee. I could try to call Molly again; she's still not replied to my texts. I wonder if Ian passed on my message.

I come up to a small roundabout which is clear and pull out. An Audi drives up close behind me. There's barely any other cars on the road, so I don't know why it's tailing me. A second later it overtakes at great speed, as though I'm in the way or have done something wrong, but I don't know what because I'm driving within the speed limit. Further down the road it stops and suddenly its reverse lights are on and it's moving backwards, straight at me. I check around, sweat rising up my neck and under my arms. I'm ready to swerve out of the way but then it stops again and moves forward as though nothing happened.

When I reach the lights I slow down and breathe out, watching it speed off into the distance. My head is pounding. Who was that? I didn't see the driver's face or look at the car's number plate, but I did see a sticker in the rear window with a phone number for a local company: ACE Taxis.

12

I take Tyler over to Katie's after dinner and drive to the pre-school meeting.

The reception is frosty as soon as I walk in, as though no progress was made the last time we were all there. Louise is sitting at the front and looks round when I come in but doesn't smile. It's odd after she's helped me so much with Facebook and posting the message on her page. If only I could see the responses but when I tried to search her name on Facebook, all sorts of privacy restrictions came up.

Mrs Howe stands. 'I'd like to propose a trip to Sacrewell Farm on the Friday after Halloween. There are farm animals to see and a play barn with a huge soft play area and another with all sorts of ride-on toys including tractors and fire engines.'

'We went last year, and it was a wonderful day out,' Hayley says, turning to face everyone.

'Thanks, Hayley, we thought so too. We hired a double-decker coach and had lots of parent helpers come along, which made life so much easier. I think they all enjoyed it too.'

'We did, didn't we?' Hayley says to Lauren who's by her side. A few of the parents murmur their agreement.

'So, what do we all think? Can we see a show of hands if you think it's a good idea?'

Everyone agrees so we go on to discuss costs and an itinerary and whether packed lunches should be taken or picnic boxes pre-ordered from the farm. I'm itching to say I'll help out, but it depends on my work schedule. Tyler will love the ride-on tractors and the animals though. Last year at Halloween, he was mesmerised by Frankenstein and Mummies. We chose a werewolf outfit for him from the local supermarket. I've promised we'll go trick or treating with Joseph this time, especially as last year hardly anyone knocked on our door. One of the drawbacks of living in a flat.

We agree the date and Hayley offers to book the visit with the farm administrator. Louise says she'll ring round for the best price to hire a coach, although they intend to use the same company as last year; she'll use that as bargaining power to make sure they keep the price down.

'Who would be interested in coming along for the ride, so to speak, and being a parent helper on the day? Please raise your hands,' Mrs Cooper says, clipboard in one hand and pen in the other. She counts the volunteers then ticks their names off her list.

'Who's got good people skills?' Mrs Howe calls out above the excited murmur. 'I was thinking if we hold a coffee morning at the village hall on a Saturday, at least one or two of you could come along and persuade a few more parents not on the committee to be parent helpers. We need as many as possible to take into account inevitable last-minute absences from sickness et cetera.'

I'm the only one to put my hand up for this, but I'm not sure anyone has noticed me at the back of the room.

'I have good interpersonal skills,' I say, and everyone looks round. I smile at Louise, but her face is blank, as though she's looking through me.

'She can say that again,' someone says loudly. Several people snigger. I can't see who spoke but suddenly lots of people have turned to look at me. My cheeks are burning. I didn't mean to draw attention to myself. I only want to help out. Why didn't I just keep quiet? I don't know why I'm being bullied again.

'Look at her, playing the innocent,' says a woman with hair cut severely into a bob, sitting next to Louise. I don't know her name, but I've seen her before. She wears red patent Mary Jane shoes and a bow in her hair like some overgrown doll.

Hayley and Lauren stand up, arms crossed.

'What do you mean?' I grab my bag, ready to walk out.

'Seeing Louise's husband behind her back, that's what,' Hayley says loudly. Louise bows her head into her hands and begins to cry. Half the front row rush to comfort her. The other half stand up and glare at me.

'What?' I can't believe what I'm hearing. How have they managed to concoct another story about me? 'That is not true.' I look to Mrs Howe for support, but she's frowning, in stunned silence.

'Louise received a private message with a photo of you together from a very reliable source,' Hayley says.

'But it's not true. Who sent it?'

'Emma. We know all about you and Steve,' Lauren says.

'What do you mean? Emma who?'

'You don't even know who the father of your child is, do you?' Hayley laughs.

'Could be any one of a number of men,' says Lauren.

'Okay, that's enough.' Mrs Cooper raises her hands.

'Louise, you know it's all malicious lies,' I plead. 'Have you spoken to your husband? He'll tell you the truth.'

'I don't think their private conversations have anything to do with you,' Hayley says, a smirk in her eyes. 'I suggest you leave.'

I look to Mrs Howe, hoping she'll step in and help me, but she gives me a single reluctant nod. I don't think she knows what to make of the accusations, so I can't hold it against her. I walk out with my head up, determined to find out who this Emma is, this so-called reliable source, and why they are out to destroy my life.

13

It's before school on Friday when the doorbell rings. I'm in my dressing gown, hair wrapped in a towel. I really want to ignore it, but how can I when it's obvious I'm in? Morning TV is blasting out of the living room so I can hear it in the kitchen. I grab the remote to turn it down and open the door.

Louise's husband Steve is standing there, shoulders hunched, looking dishevelled.

'Hey, you look terrible. Do you want to come in?' Part of me wonders if he slept rough last night. I picture all the gossiping mums at pre-school but right now I don't care, he needs help. He could be in a bad way because of me.

'Thanks.' He shivers and slopes inside, head down.

'Coffee?'

'Please.'

I remember he likes it black. 'You look half frozen.'

'I know this is the last place I should come, but I didn't know where else to go.'

'Have you eaten? Do you need a shower? You don't look like you've slept.' I fill the kettle and switch it on, then drop a piece of bread in the toaster for Tyler.

'Been walking around half the night. Tried to sleep in my car.'

'Oh no, what's happened?' I say, although I can guess. My stomach tightens.

'Louise has got it in her head that something is going on between us. Apparently, a friend of yours private messaged her on Facebook.'

'I heard about this at the meeting last night. They wouldn't listen to me, asked me to leave.'

'Shit. And I realise that me coming here is going to fuel their gossip, but I think we need to sort this out together. Who is this person?'

'All I know is her name is Emma, do you know her surname?'

'Louise didn't say. Too busy shouting at me.' He groans and wipes his palm down his face.

'Why didn't she come to me about it?' The toast pops up. I butter it and load it with banana then cut it into soldiers.

I call Tyler and put his plate on the table with a glass of milk, then carry our mugs to the coffee table.

'There's a photo as proof apparently.'

'How?' The pitch of my voice rises.

'I've no idea. She kicked me out before I could ask.' He screws his face up in pain.

Tyler runs in and stops dead when he sees Steve.

'Where's Jordan?' he trills and climbs onto his chair. He rises onto his knees, jiggling from side to side as he takes the biggest bite of banana toast.

'Not today, sorry mate,' Steve says. He looks a bit spooked. He must be thinking Tyler will blab about him being here, but Tyler knows to keep quiet about Mummy's private business.

'Sit properly now,' I remind Tyler, 'on your bottom and you can watch CBeebies.' I help him move his legs down then I prop my tablet up in front of him. He's so full of energy, especially first thing in the morning. I think of all the disapproving mums and what they'd say if they saw me letting him watch TV at the table, but most of them have got husbands and partners to help them out.

I turn to Steve and mouth 'don't worry', then get on with making Tyler's sandwich and packing his lunch bag.

'Look, why don't you stay here for a while. Have a shower, get your head down for a few hours. I can go and work in a café. I've got to take Tyler to pre-school in fifteen minutes.' I'm suddenly aware that I'm still in my dressing gown and it's starting to gape. Thankfully I have some underwear on underneath.

'Are you sure? I don't want to get you into any more trouble.'

'No one saw you come in, did they?'

He shakes his head. His eyes are red and puffy from lack of sleep and probably from crying all night. I wish he'd come to me sooner. The only way we can sort this mess out is together.

* * *

When I arrive at pre-school, I keep my head down. Part of me wonders if I'll be turned away. I'm not sure what I'd do if I am. I avoid eye contact with the other parents. It feels as if they'll know Steve is in my house just by looking at me. I probably look guilty. But Mrs Howe is as welcoming as usual, though I don't hang around to chat to her.

The café by the river isn't very full, so I order a large latte and sit in my favourite corner, the one with the high-backed sofa. Once I've switched my laptop on, I check my phone. There's still no message from Molly. I'll have to try to phone her again. If she doesn't want to speak to me, she needs to tell me straight, not ignore me.

As I'm putting my phone down to start work, it lights up. A message from Darren.

DNA test costs about £100 with one of the companies you sent me. A lot more for a legal test if you want it recognised by the court. We'd have to make an appointment with a doctor or suchlike for them to say it's been done properly. Is that what you want, other people poking their noses into our business?

He wants to get a cheap paternity test kit from the chemist. It would be the same result as with the government accredited testing labs, but this way when it comes up positive, he could deny it's a true reading.

Book the legal one then. I'll fit work around the appointment.

Seriously?

YES.

Fine. You should pay.

Why?

Because I know I'm not the dad.

I grind my teeth.

Half each is fair.

I'm only doing this to get you off my back.

You need this as much as I do.

Fine. I'll book something today. If it's negative, I want my half back.

He always has to have the last word. There are some things about him I don't miss.

I work for two solid hours once I've switched my mobile to silent, though I still keep it near me in case the pre-school rings in an emergency. It's almost midday by the time I get home.

I open the door quietly. Steve is asleep on the sofa with the TV on low. As soon as I switch it off, he wakes up.

'I'm sorry, I didn't mean to wake you.'

'You didn't really, I was only dozing.'

'How are you feeling?'

'Crap, to be honest.'

'It probably wouldn't help if I spoke to Louise, would it?'

'I doubt it. I don't think she's going to believe either of us at the moment. She needs to cool off.'

'Why don't you have a shower and I'll make us some lunch, then we can talk? Tuna mayo sandwich okay?'

'Yeah great, thanks.'

He doesn't move. Perhaps I should leave him a while longer.

'There's no hurry, okay?'

'Thanks, I've got no energy and absolutely no enthusiasm for anything.' He rests the side of his face against the sofa as though holding his head up is too much effort.

'I was just like that when my ex, Darren left. I festered on the sofa for days. I had no get up and go for anything. Such a huge part of my life was over, I couldn't come to terms with it. I thought we were a team, that we'd be together forever. But it won't be like that for you and Louise,' I say quickly, 'you'll be back together by the end of the day or week. I hope so anyway. I feel bad for what's happened.' *Even though I didn't do anything wrong*, I want to add, but don't think this fact will help at the moment.

I leave a towel out for him and go into the kitchen to make sandwiches and tea. An ache of melancholy balls in my chest. I miss feeding Darren, making him his favourite pastrami panini. He said I made the tastiest horseradish sauce on the planet. And he loved doing unexpected things for me, like filling up my car with petrol and buying my favourite ice cream on the way home from work. We were constantly leaving each other little love notes on the kitchen counter. Now he's nasty to me. How could it have gone so wrong?

By the time it's ready on the table, Steve is standing in the doorway in his clothes, his hair damp. I try not to inhale the warm fragrant air around him. I feel guilty for being attracted to him, but I'd never do anything about it.

'Louise texted me the photo of us together but didn't say which Emma she got it from,' Steve says and bites into his sandwich. 'Mmm.' He nods his approval as he chews.

'Can I see it?' I put my sandwich down.

He opens his phone and scrolls down, then slides it across the table. In the photo, we're in a bar standing at a round table chatting. There are lots of empty beer bottles in front of us, but they're what people have left there on their way to the dance floor. I'm holding half a pint of orange juice and soda, wearing a length of red tinsel around my neck like a feather boa. Steve is drinking a pint of lager. Both there for our work parties. He'd come into my office a few weeks before to upgrade the router and we got talking.

'Is that it?'

Steve nods.

'We're just chatting. Is that a crime now?'

'Apparently so.'

'Have you explained what we were doing there?'

'I said the truth: that we were both on Christmas work dos. I recognised you from an installation upgrade job I went to do in your office about a month before that. You were the one who showed me where the router was kept.'

'I remember. And she didn't believe you? She'd rather believe someone spreading gossip. Did this Emma person take the photo as well? I mean, who does that? Are they deliberately out to besmirch my name?'

'Besmirch?' He raises one eyebrow.

'Yeah, it's a good word.' I stifle a giggle.

'It is, I must try to use it... some day.' He scratches his head and we both laugh out loud. But a stab of guilt pierces my chest. I picture Louise upset at home while I'm here sharing a joke with her husband.

Why do I feel so guilty though when I've done nothing wrong? I need to find out who this Emma is. Could she be something to do with the other nasty messages and maybe even the fake missing poster?

14

After Steve's gone home, I get a text from Darren to confirm his appointment at his local clinic to have a DNA test. I sigh with relief.

It's almost time to pick Tyler up from pre-school. I wonder what reception I'll get this afternoon. I'm beginning to dread going. If it carries on, I might consider pulling him out of there for a while. I thought Louise was my friend, but someone is trying to come between us. Could Hayley have something to do with it? She seems determined to turn people against me. Why is Louise believing gossip and not speaking about it to me?

When I park my car outside pre-school there is a queue building. It's drizzling so I stay in the car, hoping no one talks to me – I can't imagine anyone's got anything nice to say.

My phone pings.

Hey you, how's it going?

At last, it's Molly. My whole body relaxes. I want to kiss my phone.

So good to hear from you. How are you?

. . .

I'm good. Ian said you called. Sorry it's taken a while to respond. I dropped
my phone; it's not been working.

I tell her I'm about to pick Tyler up and ask if eight tonight is a good time
to call her back.

I mention I'm babysitting for Katie, but it should be fine, I can still
keep an eye on the boys. She says eight works for her too.

For once I'm grinning as if I've won a prize. Molly and I are so
overdue a catchup.

I join the queue as late as I can. I hadn't noticed it was gone 3 p.m.
Looks like Louise is late too, because she is running across the car park. I
try not to look round. If she's here, then that must mean Steve is at home
looking after their youngest. Hopefully it means they've been talking
and working things out.

She slows down right behind me, but I don't feel I can speak to her
yet even though I'm itching to find out what exactly has been going on:
who is this Emma and why has she been spreading gossip about me?

Hayley comes out with her son and eyes me up and down. I cross my
arms and turn away, but she stops behind me to talk to Louise.

'Yeah, she's definitely got some explaining to do,' she says loudly.

'Just leave it, Hayley,' Louise responds. 'I need to speak to Steve properly first, see what he has to say for himself.'

'Yeah, but she should know we're on to her.' Hayley clicks her fingers.

I spin round. 'What is your problem exactly?'

'Show her,' Hayley says to Louise.

Louise opens her phone and Hayley takes it from her and holds it up
to me. Shit. It's another photo, this time of Steve leaving my flat today.

'Who took this?' I ask.

'It doesn't matter.'

'It does to me. Who is spying on me? Both of you must know.'

'Why was my husband at your flat?' Louise yells.

Several parents look round at us.

'He didn't have anywhere to go. Did he tell you he slept rough last night, in his car?' I try to keep my voice down.

'Why was he at your house?'

'You kicked him out because of me, and we needed to try and sort it out.'

'Match up their stories more like,' says Hayley, rolling her eyes.

'There is nothing going on. And there never has been. We met once at a work do and we got on well, is that a crime? The photo is of us having a drink. A year ago. That's it.'

'That's not what Emma said...' Louise says.

'Emma who? Who is this person? Show me her profile?' I point to the phone in her hand.

'I got a message from her as well.' Hayley holds her phone up and waggles it at me. 'She told me all about the kinds of services you're offering our husbands and partners... for money.' Hayley crosses her arms and grimaces at me.

A burst of anger erupts inside me. 'That is not true,' I yell. Without thinking, I shove her shoulder so hard she topples backwards into Louise. The other mums all gasp.

I turn around to see Mrs Howe standing with Tyler, watching me aghast. My face burns as she invites me into her office.

'I'm sorry, but I can't allow that sort of behaviour on pre-school premises,' she says once we're inside. Miss Lea is looking after Tyler in the adjacent room. 'I understand what a difficult time you're having at the moment, but I'm going to have to ask you not to bring Tyler in for the rest of the week. It's only two days but I hope it will give you a chance to sort out your differences with the other mums.'

My stomach drops. 'I'm so sorry, I shouldn't have let her get to me, but did you hear what Hayley was accusing me of? Someone is spreading lies about me online, calling me a whore, and it's hard to defend myself when I don't know who's doing it.'

'I'm sorry, Ellie. I've tried to support you, and I really do want to help, but my hands are tied. I have to consider the other parents and the children. Attacking another parent is not the sort of behaviour anyone wants their child to see. You do understand, don't you?'

I nod and thank her. There's nothing I can do or say to defend myself. I'm dealing with an invisible enemy, and I don't know how far they're prepared to go to bring me down.

15

Back at home, I sit Tyler in front of the television to watch *Numberblocks* on CBeebies. I kiss the top of his head and then lock myself in the bathroom. I don't want him to see me crying. I don't want to see myself crying. I can't look in the mirror. Everyone thinks I've brought this on myself, but I haven't done anything wrong. All those messages to the other mums about me, who writes stuff like that? I don't offer it about. I'm not a whore. What do they have against me? They think they know me, but they don't.

I grab a piece of toilet roll and wipe my eyes. Katie will be coming over soon, and I don't want her asking me what's wrong, otherwise she won't want to leave me.

I check on Tyler and go to make his favourite pasta – sausage, cheese and tomato. I'm not hungry but it's times like these that I wish I could open the fridge to a cold bottle of white wine. Blotting out my feelings was my go-to back then and it's so hard sometimes to face life without that option. I've managed it for four years. Ever since that fateful holiday in Jersey. As soon as I met up with Molly, I decided never to touch it again. I'm proud of myself. I'm glad I changed my behaviour, for myself and for my baby. I can stay strong, I know I can.

Katie arrives all dressed up in a glittery top and tight jeans. She looks so different with make-up on, I hardly recognise her. Joseph runs around me to hug Tyler before they run off to his bedroom.

'I won't stop otherwise the nerves will kick in and I won't want to go. It's been so long since I went on a date, I feel a bit sick; my stomach keeps churning. Is that normal?'

I shrug and smile broadly. It's sweet that she feels so nervous; she must really like him.

'You've not told me what he's called.'

'Harry. Solid dependable name, isn't it?'

'Yeah, and I'm sure he's lovely.'

'Not an axe-murderer's name, is it?'

'No, don't think so.' We both laugh.

Her face drops. 'I really don't feel well.' She holds her throat. 'I think I am going to throw up.'

I stand back and let her run to my toilet, and I try not to listen to her vomiting. Poor thing. I wonder if she'll still go. Her phone rings in her bag and I'm not sure if I should answer for her. She's only a couple of minutes late; he can't be wondering where she is already, can he? I open her bag and the name Harry is flashing up on the screen. The toilet flushes so I close it again. She comes out white-faced.

'How are you feeling?' She looks terrible and I'm not sure it's a good idea for her to go anywhere, but I can't tell her that.

'Not great. I don't want to let him down though.'

'Hey, don't be hard on yourself.'

'Oh God, now I'm late.'

'Your phone rang. I was going to answer it, but I didn't know if you'd want me to pick up.'

'I should have left earlier.'

'But you're not well.'

'You think I should cancel?'

'Two questions. Do you feel like eating?'

'Not really.' She touches her stomach.

'Do you want to kiss a man after you've been sick?'

'No, I do not. Oh God, I've blown it, haven't I?'

'If he's a good man, he'll understand.'

'I'll text him. I do feel really ill. I won't enjoy myself.' She takes her phone out and follows me into the living room where she types out a text.

'Why don't you go home and get some sleep? I'll look after Joseph.'

'Are you sure? That's such a help.'

'I was going to be looking after him anyway. My friend Molls is calling me at eight, so it's not a problem. They're busy amusing themselves so I'll bring him later, about nine? If they're tired before then, he can sleep here.'

'That would be so good, thank you. Are you sure you're okay too? You seem a bit subdued today.'

'Bit of bother at pre-school, but I'll tell you when you feel better.'

'Oh no, not again. I've been so caught up in my own drama. Why don't you tell me now?'

'I shoved one of the other mothers for winding me up and basically, I've been suspended. They've asked me not to come in with Tyler until next week.'

'What? What happened?'

I explain about the message on Facebook Messenger making out I was seeing Louise's husband and about Steve turning up at my house this morning in a right state, and how someone took a photo of him leaving.

'Is it some unspoken law never to speak to someone else's husband because it clearly means you must fancy them?'

She shakes her head.

'And now that same Emma has been sending messages to the other mums making out I'm offering sexual favours to their partners.'

'You are joking?' Katie laughs, before checking to see if I'm okay with her reaction, and I can't help joining in because it's so unbelievable.

'I'm not actually. But let's talk later; you don't look well at all.'

She nods and raises a hand in goodbye.

I feed the boys the pasta, but I only pick at the cheese strands. I've lost my appetite. My stomach is too full of worry and anxiety, there's no room for food. I guess the person who posted the fake missing poster about Tyler is the same person who is sending these nasty messages. It's probably not one of the Emmas I know. Whoever is doing this may not even be called Emma – I doubt they'd use their real name. But could it be someone I know? Maybe one of the other mums? I can't think why a stranger would target me. I need to suspect everyone, but it leaves me wondering, who can I trust?

16

I make myself a hot chocolate and curl up on the sofa under a fleece blanket. The boys are playing in Tyler's bedroom, their door ajar. I can just see them from the open living-room door.

Molly calls me on my mobile right on time.

'Hey Molls, how are you?' I ask, my voice lowered. I don't want Tyler to hear too much. 'It's been a while.'

'Yeah, I know, I'm sorry. So much stuff has been going on. How are you?'

'Same here but I'm okay. So what's happened? Are you all right?'

'Just me and Ian, we're not together any more.'

'He never said.' I sit up. I can hardly believe it.

'No, he wouldn't.'

'When did this happen?' He didn't even hint at there being anything wrong.

'About a month ago. But it's been long and drawn out.'

'Oh, I'm sorry. I wonder why he didn't say.'

'He was still living here, answering my phone, making out to everyone we were fine and happy together.'

'What went wrong?'

'Kept saying it was just a blip and we'd get back on track, but honestly Elle, he had our whole lives mapped out, I couldn't breathe. Marriage and then six kids. It's not what I wanted. He's only just moved out.'

'You two seemed like you were in it forever.' Although she deserves someone a million times better than him.

'I thought so too, but he wanted to know my every move, then I found out he'd been messaging other women, you know sex stuff, and I went ballistic.'

'I'm not surprised. Did he say why he was doing that?' I can't help being more than a little curious about exactly what Ian's been doing. I feel awful for thinking about myself when my friend is grieving a relationship, but maybe this could prove he's the one behind the malicious messages about me, and the fake police poster. If it's only him, I'd feel almost relieved. Relieved too that Molls is no longer with someone who treats her like that.

'Says it was nothing, just a bit of fun. Didn't meet up with any of these women apparently, but how do I know if that's true?'

'Where was he contacting them? WhatsApp? Facebook?'

'Both I think. I really didn't want any details. What I saw was enough. Anyway, tell me what's been going on with you?'

I fill her in on the fake poster and the messages about me to the pre-school mums, but now my mind keeps drawing me back to Ian. Could he be doing this because I wouldn't go out with him? What if he was trying to sabotage my relationship with Darren when I was with him? Darren says he finished with me because I was pregnant, and I know he didn't want kids at the time, but he was so sure the baby wasn't his, he wouldn't even give us a chance to work it out. And Darren said he loved me.

What did Ian say? *What has Darren got that I haven't?*

Is it possible Ian was spreading rumours about me then too?

'How ridiculous that they'd believe any of that rubbish,' Molly says. 'Don't they know you better than that?'

'Probably not really, I keep to myself most of the time. I don't seem to fit in. Lots of them have got expensive cars and fake teeth. I've got one good friend though, my next-door neighbour Katie. I'm babysitting for her tonight so she could go on her first date in ages. She helps me out a lot too.'

'I wish you were closer so we could go out,' Molly says in a lamenting tone.

'I know, I'm sorry. I sometimes wish I'd never moved away.'

'So why did you? You never really said. It was all so sudden and then you were expecting a baby.'

'I know, I know.'

I want to tell her, if I can get it straight in my head, but not over the phone, it's too personal. So much time has passed. I don't know where or how I'd begin. What will she think of me?

So instead I say, 'Darren is going to have a DNA test.'

'After all this time? What changed his mind?'

'His girlfriend persuaded him. He still denies Tyler is his and wants to prove me wrong, so I don't keep on at them about him paying maintenance.'

'He's winding you up trying to avoid paying a penny.' Molly laughs but I don't. 'I mean, you didn't sleep with anyone else so they can't honestly be shocked when they find out Tyler is Darren's son.'

I don't answer. I need to speak to her face to face about the night before our trip to Jersey. See what she makes of it.

'Why don't we meet up soon, go for a meal, then we can talk properly?'

I'm banking on Katie babysitting for me again if she can, but maybe she won't want to if it starts getting serious with this Harry bloke.

'Yeah, I'd like that. Shall we look at dates now?'

'I'll grab the calendar. You say when you're free.' I walk past Tyler's room and the boys are still playing nicely with his Lego.

'Next weekend, or the one after? Will you be able to get someone to have Tyler overnight or will he be coming too?'

'I'll have to see.' I stand at the wall calendar in the kitchen. 'You don't mind if he does come, do you?'

'Course not, whatever works for you, although I'm not sure he's old enough to get in if we go clubbing.' She chuckles.

I haven't been clubbing since Tyler was born. If he comes with me to Molly's, it means our night out won't be like the old days. I won't be able to completely let my hair down. But then how much fun will it be without me drinking anyway? I'm not sure I'm capable of letting myself go any more, drink or no drink.

17

At 9 p.m., I take a sleepy Joseph over to Katie's flat. I let both boys knock on the door but there's no answer. I text Katie but she doesn't reply. Did she go out after all? Maybe she felt better and decided to go. If she did, she could still be at the restaurant. I leave her a message asking her to call me but saying not to worry, Joseph can sleep over if she's staying out.

I usher the boys back into my flat and tell them to go and get their PJs on, then I linger in the hall looking out of the landing window down into the road. Someone is getting out of a taxi and chatting to the driver. In the dark, it's hard to see who it is, but I wonder if it's Katie. I wait a couple of minutes but there's no sign of anyone coming in, so I go inside and get the boys to bed.

An hour later there's a light tap on the door. I open it and Katie is standing there, holding on to the wall.

'Had a good time then?' I laugh but then stop when I see the state she's in. I put a hand out to catch her from swaying over as she comes in. 'Hey, are you okay?'

'Harry arrived unannounced on my doorstep. I couldn't turn him away, that would have been rude.' Her words are slurred.

'That's bold of him.'

'It was sweet really. He brought me flowers, came in and made me a coffee. I felt better after being sick that once, so after a shot of caffeine, I was fine. Rinsed with mouth wash and I was ready to go.' She smiles, pointing to her sparkling teeth.

I've not seen her this drunk for ages.

'And you let him into your flat?' I don't mean to dampen her enthusiasm, but I can't help the anxiety creeping up my throat. She hardly knows this man.

'I know, a bit reckless, but he was so concerned about me when I said I'd been sick, he wanted to come in and look after me. I didn't want to lie to him and make him go away.'

'He didn't try anything on, did he?'

God's sake, I sound like her mother. I wish I could stop worrying about every little thing.

She frowns. 'No, of course not. He was a perfect gentleman.'

'I'm sorry, I'm sure he was. I'm over-thinking as usual.'

'We talked about Joseph, he asked where he was, and I explained he was next door with you and his little friend Tyler. He thought us having children of similar ages was the sweetest thing, especially as the boys get on so well.'

'You talked about me?' I draw in a breath.

'Only polite chit-chat.' She flaps her hands and drops down onto the sofa. 'Asked how long we've been friends, how long we've lived here, that kind of thing.'

I'm really not comfortable with a stranger asking questions, but there's nothing I can do about that now.

'Do you have a photo of him?'

'No, he doesn't like his photo being taken. Asked me to keep my phone in my bag. Called it the scourge of society. Thinks smart phones are one of the ways the government keeps tabs on us.' She pulls the blanket over her legs.

'Blimey, is he a conspiracy theorist?' He doesn't sound like the usual sort of bloke she's interested in. Makes me wonder how they got chatting in the corner shop.

'I don't think so. But he's got a point, hasn't he? I went into the garage to pick up a loaf of bread the other day and ads for nappies came up on the big screen, I mean the exact same brand I'd just been searching price differences for on my phone. I might go back to an old phone that can't track where I am or see what I'm doing online.'

'Yeah, a lot of people feel like that and want to go off grid. It's not that easy to do.'

'I like that he's got old-fashioned values. Thinks women have forgotten what wonderful homemakers and mothers they are, trying to be like men all the time. He said men should be the ones getting their hands dirty going out to work every day.'

I frown. 'So he'd have you stuck at home with half a dozen kids, and you wouldn't mind that?'

'Nothing wrong with being a homemaker.' She scrunches her nose up at me.

'I'm not saying there is, just as long as it's your choice.'

'Bit old-school I know, but he's coming from a good place.'

'Look, the boys are in bed, so you may as well go home and get some sleep. I need to get to bed too. You look like you've had a heavy night.'

'I didn't really drink that much, but maybe it's because I've not been out for a while.' She tucks her feet under her and rests her head on the sofa arm. 'He is lovely.' She smiles to herself and in moments her eyes are shut. I gently pull the fleece up over her shoulders and get ready for bed.

I still can't believe she let this man into her flat when she hardly knows him. They were just next door, and I wasn't even aware. What if something had happened to her? My mind drifts back to the night at the Airbnb. She thinks I'm being over-cautious, but she doesn't know what can happen.

18

Darren texts on Monday morning to say he's got a date to do the DNA test at his GP surgery. I insist on going with him, so on Thursday morning after dropping Tyler off at pre-school, I drive over to Sandy, Bedfordshire. We go in together and after a quick swipe of the inside of his cheek by the senior nurse, we're out again. She says she'll send it straight off to the testing lab.

I'm paying a hundred and fifty pounds for this to be tracked and verified by professionals. If it's positive, there's no room for Darren to wriggle out of his daddy duties any longer.

'Do you want to go for a coffee before I head home?' I ask, feeling overly triumphant that I've finally managed to get him to do it. Assuming the test comes back positive, I need to keep him on side so we can discuss regular visits for Tyler to spend time with him.

'Okay,' he says, checking the calendar on his phone, 'I've got half an hour or so, as long as you promise not to bend my ear.'

'As if I'd ever do that.' We laugh together and walk down an alleyway to the shopping area and to an independent café. It's sunny and dry although a little cold in the shade, but we opt to sit outside.

'Remember that café in the Lake District that served huge slices of rainbow cake?' We shared a piece because it was so enormous.

'It was on a day like today. Piercing bright sunshine but freezing as soon as the sun went in.'

'That hotel we stayed in on Lake Windermere... It was something else, wasn't it?' I want to remind him how happy we were before I became pregnant, how it shouldn't have changed anything.

'Yeah, had a great four-poster bed.'

'Trust you.' I shove his hand playfully. Our high sex drives were perfectly matched. I wonder if he's found the same with Simone. I miss our weekends in bed. Eat, sleep, sex, repeat. Not a care in the world before Tyler came along. I thought we were heading for our forever together until he started going on about making sure I never forgot a pill because what a disaster it would be if I got pregnant. He wasn't ready to be a dad. I got that, I did, and falling pregnant was a mistake and I knew he'd be mad about it, but it was not some sort of plan to trap him. I didn't want to end the pregnancy like he did. It was our child. I couldn't destroy it just because it turned up unexpectedly. But now, four years later he's still fighting against it. I hoped he would have matured and stepped up to his responsibilities by now. If he'd have come back to me and Tyler, we could have been a proper family.

'So have you and Simone set a date yet?'

'She's looking at April next year.' He yawns.

'And you're okay with that?'

'Yeah, whatever she wants. She's already looking at dresses apparently.'

I nod and twist the spoon in the sugar. We never talked much about getting married. As I understood it, neither of us was ready. But perhaps he wasn't sure about me. With Simone, he seems certain it's what he wants. He's either very sure about her or he's trying to prove a point. Whichever it is, I admit I miss having someone special in my life.

'Have you talked about having kids?' The words fall out of my mouth. I don't want to talk about this, but I need to know.

'Not really.' He looks away.

'Don't you think you should... considering how you feel about them?' My mood lifts at the thought of this possible deal-breaker. If Simone wants children, he'll call off the wedding, won't he?

'We'll get round to it. She's more of a career girl. Don't think kids are on her agenda.'

Ouch. Direct dig.

'Have you thought what you'll do if the DNA test is positive?'

'You'd love that, wouldn't you?' His mouth lifts in a fake smile.

'I suppose I would.' I smile back, aware that I'm stepping on an emotional land mine.

'Sorry, but it ain't going to happen.' He leans backwards, stretching his arms out over the backs of the chairs either side of him.

My heart and stomach collide. I try not to let it show on my face, but my eyes feel heavy, swelling like clouds before a downpour. When we were together, he never used to be cruel to me. He was always thoughtful and considerate; we were in our own little bubble of love. But he's been angry with me about falling pregnant from the start. Why does he hate the thought of having a child with me so much?

'Don't get me wrong, Tyler's a good kid, but come on honestly, there's not one thing about him that is remotely like me.'

I stare at Darren as he twists the knife in. 'His nose is like yours and his feet, the way his little toes turn out.'

'Lots of people have toes like that. And his nose is dinky, not like mine at all.'

'It's the same Roman shape; it'll grow just like yours. And he likes football.' As if that decides it. But he's right, Tyler's nose is nothing like his. I should shut up. I sound desperate. I am desperate. I can't contemplate Tyler not being his child because the alternative is too terrifying to fathom. An intrusive image of the night at the Airbnb flickers across my mind. I shut it down. No! Darren has to be Tyler's dad.

He lifts one corner of his mouth, only half amused by my attempt to convince him. 'You're clutching at straws.' He reaches over and takes my hand in both of his. They're warm and I can feel the rough patches on his skin from tinkering on his kit car at weekends. My body tingles all over. It's so unfair that my body still longs for his.

'You should really think about who else it could be.' His smile reaches his eyes, mocking me.

'Piss off.' I yank my hand back and stand up, knocking the chair over behind me. His eyes crease up, and I know he feels sorry for me. How could he even think that? I've always been faithful. I don't know why he's insinuating otherwise. He doesn't know what happened at the Airbnb. I couldn't tell him.

I stare into space. What if the test does come back negative? How am I going to explain that? I've tried so hard to blank it out. But it would mean I'd have to face it.

19

I catch Katie the next morning before she takes Joseph to pre-school. At last, it's Friday, our final day of being banished. I ask her if she can have Tyler for the weekend so I can go and see Molls, but she says she can't because she's going to stay with her parents. I text Molly to see if she can come over to me.

It'll be a night in with a film, hope you don't mind?

She doesn't reply straight away, and I wonder if I've upset her.

I settle Tyler on the living room floor with his play street mat and lots of different cars and lorries from his bedroom toy box. I add in a small box of plastic animals and a farmer and his wife. He plays happily while I get on with some work at the dining table. My phone buzzes. It's Ian. I ignore it. Now I know he and Molly are not together, it seems even more possible that he's the one pretending to be me on Facebook, spreading lies and gossip. I wish I'd been more aware that he was so bitter about me rejecting him. I can't tell Molly, it will break her heart; even if she says it's over, she probably still has feelings for him.

My phone buzzes again. I turn the screen face down and open Facebook on my laptop. I search for his name, Ian Spedding, and a few men come up. I find one that looks like him and click on it. Sure enough it is him and it seems his privacy settings are open, but then I click again and it says account locked. The only way I can get in to see it is if I reactivate my account. I really shouldn't, but I need to see what people are saying about me, so I can work out if it's Ian or someone else I know behind the fake poster and messages.

It takes me over half an hour to go through Facebook's security questions and part of me wishes I could stop myself, but I'm an addict desperate for my next fix. Eventually I'm in and straight away I trawl through Ian's 'about' page and then his feed. I don't even know what I'm looking for. There are lots of stupid memes and pictures of people doing idiotic things like walking along the edge of cliffs and climbing tall buildings. Of course, if he's pretending to be this person called Emma, he's hardly going to shout about it. I've emailed the three Emmas I know, asking if they've said anything about me in their messages. Only two have replied and both seem quite innocent in their responses. One doesn't use social media, and the other is only on Instagram. I have to trust they are being truthful with me.

I click on Ian's friends tab and flick through all five hundred of his connections, people I'm sure he doesn't know in real life. Molly is still there and I click on her page as I've not looked it for ages. Her status is single and there's not much more information about her, but there are loads of photos in her albums, which I glance at briefly.

Ian tries calling again and I'm tempted to switch my phone off. I don't, which is fortunate, because at midday, Darren texts me.

The results are in. Do you want to meet and we'll open it together?

That was quick. I'm with Tyler, okay to bring him?

It feels lucky Tyler is with me today; he can be there when his dad is finally revealed to him. Darren will have to start building a relationship and come and visit every week. I don't know how Simone's going to take it. Will it break them up? I kind of hope not because much as I despise her, it might be good for Tyler to see his dad settled with a woman, unless she completely resents Tyler, that is.

I suppose so. Meet at usual place, 2.30 p.m.?

See you then.

I stop work and make Tyler's lunch. I'm too nervous to eat much, so I pick a few cherry tomatoes and celery sticks and dip them in a pot of hummus.

We're heading out the door when Katie opens her front door at the same time.

'I was hoping to catch you,' she says. 'Change of plan if it's not too late.'

'Oh, what's up?'

'My parents aren't well, in bed with bad colds so I won't be going to Stamford as they don't want us to catch it. So, I'm free to have Tyler for you at the weekend if you still want me to?'

'Oh yes. That would be great, I'll need to check with my friend because she was going to come over to me, but I'm sure she'll be pleased I can go to her after all.'

'I can have Tyler from this evening or in the morning, if you wanted to get away early. Whichever suits you.'

'I'll probably come home Sunday morning.'

Before I head downstairs and outside, I thank her and tell her I'll let her know asap, and that I hope her parents feel better soon.

I strap Tyler in my car then text Molly the change of plan, saying I don't mind driving to her house if she wants us to go to a club, because I won't have Tyler with me now.

Molly texts straight back.

That would be a lifesaver. Sorry I hadn't got back to you sooner. My car is making strange noises, I've had to take it to the garage again.

Great! I might drive down tonight if you're up for it?

I'd love you to come tonight! Can't wait to see you Elle. Xxx

Same. Hoping to have a bit of good news. Xxx

Can't wait to hear. xxx

* * *

Darren is waiting at our usual table with half a pint of lager. He's wearing the brown leather jacket I bought him for his birthday the first year we were together. I'm glad he didn't get rid of it. He still wears the signet ring I bought him too. Has Simone tried to make him chuck them out? I picture them arguing and him telling her they were gifts and that they mean a lot to him. I squeeze Tyler's hand.

'Say hello,' I tell him. Tyler mumbles something.

'You all right?' Darren fist-pumps Tyler, making him grin. This has to be a good sign.

A large white envelope sits on the table in front of Darren. A fizz of excitement bolts through my veins. He jumps up and offers to buy me a drink.

As Darren goes over to the bar, I lift Tyler onto the bench seat with me. He takes his colouring book and pencils out of his rucksack.

When Darren returns, he places the drinks on the table and then, immediately, his hand lands on the envelope, fingers spread out.

'Shall I open it, or do you want to?' He doesn't seem as worried as I thought he'd be. Perhaps he's had time to think about it properly, realised it's time to step up.

'I think you should; it's your DNA and I'm really grateful you did this... for us.' I cup the back of Tyler's head and gently stroke his silky hair.

'Okay, if you're sure.' He turns the envelope over and picks at the sticky tab. It's not completely flat. I expect he's had a quick look before I arrived then stuck it down again.

I take my coffee and burn my thumb on the scalding hot cup.

'Are you ready?'

I nod.

'Before I take out the result, I just want to say sorry for putting this off for so long. I suppose I was scared of the outcome, but that wasn't fair on you or this little chap.' He nods towards Tyler, smiling at him properly in a way I've not seen him do before.

'I appreciate that, thank you.'

He slips out an A4 sheet of paper and examines it. He frowns, eyes scanning back and forth as he reads what's in front of him. He looks up at me a couple of times and then the frown smooths out and Darren is smiling.

A trickle of ice enters my veins. Darren holds the piece of paper out to me, keeping his eyes fixed on mine. My hand trembles as I take it. Then he unlocks my eyes from his and smiles at Tyler.

I try to understand all the numbers and words, things like Child and Alleged Father swimming around in front of my eyes. Then I scan down to the number in bold at the bottom of the page.

My mouth falls open. I glance up. Darren is grinning at me. I stare down at the number again to see if it has changed, if my eyes are playing tricks on me. But no. It's clear in black bold letters.

Probability of paternity: 0%.

20

'Sorry it's not what you wanted, Elle.' The smile on Darren's face has gone. Tyler is sitting quietly, colouring in a racing car, not having noticed that something has changed, everything has changed.

I stare at the result again, check Tyler's name and date of birth at the top. The words and numbers are startlingly clear this time. There's no mistake. But Darren didn't just guess, he knew.

'How were you so sure he wasn't yours?' I examine his face. Any relief he's feeling isn't showing.

'Instinct I guess.' He shrugs, looks at me sideways then down at the table.

Was he hedging his bets telling me how certain he was? Just praying he was right? I know I've never been unfaithful to him, yet there it is again. That sinking feeling in my stomach. I can no longer deny it. I can't hide from the truth. A tiny part of me has known this would be the outcome, but I just couldn't face it. It had to be Darren. I needed it to be Darren. But now I know it's not, I can't run from the past any more.

'Have you been tested?'

'What do you mean?' He sits up straight. I check to see if Tyler is listening. If he is he doesn't show it.

'To see if you're firing blanks? Did you go behind my back? Is that how you were so certain you weren't his dad?' I lean across the table and tug hard at his sleeve, doing my best to save face, not show that I knew there was a possibility Tyler wasn't his.

'Calm down. No, of course not.'

'What if you are?'

But it doesn't matter, he isn't Tyler's dad. I can't escape the truth; someone else made me pregnant. Tyler looks up at me and my heart aches for him not having a daddy. I kiss his cheek.

'I'm not,' Darren says after a beat of silence. He picks up the sugar spoon and lets the white crystals fall into the pot. 'Everything's working fine down there, thanks.' He sits back, touches his belly the way women do and looks me in the eye.

'Oh. I see.' My head swims. Nausea climbs my throat. I think I'm going to be sick. I push my hand over my lips and swallow. Darren looks at me sheepishly from under his eyelashes. 'When is she due?'

'May time.'

I nod as if it's all starting to make sense, but it's not. 'How do you know her baby is yours?'

'Whoa.' He tips back in his chair at my bluntness. 'I just do. She's not like... that.' His tone is cold, as though he's talking to a stranger.

'And I am?' I whisper loudly.

'Ellie.' He speaks in an exasperated way as if I'm five years old and doing something I've been told not to do a dozen times.

'No, it's fine.' My voice is shrill. 'What an idiot I've been. Now I know what you really think of me.' I don't even realise I'm sobbing. Big fat tears are rolling down my cheeks.

'I don't, I didn't... I'm sorry, please don't cry.'

'What do you mean you didn't? It sounds like you changed your mind.' I wipe my tears on my sleeve.

'It's nothing, I don't mean anything.' He glances at the floor. 'Look, I've got to get back to work. I'm sorry, okay?' He touches the top of my bowed head.

The squeak of the pub door tells me he's gone.

On the way back to our flat, I explain to Tyler that I'm going away for the weekend to see Molly, and he'll be staying with Katie and Joseph.

Later, at home, I pack my sports bag with a change of casual clothes, a dress and a pair of heels. I glance in the mirror and try to tidy up my red eyes. I text Katie to say I'll be round in a few minutes and can she feed Tyler? Then I text Molly to update her on my travel plans.

When I'm ready to leave, Tyler is waiting for me by the front door, his backpack on and his favourite teddy in his arms. Seeing him there, my heart cracks in two. I'm not sure I can go. His face is so sad. I don't know how much of my conversation with Darren he understood, but I've let him down. I thought I was bringing his daddy back to him once and for all. But I have to face the truth – Darren is not his daddy.

And now I've got to work out who is.

21

Katie is waiting for us, her door open. Joseph runs out and hugs Tyler. This goes a long way to me feeling better about leaving him.

I go inside for a few minutes and tell Katie what I just learned, the test result and how gutted I am.

'I'm so sorry.' A frown crosses her brow for a nanosecond and I think she's about to ask me who I think the dad is. But she doesn't and I'm grateful because I don't have an answer.

'Are you sure you're okay having Tyler for two nights?' I hand her his toothbrush and toothpaste in a clear bag.

'Of course I am. I'm hoping you'll do the same for me sometime.' She raises an eyebrow, and I can't help smiling. At least her love life is going well.

'You'll call me if he asks for me or if there's any problem, won't you? Even a little cough or temperature?'

'I will. I promise.'

'I don't mind you calling me anytime. If he wants to speak to me or say goodnight, please let him.'

'I will, now stop worrying.'

'Thank you.' We both lean in for a hug.

'Try and enjoy yourself, okay?' She understands how it is, why I can't help checking every little thing. We've talked about how hard being a single parent can be, so many times. How we try to do the job of both parents and can't help feeling double the weight of responsibility too. It takes extra effort to make sure our children are as happy and emotionally comfortable as possible. The guilt is constant, trying to make up for their absent dads. Tyler has never known what it's like to have a daddy around, but Joseph does; it must be harder for him when his dad turns up without warning then leaves again.

For weeks Tyler would cry every time I left him at pre-school before he settled in. He's so used to it just being the two of us. This weekend without me will be a big test for both of us.

I drive for the next hour, stopping and starting in the rush-hour traffic, blasting some favourite tunes out of the car radio. Halfway to Bristol, at 6.30 p.m., I pull into the services to grab a coffee and go to the loo. It's busy – full of families and office workers in smart suits talking into their earpieces, looking at first glance as if they're talking to themselves. Almost everyone seems to be with someone or going somewhere.

I text Molly to update her on my journey and expected time of arrival, taking into account the heavy traffic ahead. She texts straight back asking if I've eaten and saying that she can't wait to see me. It's been a while since we last saw each other and I feel strangely nervous. I'm hoping she'll listen to my story without judging me.

I drive on for another hour, and think about everything that's happened today. How deluded I've been to assume Darren was Tyler's dad. What do I do now? Sometimes I feel like I'm the only person on the planet with a fatherless child. What sort of person can't remember how they got pregnant for God's sake? But I can't avoid it any longer. I've been dreading and denying this day in equal measure. I need to work out who his dad is, for Tyler's sake. Part of me wishes I could speed down the fast lane with the window open, burn off this rage building inside me, but I can't do things like that any more, I have Tyler to think about now.

I call Katie to see how Tyler is without me, and it's a relief to hear him playing in the background.

'He's absolutely fine,' she says. I take the opportunity to confide in her about the night at the Airbnb and ask her if she thinks I should go back there.

'If it helps you piece together what happened, then it's probably a good idea. You might recall something important.'

It's gone 8 p.m. when I pull into Molly's road on the outskirts of Bristol. I park outside her block of flats, a building with unflattering brown boxy bay windows. The road is busy with a parade of small shops opposite and lots of teenagers in groups hanging around an off licence.

I grab my sports bag from the passenger seat and climb out. Almost immediately, a group of hooded youths bump into me, pushing past on the narrow pavement, making whistling and grunting noises. I try to flatten myself against the side of my car, terrified they're going to hurt me. They laugh and look round at me with catcalls as they strut away. I'm shaking and trying to catch my breath.

Molly bursts out of the main door to the flats. 'Are you okay?' she calls as she rushes towards me, arms open. I fall into them, crying. That was the last straw to the most stressful day. We stand there for a few minutes until I pull away.

'What happened?'

'Some teenagers were jostling and catcalling me. I've had such a bad day, but it's so good to see you.'

'You too, although I hate seeing you like this. Come on, let's go in.'

I pick my bag up and follow her into the brightly lit hallway. We have to walk up two flights of stairs because the lift is out of order – has been for weeks apparently.

Molly's studio flat is small but tidy. There's a bedroom area off a good-sized living room, with a kitchen along one wall and a bathroom a step or two opposite the front door.

'You can have the bed or the sofa bed, it's up to you.'

'Sofa bed will be fine, thank you.'

'Leave your bag here or in the bedroom area. Can I get you a drink?'

'I'd love a cup of tea please.'

'You're still off the booze?' She switches the kettle on.

I nod.

'I'm impressed. I must admit when you said you were going to stop, I thought you'd last a week, a month at most.'

'Really? You never said.'

'Don't you remember what you were like?' She laughs.

'I know, I drank too much.'

'Erm, just a bit.' She drops the teabags in and fills up two mugs with boiling water.

'It bothers me that I don't remember a lot from back then.' I pass her the milk from the fridge.

'That's hardly surprising.'

'Did I ever black out?'

'You'd fall asleep. I'd have to wake you up to get you home, tuck you up in bed and you'd have the mother of all hangovers in the morning.'

'Thank you for doing that. Looking out for me. I was so stupid.'

'That's all right, that's what friends do. So how long's it been now?' She squashes the teabags against the side of the mugs.

'Four years. Since we went to Jersey together.' I wince at the memory.

'Oh yes, I remember. I thought you were having me on. Was a bit lonely drinking on my own.' She pushes her bottom lip out. 'But honestly, good for you, it's seriously impressive.'

I take the mug from her and we sit in her living area where we order a large meat feast pizza, cheesy garlic bread and a side of cookies. I check my phone. No messages from Katie.

'Do you want to go out later? There's a new club along the high street.' Molly finishes her tea. She always gulps it straight down.

I shake my head. 'I'm sorry, I feel exhausted. Could we go tomorrow?'

'Course. You said you've had a bad day; do you want to talk about it?'

'Can I tell you later? I just need to clear my head, chill for a bit first.'

'Of course. Let's find a film to watch.'

We watch *Bridget Jones's Baby* and do our usual thing of making silly comments all the way through, especially as we know it so well. The doorbell rings not long into the film and Molly jumps up to collect the food, filling the whole studio flat with the aroma of pizza and warm cheesy garlic bread. It fills my nostrils as though it's the best smell I've ever inhaled. I didn't realise how hungry I was.

'Is it really important for Bridget to know who the baby's dad is?' Molly asks when it cuts to the advert break. 'I mean from a paying maintenance angle, of course it is, but biologically, is it essential or is it more about your kid knowing their heritage?'

'I think it is, for the child and mother for both of those reasons. The father needs to take some responsibility bringing up the baby. It's hard work.' Bridget's dilemma feels horribly familiar. I wish we'd picked a different film.

'But loads of people don't know their father. People are adopted every day and never know who either parent is.'

'That's sad though, isn't it? And how about the ones like me who didn't plan on getting pregnant? What then?'

I look away.

Molly pauses the TV. 'Are you okay? Do you want to talk about it?'

I tell her about the DNA test result, the missing poster of Tyler and the nasty messages online, even about all the trouble at pre-school, but I hold back mentioning the night at the Airbnb.

'If Darren's not the dad, then who is?'

I smile inwardly. This is why I've taken so long to tell her. There's no going around the houses with Molly, she says exactly what she's thinking.

'I need your help because... I don't know.'

Her eyebrows shoot up. 'Oh, okay. Is that why you asked about blacking out? Because you can't remember who the father is?'

'Maybe? I don't know. I didn't sleep with anyone else. At least, I don't remember it. I have no idea who the father could be.'

Molly frowns.

'Did I always come home with you at the end of the night?'

'Not always. Sometimes you went off with whichever guy you'd been chatting to. I didn't always see who.'

I groan. 'They weren't bad dreams then. Waking up in the morning not knowing where I was.' My hot face fills with shame that I could have behaved so recklessly.

'Hey look, you went home with someone, and had sex with them. It's not a crime. I did that too, once or twice.' She gently rubs my arm. 'And I'm pretty sure that was before you met Darren.'

'I wasn't unfaithful to him.'

'But there's only one way of getting pregnant that I know of, and it's not from a toilet seat.' She's trying to cheer me up, and I can't help lifting a smile at her.

'I know. I keep thinking I must have got drunk and slept with someone that night at the Airbnb on the way to Jersey. Trouble is I can't remember anything.'

'Why that night?'

'Because I had too much to drink and must have blacked out. Nine months later, Tyler was born. Maybe I'm lying to myself and I've blocked it out, but I honestly can't remember being with anyone.' My eyes are sore, on the verge of tears. 'I've no idea what I'll say to Tyler when he asks me who his daddy is. How will I ever find out?'

'What do you mean? What happened at the Airbnb?'

'I had a couple of cocktails with a few guests in the garden. It was a gorgeous warm evening, the patio was decorated with fairy lights. More people arrived so it turned into a bit of a party. I stayed out there for a few hours, but I didn't think I was that drunk. I felt really tired though, so went to bed fairly early.' I stare down at my trembling hands.

'And what happened after that? Was someone with you?' Molly touches my arm. I shake my head once.

'I went up to my room alone, but I woke up in the night, and it was so weird.' I swallow hard, unable to say it. My breathing quickens. I've never told this to anyone.

'It's okay, take it slowly.' She gently rubs my back. 'Try and tell me what was weird.'

'There... there was a man watching me. He was standing at the end of the bed wearing a clown mask.' I'm shaking just picturing it.

'What?' Molly grabs my arm, eyes wide.

'I thought I was having a nightmare, but then I heard myself screaming. I've no idea how long he'd been there.' I break down in Molly's arms.

'My God, Ellie. How did he get in?'

'I don't know. I'm certain I locked the door, but what if I let him in?'

'What did you do?'

'I screamed and the landlord came to help me. He got the man out and brought me a warm drink to calm me down. He was so kind to me. I don't remember much else from that evening.'

Molly frowns and shifts to the edge of the sofa so she's facing me. 'Are you saying you think you slept with this masked man, and he could be Tyler's dad?'

I nod, tears falling from my eyes.

22

Molly leans forward and hugs me. 'I wish you'd told me this at the time. I could have helped you try to find out his name.'

I bury my head in her shoulder. All the dreams about a clown I've been trying so hard to suppress come from that night. From not wanting to admit to myself that I'd drunk a lot more than I thought, and not remembered being with this man.

'Did you recognise him from the party, the clothes he was wearing or his hair?'

'I'm not certain but I think he was the guy I'd been chatting to in the garden, who kept topping up my glass. I think I remember someone helping me upstairs; I was swaying all over the place. Maybe it was him. What if I was so drunk, I invited him in? Or perhaps he left and broke into my room later. If only I could remember.'

'Oh my God, Ellie.' Molly sits back, worry creasing her face.

I swallow back my shame. 'All this time I've denied to myself that I'd drunk too much, slept with someone then blacked out.' I've pushed away the niggling doubt to the back of my mind that I behaved like that, not wanting to admit that I cheated on Darren.

'I'm sorry I didn't give you a chance to explain. I was so mad at you.'

And she was. Molly gave me the silent treatment for the rest of the journey.

'No wonder you stopped drinking so suddenly. I'm sorry I wasn't more supportive.'

The tears come again, just from remembering how ashamed and strange I felt waking up in that room. The draft of cold air from the sash window that wouldn't shut, the sour beer smell of the man's breath and the grainy texture of the cotton sheets on my skin.

'I'm so sorry, Ellie. I'm such an elephant sometimes, stomping all over the situation, not reading the room.'

'It's not your fault. You had every right to be annoyed.' Although I secretly wish she hadn't been, because then I might have plucked up the courage to tell her.

'But I ruined the holiday. We didn't really get on like we normally do after that.' She's right, we bickered about everything, what time we were going to bed and when to go down to breakfast. My head was still in such a muddled daze. I tried to fit in with whatever she wanted to do, but nothing I did or said was right.

'You said you'd got drunk and overslept so I thought you didn't care about meeting me at the ferry on time.'

I remember deciding it was easier to tell her that. I didn't want her asking me questions because I was still trying to process what I thought happened.

'It's both our faults.' I wipe the tears away with my fingers. The truth is, our friendship changed that day. And afterwards, when I moved to Huntingdon, it felt like I was running away from Molly. Of course, I did it for Darren. He moved there for work and I wanted to be nearer him, convinced that the baby was his and that one day he'd come to accept it. But then he met Simone.

'Can you remember anything else from that night?'

'After the landlord came in and pushed the other man out, I heard them arguing. The party was still going on in the next room, music thumping through the wall. I'd taken my earplugs out, although I can't remember doing that. If the masked man broke in, I didn't hear him because I'm guessing I'd blacked out.'

'That doesn't sound right at all. Is there something you're not telling me?'

I stare down at my legs. 'I woke up in a sticky sweat. I think... I think he took advantage of me.' Fresh tears are running down my face.

'Shit, Ellie. You didn't give your consent?' Molly's face is scrunched up.

'How could I?' I cry.

She reaches over and pulls me to her.

'What did the landlord do? Did he call the police?'

'He tried to calm me down, said there was no need to call them. He thought the man was just one of the partygoers who'd gone in the wrong door thinking it was the bathroom. I tried to explain that the door was locked but he told me he didn't see how the man could have broken in, because there was no damage. He was really patient with me and offered me a drink, a hot chocolate to calm my nerves. I remember drinking it and him saying he'd stay a while if I wanted him to. I don't remember saying yes exactly but he was being so kind and I felt safe.'

'Bit weird, isn't it?' Molly folds her arms.

'Not really. He was just this older guy, looking out for me. I was really upset.'

'Elle, did he touch you?'

'God no, nothing like that. It was all above board. When I woke up, he was still there, lying on the bed on top of the duvet fully clothed next to me, guarding me all night.'

'Oh my God, you're joking?' Molly covers her mouth with her hand.

'It seems a bit silly now, but he was watching breakfast TV. He even had his shoes on.'

'What did he say?'

'Something like, *morning, do you want a cup of tea?* It was so casual, like he should still be there, and I shouldn't think twice about it.'

'Jesus. I don't like the sound of that. He'd been watching you sleeping the whole night?'

'I suppose so. But I felt safe.' I frown. He was a nice guy, got me a cup of tea and toast and made sure the bathroom was free so I could have a shower. It had been such a humid evening. The damn window was jammed and wouldn't open or shut completely, so cold air was blowing through the gap the next morning.

'I should have found out what had happened, why you were so late.'

'I was a bit shell-shocked seeing him there at first, but grateful too that he kept the masked man away.'

'What did you say to him?'

'I asked him what he was doing there. He said I asked him to make sure that bloke didn't come back, make sure I was safe. I should have asked him so many more questions, but I felt vulnerable lying there next to a stranger.' I stop speaking. Now that I'm hearing it all come out of my mouth, I can see how odd it looks but he wouldn't have been there if I hadn't asked him to stay.

'It does sound like the landlord was trying his best to help you. He wouldn't have stuck around if he was the one who'd attacked you.'

'That's what I thought. He was a real gentleman.'

'Tell me again how much you'd had to drink?'

'Only two, maybe three cocktails. I hadn't wanted to get drunk because I was getting up early to meet you for the ferry. I thought the cocktails must have been stronger than I realised.'

'And you said you think the man in the clown mask could have been the same person who made your drinks?'

'I think so, the Hawaiian shirt he was wearing was partly covered by a jacket when he came into my room. But the more I think about it, the more I'm convinced it was the same shirt and the same man.'

'And presumably he hadn't been wearing the mask when you were drinking with him in the garden?'

'No, but other people were messing about wearing different masks.'

Molly bites her lip. 'Did you have any physical signs of being attacked?'

'Nothing certain. Just a feeling that things weren't quite right.'

'And you don't remember anything else from that night?'

'Only what I've told you. It's a complete blank.'

Molly leans back, her face serious. 'I think the man who made your cocktails drugged you, then once you were out of it, it's possible he raped you.'

I blink at her. Then my stomach clenches as though I'm going to throw up. Molly has spoken my darkest thought. The one I've packed away to the back of my head, never to be uttered aloud.

'It has to be. It's the only thing that explains it.'

'You really think that's what happened to me?' I hug the cushion in my lap. Molly puts her arms around me and we stay there for a while in silence. I break away first and finish my drink. I shut my eyes as exhaustion hits me in a huge wave.

'Have you thought about how you're going to find out who this man is?'

'I think I should go back to the Airbnb, see if I can track the landlord down. He's the one who saw this man, who can hopefully find him for me.'

'Do you want me to come with you?'

'I was hoping you'd say that.'

I hug her.

'You want to go in the morning, don't you?'

'Could we?'

'Yeah, of course.'

'Shall we have a quick look online first?'

Molly refills our drinks while I look up the screenshots on my phone of the original advert and confirmation email I found at home.

I show Molly and she opens her laptop and types the postcode into Google Earth. The house is quite near to Southampton town centre. A familiar-looking building comes into focus as she zooms in. The old-fashioned style with the black and white tiled pathway is imprinted on my brain.

'That's the one. I'd like to go down there and look around,' I say.

'Fine, let's get an early night and we'll go in the morning.'

23

We're up at 8 a.m. and by 9 a.m. we're showered and have made sandwiches and a flask of tea. We decide to take turns driving. It will take approximately two hours from Bristol to Southampton, depending on traffic. Molly drives first so I can have a chat to Tyler, see how he is after his first night without me.

'He was such a good boy,' Katie tells me on FaceTime as she walks into the living room. 'He got up in the night for a wee, didn't you, Tyler?' He nods and bites into a piece of toast and Marmite.

I tell Katie what our plans are. I wonder if Tyler will be okay, but I have to make the most of my visit, find out as much as I can on my search to find out who his dad is, and who attacked me.

'I'm taking the kids to the play park this afternoon, if that's okay with you? I'm meeting a couple of the other mums.'

'That's fine. Hope you have a good day. I'll speak to you later. Bye-bye little pickle,' I call out to Tyler and he waves and grins, his mouth full of half-chewed toast and Marmite, which he refuses to eat at home.

'You too. Say bye, Mummy.'

By 10.15 a.m. we're over halfway there and we've eaten our lunch already. I'm dying for a strong cup of coffee. The tea in the flask is not hot any more, but warm. It's milkier than I usually like it and sickly because Molly had to add sugar.

As soon as we pull onto the road I remember in Southampton, I recognise the houses – the style of them, at least. It takes a while to slowly drive up and down the long road, but eventually I spot the house I stayed at. The black and white chequered path and three worn steps up to the front door made it stand out. We park up and walk along the pavement until we reach it, number 149.

From what I can remember, it doesn't look like it's changed much, except there's a Toyota Yaris parked on the drive where the bins used to be.

There's a crack in the white tile by the gate. I remember thinking at the time it was a shame it hadn't been fixed.

I stand in front a few moments longer, taking in the beauty of the ordinary sunny autumn morning, the seagulls wheeling around the sea front across the esplanade.

I feel light-headed, more nervous than I thought I'd be. Molly must sense it because she squeezes my hand. We glance at each other then walk up the steps and knock on the door. While we're waiting for an answer, I become certain this is the right place. I can remember myself hurrying out of the front door and down these steps.

A woman I don't recognise answers the door. Her dark hair is short and sticking up on one side as if she's just woken up. Her mobile is tucked under her chin, and on her hip she's holding a crying baby in a nappy and vest.

The woman frowns and turns away. 'Call you back.' She has a strong east European accent, the letter L sounding long. She slips the mobile in her jeans back pocket. 'What do you want?'

'Do you still rent out rooms?' I ask, gripping my handbag tighter.

'What?' She frowns.

'I... I stayed here, about four years ago.'

'You can't have.' She frowns and jogs the grizzling baby up and down, its fingers in its mouth.

'It was advertised on Airbnb.'

'You've got the wrong house.' She starts to shut the door and I surprise myself by reaching out to stop her.

'There was a man here. Philippe? Short blond hair, French accent.'

She shakes her head. 'That's not possible. This is my house.'

'It was definitely here,' I say more firmly. 'There was a party, and the neighbours were banging on the wall.' I step back and stare up at the sash window on the first floor. It was advertised as a room with a view of the sea. Seagulls are screeching loudly overhead, just like they were when I woke up that day. I thought they were trapped in my head. I tried to open the window, but it was jammed, cold air blowing through the gap onto my sweaty skin.

Dizziness comes over me. I've not remembered that so vividly before. I look at the ground and blink a few times until it passes. Molly puts a hand on my arm.

The woman tilts her head at me. 'Are you done?'

I tap on my phone and hold it up to show her the Airbnb advert but she doesn't even look and instead shuts the door. I'm taken aback by the force of it. I go to ring the bell again, but Molly pulls my hand down and steers me back along the path.

'Let her cool down, we'll come back later.'

I nod, my thoughts all over the place, as I try to work out how I could have stayed here when she's saying she never rented out a room. I let Molly lead me back to the road. We cross over and walk towards the beach front. A few shops and cafés are open. We find somewhere, have a pot of tea and a full English.

'If the owner doesn't think it's her house, how can it be?' But I can't help shuddering every time I look at the photo of the modern style double bed with a chunky dark wood slatted headboard. The other photos are of a low three-drawer chest of drawers with a TV on top, and a chair and small table with a lamp near the sash window.

Private room in a family home hosted by Philippe. Up to two guests, one bedroom, one double bed.

Underneath, my screen shot has captured the whole advert.

Great for remote work. Fast Wi-Fi plus dedicated space in a private room. Philippe is a Superhost. Superhosts are experienced, highly rated hosts who are committed to providing great stays for their guests. Philippe has sixty-seven reviews for other places. £53 night. 14-15 Aug.

'Where you'll be' is the heading above the map on my second screen shot, which has a small red house symbol to show the general location of the property within a pink circled area with the note: 'Exact location provided after booking', and a calendar with dates I selected.

'You need to try and show the woman this again. If she looks properly, hopefully she'll recognise it. It should be enough to persuade her you're not making this up.'

'I'm confident it's the right place. I really need to go in there, have a good look around to make sure.'

'Finish up here and we'll try her again. If she sees how serious you are, that you have the advert from the Airbnb website, I reckon she'll let you in.'

We pay the waitress and leave a tip on the table. My head is thumping. I just want to be believed. Something bad happened to me in that house, and I need to find out what and who's behind it.

24

This time Molly rings the bell and stands in front, protecting me. The woman comes to the door again, still holding the baby.

'What is it now?' she says, and I feel like turning away.

Molly explains everything to her again in quiet tones, this time including my rape suspicions.

I stand next to Molly so the woman can see me. She glances at me, and her face softens. My eyes are drawn past her and the baby's chubby arm, to the kitchen at the end of the long hallway. The cocktails must have been prepared in there. I shudder and take a step back and point up. 'Did you ever get the window fixed?'

'How'd you know about that?' The woman's eyes narrow as she wrestles the grizzling baby to her other side. I show her the screen shots of my Airbnb bedroom on my phone, and think I detect a flicker of recognition in her expression.

'This is your room, isn't it?' I narrow my eyes at her.

She doesn't answer but takes a step back to consider us, looking us up and down, all while jogging the baby on her hip. It cries out and she kisses its hot red cheeks.

'I think a man attacked me. We've come a long way because I need to find out who he is. I have a child too. Please, could we come in?' I say quietly.

She still looks unsure but she steps aside and leads us into the front room, a large square space with a corner sofa and toys strewn across the floor and quilted play mat.

'Were you living here four years ago?' I ask.

'Yes, we've been in this house five years.'

'And when did you let out a room on Airbnb?'

'We didn't.' She picks up a half-finished bottle of milk from the table and offers it to the baby who takes it into its mouth and sucks hard. Molly and I look at each other.

I gaze around the room and at the mantlepiece where there's a recent photo of this woman with a man and the same baby. I step closer and peer at it, but I don't recognise her husband. It is not Philippe.

I show her the screenshot again of her bedroom, then swipe through all the photos: the bedroom and bathroom. The tiles are the same geometric style pattern I remember. There are no photos of the front of the house or the outside space, but it does mention use of the kitchen and lighted patio area is included in the price.

'This can't be our house. We've never rented out a room.'

I look at her squarely to consider if she could be lying. If she recognised the bed or furniture, she'd say, wouldn't she?

'But this is the room I remember staying in' – I point at the picture – 'with the window that wouldn't shut. There was a host here called Philippe.'

'That's not possible.' She shakes her head even though she clearly knows about the window. It could be a coincidence. Lots of old sash windows must be broken. But she gives no explanation.

'Please, can I just go upstairs and look at the room?'

She sighs. The baby is quiet now, except for the sound of it sucking on the milk. Tears are caught in its eyelashes.

'Okay, but I'll come up with you.'

We follow her upstairs, the baby still attached to her hip. The carpet and wallpaper are different to the photo, and I worry that my memory is letting me down and she's right, I've got the wrong house. But I keep coming back to the broken tile on the path and the house number in the email, and they assure me I haven't.

We stand on the landing. There are four rooms. My legs weaken and waver. I slip my arm through Molly's to steady myself. We exchange a glance and she holds me tighter. I can't face the room I stayed in straight away, so I go into the largest room, which was the one where the party was being held. There's a double bed, a wardrobe, dressing table and a sofa in the bay window which overlooks the back garden. I look down at the lawn and there's still a string of lights in the trees and hedge. My mind flashes back to them lit up, twinkling in the half-light as it got dark, while music pumped out of two tall speakers.

When I arrived, Philippe was dressed in faded jeans and a beige short-sleeved linen shirt. He took me out to the patio area where the party was warming up, already full of guests. Then he showed me to my room, leaving me with the key. He told me to come down when I was ready, for a cocktail. I left my bag, small suitcase and jacket in the room, freshened up and joined the other guests. A man with dark hair wearing a Hawaiian shirt made me a brightly coloured Aperol Spritz cocktail in a balloon glass with a slice of orange. After a while, he refilled my glass once, twice, maybe three times, and it wasn't long before I felt a little tipsy. I told everyone I was chatting to that I needed to get up early to catch the ferry, so I said goodnight. Did the dark-haired man help me or follow me upstairs? I can't remember much of what he said to me before that. The party continued throughout the house and was in full swing in the bedroom next door too. I'm sure I locked my door before going to bed, but by then I was swaying all over the place. I remember bumping into the wall and someone laughing. Was that me or the dark-haired man? I remember saying I didn't want someone wandering in by mistake. Or did I say that to him jokingly before he pushed his way in?

That was the last alcoholic drink I ever drank. I've blamed myself all this time for getting drunk, losing control, and possibly letting a man take advantage of me. At the time, I even thought that the drink must have had twice the amount of alcohol in it because I felt so out of it. I practically fell into bed.

The woman sits on the sofa next to a Moses basket on a stand. She rocks her child in her arms as it drifts off to sleep. I'm hesitant walking into the next room. My room.

There are bare floorboards where there was carpet and a different double bed with a wrought iron frame in the middle of the room. Bedside tables are on either side but apart from that the room is bare. My breathing quickens as I picture myself waking up that day wearing only a T-shirt and drenched in sweat. The TV that was on a chest of drawers opposite the bed has gone, but it was there, switched on and Philippe was on the duvet watching the breakfast programme. My clothes were strewn across the floor. I got up, aching all over, barely able to walk to the bathroom. Hours had gone by that I couldn't recall. I remember the key was in the door which was slightly open.

I check now and there it is, the same ornate key on a short string. I turn it as if I'm locking the door and it clicks, but no bolt shoots out, no mechanism to secure it shut. I bend to inspect it closer, and it does click but the surface of the metal is bumpy where it's been hacked off. I draw in a breath. Something bad happened to me here. Whatever it was, I have no recollection of it, but my body remembers because fear is carving out my insides.

'What is it?' Molly whispers, trying not to make too much noise as she walks on the bare floorboards. 'Is this the room?'

I nod once, unable to speak. Hot tears spill from my eyes. I can't stop myself shaking.

'The lock,' I manage to say in disbelief.

'What do you mean?' Molly puts her arm around me as I turn away, sobbing.

'It's broken.'

'What are you saying?'

I swallow hard and muster all my strength to speak. 'It was never possible to lock this door. I was never safe.'

25

'What do you mean, Elle?' Molly puts her arm around me, and I sob into her shoulder.

'Can I help you?' The woman appears on the landing without the baby, looking in at us.

'This door lock, has it always been like this?' Molly asks while I wipe my tears on my cuff.

'Like what?'

'Broken. Has it ever locked?'

'I don't know, we've never needed to lock it.'

'I was in this room. I stayed here. And I think someone attacked me,' I tell her.

'That's not possible. How can it be? This is our family home. We don't know you.' She looks from Molly to me, probably wondering if we're con artists. 'I think you should leave.' She ushers us to the top of the stairs.

'Wait, please. If I can tell you the date, would you be able to tell me if you were here then?'

'Possibly, but four years ago? Like I said, we were living here. I don't know what else I can tell you.' She follows us downstairs.

My gut clenches. This can't be the end. I was in that room. Either she's lying or she wasn't here.

'Do you keep a diary on your phone?' I ask her halfway down the stairs.

'I've probably had a new upgrade since then.' She sighs.

'How about on your computer?'

'I don't suppose so. I archive old emails going back a few years, that's about it.'

'How about keeping photos in a cloud on your phone, a kind of image diary?'

'I have that, why?'

'Can you remember the exact date?' Molly asks me.

The date is embedded in my brain. 'Fifteenth August. I still have a screen shot of the ferry ticket on my phone.'

'Of course you do.' Molly smiles.

'I took it in case I lost the ticket. I always screen shot things.'

When we reach the bottom of the stairs, I take my phone out and scroll. I already checked I still had the image before we left Molly's house. I found photos of our holiday in Jersey too. I flash the screen up to Molly, then hold it up for the woman to see.

'Fifteenth August 2018. Were you here on that date?'

The woman looks at me blankly. Then her gaze shifts from side to side as though that date has triggered something. She pulls her phone out from her back pocket and opens the app with all her photos. She flicks through hundreds of images, and in moments she's reached 2018.

'We were in Florida then, for six weeks. Toured all the studios and the theme parks.' She holds up a photo of her and her husband standing with a line of Storm Troopers. 'We'd only moved in here about eight months before that. My granny died and left me a bit of money. I always wanted to go to Florida as a kid and she wished she could afford to take me, so that's where we went, in her memory.' She looks down at the baby's coat on the newel post, and I wonder if she's planning to take her son there when he's old enough.

'So you weren't here at all for those six weeks.' I can't square that in my brain. No one was here, yet I was here and a whole bunch of people having a party. Someone called Philippe was acting like he owned the place and clearly, he didn't.

It doesn't make sense.

As we turn to leave, there's a light scratching sound at the back door.

'What's that?' I spin round.

'It's okay, it's only Rufus our little terrier.'

'Was he here four years ago?' I ask her.

'He's only one and a half. We had two boxers back then. They were our first babies. Rocco died last year and Stanley the year before that.'

'I'm so sorry,' Molly and I say at the same time.

'Thank you. Actually, I'd forgotten about that: we almost didn't go on holiday because of the dogs. They were getting so old, struggling with their joints. I didn't want to leave them. I was terrified they'd die while we were away. I couldn't bear the thought.'

I'm only half listening, still wondering if my memory has betrayed me or if I dreamt about this house. Is that possible? Did I watch some creepy movie and it's seeped into my brain and somehow melded with reality? I've been certain about this for so long, I'd have put my life on it being true. Could there be some of my DNA in that room to prove I was here? But the room has been changed so much. And it's been four years. There's no carpet any more and all the furniture is different. The walls were painted sage green then. Maybe there's a trace under the new wallpaper. But if the owners were away on holiday, I *could* have been here. How was Philippe here without their knowledge? Who is he?

The woman opens the front door.

'Thank you for letting me have a look around. I really appreciate it. You must think I'm a bit mad.'

'No honestly, it's fine.'

I step outside but Molly hesitates. She does this thing of tapping her fingers on her chin when she's thinking hard about something.

'So did you find a good kennels for your elderly dogs, so you could go on this big holiday?' she asks.

'No, we didn't. We looked at loads, but I couldn't bear the thought of them being locked up in a stable when they were so used to their home comforts.'

'So what did you do?' I ask.

'A friend came up with a much better solution. I've no idea why I didn't think of it myself. It really gave us peace of mind. There's no way we could have gone to Florida otherwise.'

'That must have been a relief. Can I ask what it was?'

'We hired a house sitter.'

26

I twist round and blink at Molly in disbelief.

'A house sitter was living here while you were away?'

'Yes, that's right. We went to an agency that specialises in house and dog sitting. It's such a good idea. It means the dog can stay with their home comforts. We wrote a huge manual with all their routines in detail, feeding times, walking times, medication. It was an enormous weight off our minds to know someone would be here with them.'

'And who was the person they sent?'

'He was quite a young man. I must admit we were expecting someone older, a retired couple maybe, but the agency said he was one of their most reliable house sitters. And he adored dogs.'

I don't remember seeing any dogs.

'And everything was in order when you came back?' I ask.

'Yes, no problems. Dogs were happy. Place was spotless, even the utility area. So you see you can't have stayed here, because he wasn't allowed to have anyone in.'

'Did you check up on him?'

'Why would we need to do that? He had instructions to contact the agency if one of the dogs became unwell and they would contact us immediately. Both dogs were fine, thankfully.'

'But you trusted him to be here alone for six weeks?'

'That's right. That's what he was paid for. They sign a contract, you know.'

I glance at Molly. Her eyes are wide. At last, we're getting somewhere.

'Are you trying to suggest he went against the rules and let you stay here while we were away?'

'I don't know how else to explain it.'

'You think he came here to look after our dogs and house, then advertised our spare room on Airbnb?'

'I think it's possible.'

'Why would he do that?'

'To make money. He must have held a party here that weekend, maybe the following weekend too.'

'I don't think so. I'd have known if lots of people had been in my house.'

'How would you? You said yourself you weren't checking up on him and the place was spotless when you got back. He probably paid people to clean it up.'

'So how many people are you suggesting stayed here?' Her voice has risen. She crosses her arms.

'I don't know but there were a lot of people when I arrived. Maybe they crashed out wherever they found a space. You've got four bedrooms and an attic room I think?'

'Yes, but that doesn't mean anything. I didn't find one thing out of place.'

'Don't you think that's a little odd?'

She sighs. 'Right now I don't know what to think.'

'Didn't the neighbours complain to you about the noise?'

'None of them talk to us, they don't even wave.'

'Maybe you should ask them about it.'

She shakes her head. 'It's so long ago.'

'If you still have the name of the house-sitting agency, please can I have it so I can contact them, find out who he is? Can you remember his name?'

'I think his name was Jim, but I can't remember a surname.'

'That's odd. My host was called Philippe.'

'Don't remember that name. The company we used was Mind My Home. I don't want to get anyone in trouble though.'

'You won't be. I just need to ask him a few questions. He may have an idea who attacked me.'

'Will you let me know if he did hold a party here? I'm really not okay with that. I completely trusted him, and the agency. They say they vet everyone, and he's supposed to have had a proven track record. He shouldn't be doing this kind of work if he's not trustworthy.' She looks up the agency number on her mobile. I ask her to text it to me, then we'll have each other's numbers too. She tells me her name is Leah Buckworth, and I can mention her when I call the agency.

Molly and I wander back to the café we went to earlier and order coffee in a large cafetiere. I call the agency and ask about Jim and give the details of the house and its location, but they tell me they can't give out confidential information.

'What now? Jim is not even the name of the person who hosted me.'

'You need to find out his surname; without that you'll never be able to track him down. He must know the Airbnb host because it seems they were at the house at the same time.'

'Do you think he'll still be operating? Maybe I need to search Airbnb for all hosts with the name Philippe.'

'There'll be too many though, won't there?' Molly knocks back her coffee and refills it from the cafetiere.

'Probably.'

'What if Leah's got the name wrong? She must have some emails from the transaction. It'll have his full name on that, won't it?'

'Good point.' I sip my coffee, still too hot for me.

The phone only rings twice before Leah picks up and I feel bad, wondering if I've woken up the baby. I ask her if she can look up her contract for when the house sitter stayed.

'Any personal details of his would me help me track him down,' I tell her.

'Okay, anything important like that I'd have printed out. It'll be in an archive box in the loft. I'll go up there later and have a look. I'll phone you.'

'Thank you, I really appreciate it.'

My phone rings as soon as I end the call.

'Ellie, it's Katie, something's happened.' She sounds out of breath.

My blood pressure shoots up from nought to sixty. 'What is it?'

'Don't panic, but I'm at the hospital.'

'What?' I sit up.

'There's been an accident.'

27

'It's Joseph. He fell off the climbing frame at the park. It's okay, Tyler is fine.'

'Oh no. Is Joe badly hurt?' I press my fist against my forehead, feeling guilty that I'm grateful it's not Tyler.

'They think it's concussion. He may have to stay in overnight so they can keep an eye on him.'

She leaves the statement hanging. What she means is, she'll need to stay in hospital with Joseph. Panic crashes over me.

'Is Tyler with you?' My voice sounds constricted. Katie is silent and I wonder if I should repeat myself.

'I'm sorry, I couldn't bring him with me. I had to go in the ambulance with Joe.'

'Where is he now? Who's he with?' I try to keep my voice steady, even though my pulse is rising fast.

'He's fine. Harry's looking after him.'

'Who?' My heart is pounding out of my chest. I can't think who Harry is. I stab my finger at the door to indicate to Molly that we have to leave.

'The guy I've been seeing, remember?'

'But I've never met him.' I press my throbbing temple with the heel of my hand. My head feels like it's going to explode. I leave Molly to pay and hurry outside.

'I'm so sorry, there was nothing else I could do. None of the other mums could have him and the ambulance wouldn't let anyone else come with us.'

'Wasn't there anyone there I know?' I wonder if it's a case of they didn't want to look after him because he's my son.

'I doubt it. It was mainly mums with babies, from nursery.'

'So what's going to happen to Tyler tonight?'

'Harry said he'll stay with him. He's got a spare key to my flat. He's going to take Tyler back for his dinner.'

'But you hardly know this man, and I don't know him at all,' I shout. I can't stop myself.

'What else am I supposed to do?' She sobs. 'Joseph is about to go into surgery. He's got a gash on his head they need to sew up; I can't leave him.'

'I know, I'm so sorry for yelling. I'm going to drive back. I'll contact Louise and Steve, see if they can go over to yours and take over from Harry.' Katie and Louise have been friends since they were at the village primary school together. I just hope Louise is speaking to me.

'You really don't need to. He's been absolutely brilliant with the boys today; they adore him.'

'I'm sorry but I'm not comfortable with Tyler being with someone we don't know. I'd be much happier if he's with Louise and Steve.'

'Okay. I'm really sorry, Ellie.'

'It's not your fault. I hope Joseph is okay.'

I say goodbye and end the call. I can't blame her. I don't know what else she could have done, but it doesn't take away my fear that Tyler is being looked after by a man I've never met. I call Louise and thankfully she answers, and being the kind person she is, she puts aside whatever she might be feeling about me and agrees to go over to Katie's flat and take Tyler to her house. I don't much fancy meeting a stranger alone in her flat in these circumstances. It makes me look like a terrible mother. Going away for the weekend without my son. Not having plans in place for emergencies like this. This is the problem with not having made many friends in the area.

'Are you okay? What's happened?' Molly asks as soon as she comes out of the café. I explain everything.

'I need to get home as soon as possible. I can't bear the thought of Tyler alone with this man he only met this afternoon. He's not used to being with strangers, especially a man. I should have brought him with me. I never considered what Katie would do if Joseph had an accident.'

'It'll be okay. If Katie trusts him, that must mean he's a good bloke.'

'I suppose so, but I still need to get home.'

Molly drives me all the way back to hers without stopping. By the time I've grabbed my toothbrush and clothes from her flat, said goodbye and got on the road, it's gone 3 p.m. The sky is darker than usual for this time of day. A storm is picking up bending the trees backwards and forwards. Rain comes down in gusts of wind, as though someone is tipping buckets of water just to slow me down. My car is being pushed sideways and I'm forced to concentrate harder than usual to keep within the motorway lane. I will not be stopped. I need to get home tonight to look after my son. I shouldn't have gone so far without him. What was I thinking? Molly said she wouldn't mind me bringing him with me, so why didn't I listen? I suppose I wanted things to be the way they were with her before Tyler was born. Going out together, getting dressed up, feeling carefree. But it's never going to be like that again.

Having Tyler pushed us apart. I'm a different person now yet I need her more than ever. She's my best friend, the one who knows everything about me, has never judged me. I push my foot down harder to the floor, and speed all the way home.

28

By the time I've parked and reached Louise's, it's almost 6 p.m. When I knock on her door, all I can hear is Tyler's voice shouting, 'Mummy.' Louise opens the door and Tyler comes bowling out, arms open. He wraps himself around my legs and grips me tight.

'Hello Pickle. Are you okay? What a lovely welcome. Maybe I should go away more often.' I laugh but immediately the tears come, and I hug him tighter. He pulls back.

'Please don't, Mummy.' His pained face tips up to me, bottom lip out. He's about to cry. I hug him again then he runs upstairs with Jordan, presumably into Jordan's bedroom.

'Come in and have a cup of tea, you must be tired after all that driving,' Louise says.

'Thank you, and thanks for looking after him. I'm grateful.' We look each other in the eye.

'Steve explained to me how you know each other.'

I nod, waiting for the but. She shuts the door behind me.

'And I believe him. I'm sorry for flying off at you like that.' I follow her to the kitchen where she's made a pot of tea.

'I'd probably have done the same, but someone is out to get me.' I'm relieved Steve was able to put her straight.

'Whoever it is, I will do my best to help you find them. They could do this to anyone. It's disturbing how easily they can bring someone down.' Louise carries the pot and three small mugs on a tray into the living room.

'Thank you. I'm so glad we're fine again,' I say, following her. We are mothers first and foremost, looking out for each other. I sigh, grateful to have both of them on my side. 'Any news on Joseph?'

'He's had his head stitched up, but they need to keep him in overnight. It was quite a fall apparently.' She looks to where Steve is standing, holding the TV remote.

'How are you?' he asks. 'You must have been worried sick.'

'Just a bit.' I sit with them in the living room, cradling a mug of tea. 'Do you know what happened?'

'According to Katie, Joseph was climbing to the top of the frame then got on the outside of it with another boy. Harry was standing underneath, and tried to reach up to help, but Joseph kept kicking his hand away, quite aggressively apparently.'

'That's not like Joe at all.' I frown.

'The next minute Joseph had fallen.'

'So he slipped?'

'I suppose so.'

'Hopefully we'll hear more about it soon. As long as he's okay. Katie must have been beside herself.'

'I think she was, and she was so worried about Tyler, but Harry stepped right up apparently.'

'That's good of him. You both met him then? What did you think, did he seem all right to you?'

I don't mean to sound paranoid, but the question is out before I can stop it.

'I think so,' Louise says.

Steve glances at the floor then back at me. 'I don't know. He's either the perfect man or he's insecure. He was trying way too hard.'

'What do you mean?' I lean forward.

'One of those annoying blokes who talks to kids like he's their mate, like he's got them sussed, on their level. But how's that if he doesn't have any of his own?'

Louise is frowning. 'Really? I thought he was making a heroic effort to connect with Tyler. You can't hold that against him, surely? He might have nephews and nieces.'

'I suppose he could have been a man who doesn't take to kids at all. That would have been worse.' I sip my tea. I don't want to take sides.

'Exactly.' Louise swivels in her seat so she's facing Steve. 'When I spoke to Katie on the phone, she said Harry was straight in there playing football with the kids, chatting to them like they were all his best buddies, which I think is lovely. He organised a goal and two small teams and they were off. She said she's never seen anyone like it.'

Steve shrugs, clearly envious. I wouldn't have expected it of him, but not all men feel comfortable around other people's kids and the ones who do are sometimes viewed with suspicion or envy.

I change the subject slightly. 'Wasn't there anyone else at the park who could have had Tyler for me? No offence to Harry but I've not actually met him yet. I mean, wasn't there someone I know?'

I stare into my tea. Why can't I be more like one of those popular mums, full of confidence and energy, always smiling and helping people? Instead, I'm sad, lonely and single.

'I don't think so. Apparently, Katie was mostly with new mums you wouldn't know. Ones she's met at the anti-natal clinic or the nursery. Harry said she didn't have time to ring round and anyway he offered.'

Maybe it's me being overprotective or maybe it's because I'm not used to leaving Tyler with anyone. We're a team, just the two of us. I was expecting too much of him staying over with Katie. It was hard enough leaving him at pre-school for those first few weeks. I wondered if I'd have to give up and try to work around him at home, but then everything got easier for him. He made friends and each time he left, he knew I'd come and collect him after a few hours. It's unusual for him to be comfortable with someone so quickly. But how would I even know that? Perhaps he wasn't. That was quite some welcome and he seemed... relieved that I was home.

I tell them about Darren's negative DNA test and how I'm trying to find out who Tyler's dad is. It's bad enough having to admit that I don't know. The implication of that is not pretty. It could make all that gossip about me on Facebook seem possible. But I'm not ready to tell anyone else I think I was attacked. Not when I have zero proof.

'You have an idea who it is though, and you're trying to find him?' Louise always wants the cleanest most straightforward outcome.

'That's right.' I side-eye Steve. He's someone I could confide in, because he's not easily taken in. He wouldn't judge me. Much as I like Louise, I know she's susceptible to gossip. She'd easily assume I slept around given the right context. After all, look what happened with the rumour about me and Steve.

Steve shuts his eyes and nods, as though he understands my predicament. They're sitting close, legs touching and it's good to see they've made up. I'm grateful Louise is talking to me again.

'So come on, tell me what Harry is really like?' I ask as I stir a spoonful of sugar into my topped-up tea.

'He seems really kind and bubbly, doesn't he?' Louise turns to Steve who nods. 'He was concerned about Joseph. Didn't seem sure what had happened. Said that one minute Joe was on the top of the climbing frame kicking Harry's hand away and the next he was in a heap on the ground, head thudding the tarmac.'

'God, how awful. Could have been so much worse.'

'Harry seemed quite shaken too.'

'And he offered to look after Tyler then brought him back here by himself?'

'I think so. We arrived here about half an hour later. Tyler was absolutely fine. He was in Joseph's bedroom playing when we got here. Harry was watching football.'

'They weren't spending time together?' There's something odd about that – the man who's so brilliant with kids. Maybe he'd had enough for one day. Tyler should have been with an adult he was familiar with during those first few hours after the accident, in case he was upset about what had happened to Joseph. He barely knows Harry and may not have felt comfortable asking him questions.

'There was a relaxed atmosphere when we came in if that's what you're worried about. Tyler wasn't hiding or anything.'

'They did seem to get on really well,' Steve adds.

'What do you mean?'

'When Harry left, he high fived Tyler then gave him a hug. It was so sweet. Katie was right, you honestly had nothing to worry about leaving Tyler with him.'

I smile and nod, not sure if that's true, because my gut is telling me something different.

29

After Louise and Steve have gone, I text Molly to let her know I'm back, and Tyler is okay. While he's brushing his teeth before bed, I can't help asking him about the accident.

He spits out the toothpaste and wipes his mouth with the towel, leaving a white line on the fabric. The dentist has told him to keep the fluoride in his mouth and he takes it very seriously.

As I help him into his pyjamas, I briefly go through what Louise told me about the accident.

'Did Joe slip by himself?'

Tyler shrugs. 'Harry shouted, "Get down this minute, Joseph. I won't tell you again."' Tyler mimics Harry's deep angry voice then roars like a lion.

'So do you think Harry might have scared him?'

Tyler nods and repeats his impression.

'Where was Katie when this happened?'

'With Amy's mummy.'

'Chatting?'

Tyler nods.

God, I've done that myself. Looked away for a second and Tyler had let go and fallen off the roundabout, scraping his knees on the rubber tarmac.

'Oh dear. But Harry was watching him for her?'

Tyler carries on nodding then begins to move his head round and round playfully. I tickle him under his arms, and he squirms in fits of giggles.

We hug and I kiss the top of his head.

'The doctor is going to fix Joseph, isn't he?' Tyler blinks rapidly, tears welling up in his eyes.

'They're going to try. Because he hit his head, they need to keep an extra close eye on him, so they'll have to wake him up every couple of hours to make sure he's okay.'

'Will he be better?'

'I think so. He's being well looked after by all the doctors and nurses.'

I pull him to me and hold him tightly in my arms, grateful he's not hurt too. Thank goodness I was able to come home this evening.

'We can't always stop accidents happening even if we're right there. If Joseph was determined to stand on the top of the climbing frame and not hold on, there wasn't much anyone could have done except try and stop him from falling.'

'He did hold on.'

'Did he?' I frown.

'Will the police take Harry away?' Tyler says.

'Er, no I don't think so. Why would they do that?'

Tyler shrugs and picks up a dinosaur from the side. He stamps it up and down on top of a teddy, making growling noises. Perhaps he blames Harry for not stopping Joseph falling. Does Katie know that her boyfriend shouted at her son? I text Katie to see how it's going at the hospital, if there's anything I can do to help.

I switch the TV on but mute it straight away and go to make a cup of tea. What if I hadn't been able to come home tonight? Would Louise and Steve have been able to take Tyler for me, or would Katie have insisted Harry could cope? I shudder involuntarily. Tyler would have been left alone all night with a man he barely knows. That's terrifying for a child. Katie seems to think Harry can do no wrong, but Tyler says he shouted at Joseph. Is it possible he caused him to fall? Was Joseph so scared at being yelled at that he lost his grip?

Maybe I'm catastrophising again. I sit in front of the TV with my tea and unmute it. I squint at the screen. It's on the input menu. Why is that? I click it back to live TV. Tyler must have been fiddling with the remote control. The last thing I remember watching was *Bake Off*.

My phone buzzes. A text from Katie.

Joe's fine thanks, all stitched back up and resting. We don't need anything thanks. Harry's already brought our overnight things. I hope Tyler's okay. Harry says he was a really good boy.

I chuck my phone on the table. Who does this Harry think he is? Of course Tyler was a good boy. And why did Katie need Harry to take their things to the hospital? It doesn't feel right that he's getting so involved when he's only been around five minutes.

I take a breath and calm myself. It's not really my business. They are in a new relationship, and not everyone has the trust issues I do. This is clearly okay with Katie, and I respect her; although her judgement when it comes to boyfriends in the past has not been great, I need to have more faith that she's found a good one.

I reach for my phone and type back.

That's good to hear. Tyler's so pleased I'm home. He's really upset about Joseph and hopes the doctors can fix him. Do you know what happened exactly? Please thank Harry for looking after T for me.

I will, thanks. Harry shouted at Joseph to get down when he went up over the top of the climbing frame and wasn't holding on. Harry's blaming himself, wonders if he scared him when he shouted, making him topple over. He tried his best to catch him.

Sounds similar to Tyler's story, so it must be what happened. Harry's probably an okay guy. It's just me thinking the worst of an innocent man. Not all men are out to hurt women, I remind myself. My dad was kind and generous. Always thinking of other people. Loved his allotment and sharing out his vegetables with the neighbours.

I ought to ask the doctor about having some therapy. I never used to be like this. I need to stop thinking the worst, but it's so hard. I take in a deep breath and let it out slowly. I'm following an account on Instagram about not letting a trauma take over your life and change your personality. I need to be brave, find out what really happened to me that night and deal with it, otherwise I'm going to be alone forever. There are lots of good men out there, kind and gentle people who I can trust and rely on. I need to start believing I can meet one of them.

My phone beeps. A text from Leah, the woman from the Airbnb house. She's gone through her archived emails. The man who signed the house-sitting contract was called Jim Ball. That doesn't add up. Unless Philippe was working for someone else that night. I search the name on the internet but there are lots of men with that name. Leah's given me an address for him in Islington. I search that too and when I zoom in on Google Maps, the property shows up as flats on Liverpool Road.

I decide to go there and find out if Jim Ball knows Philippe, or if – as I suspect – they are the same person.

30

As soon as I've dropped Tyler off at pre-school on Thursday morning, I park at the train station and catch a train to Finsbury Park. From there, it's a couple of stops to Highbury and Islington. I'd wanted to make this trip to Jim Ball's address straight away, but I had work to catch up on and any spare time I've had, I've been helping Louise make Halloween decorations for the pre-school party on Monday afternoon.

I'm there in one hour and fifteen minutes. Then it's about half a mile walk to the address Leah gave me in Liverpool Road.

I look up at the block of flats, my stomach jittering. I didn't exactly think this through. I found the quickest way to get here and jumped on a train. I should have brought someone with me, because I don't want to go into a man's flat on my own. What if it is Philippe living here under this other name Jim Ball? Is he using another name because he's a criminal, trying to hide who he really is? Will he come outside to speak to me if I ask him to? Or am I putting myself in danger?

There's a column of buzzers with numbers on, most of them with typed or scribbled names. I check the piece of paper in my pocket: Flat 5. There is no name on the label for flat 5. I press the buzzer and wait. No answer. I try again a few times, pressing and pressing but when there's no response, I press numbers 3 and 4. No answer from them either. It's

10.20 a.m. Most people will be at work. I could kick myself. I press the button for flat 5 again. After a pause, there's a crackle and a man's voice asks, 'Who is it?'

'Are you Jim Ball?'

'Who's asking?'

'My name's Ellie Hunter. I wonder if I could speak to you?'

'What's it about?'

'It would be easier if I could talk to you face to face.'

'All right, hang on. I'll come down.'

The intercom crackles and goes dead. Moments later, a tall man with scruffy fair hair and beard stubble opens the main door.

'What's this all about then?'

If he's Philippe, he's not as I remember him, but then, I didn't really look at his face in any detail and it has been a while.

'The owner of this house in Southampton gave me this address for a Jim Ball.' I show him a screenshot. 'Is that you? He was her house sitter.'

He takes his time, looks me up and down. 'Yeah, that's me, why?' He folds his arms and leans against the door frame.

'It's just that I stayed there four years ago but the landlord I dealt with was called Philippe. He had a French accent. Was that you too?'

He lets out a half-hearted laugh. 'That's my nickname.'

'So you advertised a room on Airbnb without the house owner being aware?'

'Yeah but no harm done. You're not grassing on me, are you?'

'Why did you do it and why the accent?'

'That was my mates getting me to make the parties seem a bit more exotic.'

'Oh, I see.' I don't know what to make of that, so I explain about the man in the clown mask who broke into my room and ask if he knows his name.

'I remember that; what an arsehole. But sorry, I've no idea who he was and no one else seemed to either. He just turned up, as people do when they get a sniff of a house party. Never saw him again.'

My heart sinks. 'If anything does come back to you, please can you contact me?' I scribble an old email address on a piece of paper from my handbag and pass it to him. 'I'm grateful you looked after me that night, thank you.'

'It was no bother.' He takes the piece of paper then shuts the door.

Who was that man in a clown mask and how am I going to find out?

* * *

As I turn to walk to the station, a black cab pulls up next to me and a man in a suit steps out, leaving the door open. He asks me if I need a lift, then hurries away across the road. I was going to walk but I may as well take a ride as it's right here, so I climb in.

The doors lock. It's an automatic safety feature, but my stomach still clenches.

The driver barely acknowledges me. He's busy chatting into a headset in a language I can't quite work out. He pulls away without asking where I'm going. His phone is in a cradle and there's a map on the screen with a flashing marker showing the vehicle's location.

I shift to the edge of the seat and speak as loudly as I can without appearing rude.

'Can you take me to Islington and Highbury train station please?' I tap on the partition window but still he doesn't look round. He doesn't seem to hear me and he's wearing a baseball cap on sideways which obscures his face. Continuing to talk on the phone, he turns us left at the lights and I'm sure we're going in the wrong direction.

'Where are you taking me?' I shout and thump louder on the window, standing now so he can't pretend he hasn't seen me.

Still no reaction.

I try to reach over the cash tray, through the small opening where customers pay him. My hand barely gets through before I'm stuck. He brakes suddenly at the lights and I jolt forward, crashing against the partition and almost losing my footing.

In one swift movement he twists round and grabs my hand, covering it with his hot rough skin. He presses something small and sharp into my palm. It's a screwed-up piece of paper, the edges sharp blades on my hand. I close my fingers around it and yank my hand back, scraping it through the small hole. I turn away to open the paper.

'No!' he shouts at me and shakes his head. His dark squinting eyes pin me to the spot. I recoil at the unsightly burn on the side of his face.

'Let me out!' I scream and kick the door. I press the button to open the window but that's locked too. 'Let me out!' I screech.

A group of students outside a café look my way, then at each other and start striding towards us. The doors suddenly unlock with a loud click.

I grab my bag, open the door and leap out. I mouth 'thank you' to the students. I've not paid the man, but he doesn't try to stop me.

I run all the way down the street, sweat prickling under my arms and all over my head. What is going on? Who was that man? I glance over my shoulder only to see the taxi driving up behind me. I run faster, my breath burning in my throat. When I look again, he is taking a right turn away from where I am. I stop to catch my breath, doubled over with relief, and then keep going. No time to be distracted in case he comes back. I need to get away. I stuff the folded piece of paper into my pocket and check the direction to the train station on my phone. I'm a mile away from where I was.

Where was he taking me?

I half walk, half run and by the time I reach the station, my whole chest is burning. I'm going to be late picking Tyler up if I don't catch the next train.

I stand in a quiet spot near the waiting room, making sure no one is near me, then take out the piece of paper the man planted in my hand. I carefully unravel the small square. There's something written in the middle in black biro. I turn the paper around and read it. A silent gasp escapes my lips.

Be careful what you wish for.

31

I arrive at pre-school five minutes late but thankfully the queue is still there. Maybe it's one of those days when they didn't open the door on time because not all the children were sitting quietly, or they forgot to hand out a letter for the parents. There's a committee meeting tonight about the trip to the farm next Friday and the pre-school Halloween tea party on Monday afternoon. There's the bigger community party later that day for all the children in the village. The clocks go back an hour on Saturday night, so it'll be getting dark by about 4.40 p.m. on Monday. Dark and spooky for when the main party starts at 5 p.m.

'How's Joseph?' a voice says behind me. It's Louise, with Callum in the pushchair and Jordan holding her hand.

'Joseph had a good night, but he has to go back in for a check-up.'

'That's a relief. Are you coming to the meeting later?'

'I may need to bring Tyler with me. Katie will be busy looking after Joseph.'

'Steve can have him for you. He'll be looking after ours anyway so he won't mind an extra one.'

'That's kind of you, thank you.'

Back at my flat, I check my phone and I have a text from Katie saying she's back at the hospital; she thought they'd be in and out but then Joseph started feeling dizzy and nauseous again, so they're keeping an eye on him. I ask her if she needs anything, but she replies as I expect.

Thanks, but Harry popped back to my flat earlier to pick up a couple of things for Joseph, to keep him amused.

I don't know why I'm letting it bother me so much. I suppose as single mums, we've come to rely on each other, but the truth is, with Harry around I'm not needed.

I don't really have time for a shower. Maybe I'll have a bath later when Tyler is asleep. I need to relax after the day I've had. Plus, I'll need to catch up on the work I was supposed to do today.

I grill fish fingers and potato croquettes for Tyler and microwave a small cup of peas. Once he's eating, I make myself a fish finger sandwich with mayonnaise. I didn't realise I was hungry, and wish I'd made enough for one more.

In my bedroom, I sit on the bed and apply a light pink lipstick in front of the mirror, then brush my hair. One of the dressing-table drawers is slightly open. I stand up and push it with one hand, but it's wedged and I have to tug it out then push it in straight to close it. I know it gets stuck easily, so I wouldn't have left it like that – it was my grand-ma's dressing table, and she always taught me to rub a bar of beeswax on the wood under the drawer to help it move smoothly – but I don't know who else would have touched it. I don't think Tyler has the strength to pull it open. But it must have been him. It couldn't have been anyone else.

I confiscated Tyler's Batman figure this morning when he refused to brush his hair so he must have been looking for it, I decide. I've hidden things in that drawer before, but ever since he discovered that hiding place, I've stopped putting his things in there. I take the Batman toy out of the airing cupboard, hidden on the top shelf under a towel and take it into the kitchen. Tyler has finished his dinner and is drinking the beaker of squash in one go.

'Good boy for clearing your plate. Was that nice?'

He slams the cup down with a satisfied smack of the lips and shows me his open mouth, which is orange-rimmed.

'As you've been so good, you can have your Batman back.' I put it on the table in front of him and take his plate. 'Were you looking for it in my bedroom?'

He shakes his head as he picks it up.

'Did you look for him in my dressing-table drawer?'

He doesn't answer. He gets down from the table and kneels on the floor next to the den he's made from old cereal packets. He takes Robin and the Batmobile out of the cave.

'Did the drawer get stuck, Tyler?'

He ignores me.

'Tyler, I'm talking to you. Did you go in my dressing-table drawer?'

'No, Mummy.' He emphasises the 'no'. He doesn't normally lie, and I don't know why he would now. Maybe he's forgotten. It was this morning, after all. Katie's the only person who has a spare key, but it can't have been her as she's been at the hospital all night and day.

Thinking about it, I decide it must have been me. I was in a hurry. Some actions are so automatic, my brain doesn't always acknowledge I've done things.

I drop Tyler at Steve and Louise's and walk with her down to the pre-school. For once, the meeting goes smoothly and people seem to have forgotten how angry they were with me before. It would be nice to get an apology, but if they haven't got proof, I suppose that's not likely.

I let everyone know I have to duck out of being a parent helper on the farm trip next week because I'm still so behind with work and preparing notes for the annual trade conference. There are plenty of other parents who are willing to go, so they won't miss me. I keep a low profile in general, but especially now, never sure whether whoever is targeting me is going to post another nasty message on Facebook. It seems to have died down for now and I'm still not sure why it was going on in the first place, who has it in for me.

As soon as I've picked Tyler up from Steve and Louise's, I come home and get him to bed. I've been dreaming of having a relaxing bath all afternoon, so I put the chain on the door, light a candle and switch the small portable radio on. They're playing a medley of jazz which fits the mood I'm after perfectly. In the back of the wardrobe, I dig out a mini bottle of Molton Brown's Rosa bath and shower gel. I've been saving it up since last Christmas when I won it in a cracker at work. I recently read on Instagram not to save things for a special day, because that day is today. A perfect day may never come. I think about Nan's porcelain tea set she saved for best. Her mum and dad gave it to her on her wedding day, but she never used it. Mum thought it was such a shame when she found it in Nan's cupboard after she died.

I pour a generous amount of the dark crimson gel into the hot running water and breathe in the exotic aroma. A soft mound of bubbles begins to build and I slip naked into the water and submerge myself completely.

My phone rings and I glance over at the washing basket lid and see Ian's name come up. What does he want now? I let it ring out. Hopefully he'll get the hint and give up, but my phone beeps again, this time with a notification of a voice message. I stand up to soap myself down with my loofah. The bathroom is full of steam. I catch a glimpse of my hair piled on my head in the mirror over the sink. It's mostly misted up but I stop in my tracks, transfixed for a long minute, my arms wrapped around myself, trying to take it in. I shiver, my damp skin cold now. I blink but it's still there. I'm not imagining this. I don't think it's something Tyler is capable of. It's too high up for a start. A chill sweeps through me as I look again at the words that have emerged on the mirror.

Watch Out

Someone has been in my flat.
The bathroom door flies open, and I scream.

32

Tyler looks round the bathroom door at me, eyes wide at my reaction.

He hesitates before saying, 'Mummy?'

'I'm so sorry darling. Mummy was spooked.'

'Someone's on the phone, Mummy.' He lifts up the portable house phone, which is too heavy in his small hand.

'Who is it?' I mouth at him.

He shrugs.

'Can you tell them I'll call back? I'm just getting out of the bath,' I whisper.

Whoever it is has just heard me scream. I hope they're not panicking. Tyler speaks into the phone – the wrong end – as he closes the door behind him. I'll deal with it in a minute. I sit back down in the bath and rinse, then grab a towel and dry myself. I take a quick photo of the writing on the mirror before it disappears.

How did someone get into my flat to do this? They must have been the one who went through my drawers too. And there I was accusing poor Tyler. He'll think Mummy's gone mad with all this strange behaviour.

I can't remember giving anyone other than Katie a spare key. I pad along the hallway and check the hook behind the front door. The one I keep there has gone. Maybe Steve borrowed it and forgot to give it back. Could it be an early Halloween prank? If it is, it's certainly bloody worked.

I put my dressing gown on and go to see if Tyler is okay. He's gone back to bed. I didn't even hear the phone ring. I check on the last number call list, and surprise, surprise it was Ian.

I listen to the message he left on my mobile earlier. He doesn't say much, just to call him back.

I call Molly instead.

'How are you? I was just wondering if you're free for a quick chat?'

'Yes of course.'

I tell her about the message on the bathroom mirror and she also suggests it could be Katie, trying to scare me for Halloween. Except she's been so taken up with looking after Joseph, I wouldn't have thought she'd have had time to even think about it. She does love Halloween and she's pranked me before, sneaking into my flat and even one time leaving a severed hand in my fridge. It looked so realistic, I screamed my head off until I realised it was made of rubber. I mention about the dressing-table drawer, but she's not sure that's proof anyone's been there. I hope she doesn't think I'm getting paranoid. Best to put it all out of my mind for now.

'Leah from the Airbnb house got back to me.'

'That's quick. What did she say?'

I take the phone into the kitchen and tell her about going to Islington, while I make a mug of hot chocolate. 'Philippe was there. It's his nickname; his real name is Jim Ball, same as on Leah's house-sitting contract. He remembers the man in the clown mask but doesn't know who he is or his name. How am I going to find out who he is and what he wants with me?'

'I've no idea.'

'I don't know anyone else who was at the Airbnb that night.'

I carry my drink through and sit in front of the TV. I take a deep breath and tell her about the taxi waiting outside the flats, how the man got out and offered it to me, and how the driver grabbed my hand and gave me a note.

'That sounds terrifying. What did the note say?'

'Be careful what you wish for.'

'Oh my God, Ellie. It sounds like this whole taxi thing was planned. Why didn't you take someone with you?'

'Who?' I sip the creamy chocolaty drink.

'I don't know, one of the mums from school? Did you get the taxi's licence number?'

'No.' I groan. 'I didn't even think to look, I just wanted to get away as quickly as I could. I thought I was being brave going to London alone, overcoming my fears.'

'I know, honey, but it's not always that simple, is it?'

'I should be able to walk down a street or get in a taxi on my own in the middle of the day and feel safe, be safe, shouldn't I?' I get up and go to the window.

'You should, we all should.'

'What do you think the note is supposed to mean? Maybe the driver was sent to warn me off?'

'By who? Seems strange it was outside Jim Ball's flat. Whoever left you that message knew you were going to be there. This feels dangerous. I'm worried about you, Elle. This whole thing has already taken a huge toll on you.'

'How would anyone have known I was going to be there and why would it matter to them?'

'Maybe Leah isn't telling us the whole truth. She could have got in touch with Jim Ball and warned him that you're searching for the person who attacked you.'

'But I'm sure she was being straight with me. And why would she do that? She's been so helpful.' I drag my hand through my hair. I can't seem to make any sound judgements about people any more.

'She's the one who told you that address. You're accusing someone of attacking you in her house. She might not be able to keep that to herself.'

'Maybe. I keep thinking about the man who offered me the taxi. It wasn't an accident that it pulled up at that precise moment. I was meant to get that message. I need to work out what it means, and who had me followed.'

33

The clocks change early on Sunday morning, and I wish I could have more than an hour to catch up on my sleep especially after having another nightmare, but Joseph has stayed the night and I can hear the two are up already even though it's only 6 a.m. It's a relief that he's recovered from his fall, and he seems to have no lasting effects. They made a den last night, draping old sheets between the backs of two chairs. They slept underneath in sleeping bags. I let them have a small torch each and books, but no sweets. They'll be getting enough of those tomorrow evening trick or treating.

Katie asked if I'd have Joseph so she could take Harry out for dinner to say thank you for everything he did for her after the accident. After my initial reservations, he does seem a kind man, I decide, although I've still not had the chance to meet him yet, but hopefully I will at Halloween tomorrow night. I've promised myself I won't take it personally that she's spending so much time with him. Maybe she senses my jealousy and that's why she's not gone out of her way to introduce me to him. If I met someone special, I wouldn't want her to feel pushed out. And she's not pushing me out, she's very much still including me in her life. And now he's a big part of her life too, I need to accept it.

In the bathroom, I stare at the mirror, the message invisible now. I spray glass cleaner on a cloth and wipe it down again anyway. Looking around, I can't see anything else that's odd or out of place. No other sign that Katie or Steve or anyone else has been in here. Although there are enough signs: the dresser drawer, and the TV was in the wrong mode. That was strange. But maybe I'm overthinking. Am I letting this whole Airbnb business make me read too much into every little thing?

Katie knocks at about 11 a.m. to collect Joseph. I half expect her to bring Harry over to meet me, but he's had to rush off to visit his aunty in hospital.

She sits in the kitchen with me while the boys finish their game of hide and seek.

'Are you still up for getting a tattoo on my birthday?' I open the website on my tablet and swipe through the customer gallery.

'Yeah, I am. What about you, have you decided what to get?'

'Tyler's name I think.' I touch my wrist. 'What about you?'

'Not sure yet. Something in memory of my nan. Shall we pop in there and chat to them before we book it?'

'Good idea. So come on, spill, how's it going with Harry?' I switch on the coffee maker and fold my arms, leaning against the counter.

She crosses her legs and smiles, dipping her head. 'Good, I guess.'

'It's getting pretty serious then?'

She tips her head from side to side. 'Maybe a little.'

'So soon?' The words trip off my tongue unplanned.

'I don't want to rush it, but he's really keen, put it that way.'

'Will he be here tomorrow?' I fill our mugs with black coffee.

'Yeah of course, he loves Halloween as much as I do and he's got the most incredible outfit. I can't tell you. Wait until you see it.' She sniggers.

I nod, trying to look as enthusiastic as she does.

'I'm really pleased for you. Be good to meet him.' I sip my drink even though it's too hot. My lips burn.

'He can't wait to meet you either.'

'Oh. What have you said about me?'

'Nothing really, don't look so worried.'

I can't help but imagine the worst; him thinking I'm one of those women who used to be an alcoholic, has no idea who her child's father is, and that's why I'm single.

Katie raises an eyebrow and for a second, I think I just said that out loud.

'Only that you're my bestie, you're Tyler's mum and you live next door.' She's full of smiles.

'Oh. Thank you.' I try not to sound bothered because I shouldn't be. My paranoia is tapping on my brain, trying to tell me different, but I'm learning when to ignore it. To distract myself, I open a packet of cookies and offer her one.

'Honestly, Ellie, I've arsed about for so long with the wrong men, and finally, now someone like him has come along, I wasn't expecting it.' She takes a cookie and bites into it.

'It's about time you found happiness. You deserve it.'

We hug. All the rubbish she put up with from her ex seems to melt into the past. I gently pull away from her. One day this will be me. If I can ever trust a man again.

'You starting early this year then?' I try to keep a straight face, watching for her reaction. She must have been desperate all week to find out if she scared me.

'What do you mean?' She takes another biscuit. She's hiding it well, considering she's been waiting for days for me to say something.

'You know.' I want to smile because she really spooked me this time, but I try to hold it in.

'Do I?' She frowns.

'The message on the mirror in my bathroom?'

'What?' She holds the biscuit in front of her lips.

'Bit early, even for you,' I quip.

'What are you going on about?' She takes a bite and crunches loudly.

'It's okay, I accept your apology in advance. You don't need to pretend it wasn't you sneaking in here, trying to scare the bejesus out of me.'

She shakes her head, wide-eyed, as if I've accused her of leaving a headless body in my bath.

'And the dressing-table drawer shoved in any old how so it was left stuck.'

She laughs.

'Very clever,' I continue. 'I half thought it was Tyler at first, but there's no way he'd have the strength.'

'You've finally lost it, haven't you? I have absolutely no clue what you're going on about.'

'Mmm, you're bound to say that, aren't you? Like the time you left the bloody hand in my fridge. Took you ages to admit it.'

She starts laughing again. A sure sign of guilt. There's no one else it could be. Even if Steve borrowed my key, there's no way he or Louise would have done this. They don't know me well enough, and Louise would be horrified at the suggestion. I knew it must have been Katie. She loves nothing more than pranking me at Halloween.

'I don't know how or when you got in, but you are good.' I point at her. 'You scared the shit out of me.'

But now she's shaking her head. She's not smiling any more.

'No Ellie, listen. I mean, I really don't know what you're on about.'

'What?' I frown, searching her face for a smile, but there isn't one. 'Someone wrote *Watch Out* in steam on my bathroom mirror. But if it wasn't you, then who was it?'

34

On Monday, I take a couple of hours off after lunch to help out with the Halloween party at pre-school. I've arranged to take Tyler trick or treating with Katie and Joseph at 4.30 p.m. when it'll start to get dark. Harry is going to join us, and for some reason I'm nervous about meeting him. I wonder what else Katie has told him about me. Ridiculously nice things I can't live up to no doubt.

I've made Tyler's Halloween outfit this year – Frankenstein. He's still young enough not to care if it's brand new from a shop. He's more excited about the pumpkin bucket I've bought him for all the sweets he's hoping to collect later.

All the pre-school staff are dressed as witches with painted green faces and stuck-on warts. I decided to be a witch too so I could wear my favourite emerald velvet dress, which almost touches the ground. My black lace-up ankle boots and shiny satin cape finish the outfit perfectly. Bright red lipstick, plenty of black eyeliner and a bold black beauty spot on my green painted skin.

Tyler has already seen my outfit, so when I go in, I'm relieved he's not scared. But when the rest of the children see everyone's costumes, it only takes one to start screaming and then they all scream. Mrs Howe lowers her outstretched hands, as she flaps them up and down, shushing everyone.

The committee members have helped the staff to decorate the main room with white sheets covering furniture that's not being used. We've made ghosts out of scraps of white and grey material and strips of netting and draped them over bent wire coat hangers. Mrs Howe has hung them from the ceiling on string tied up across the room. Louise and I spent ages cutting eye holes and sticking black paper behind them. Lauren managed to acquire sheets of bright orange paper from her husband's work and Hayley helped her make pumpkins with scary cut-out faces and black paper stuck behind.

'Who wants to play a game?' Mrs Cooper asks, and all the children shout 'yes' back to her. We go out to the yard and play What's The Time, Mr Wolf. I'd forgotten what fun it is. Mrs Howe encourages the children to play the character they're dressed up as and as Joseph is a werewolf, he plays the wolf for the first few rounds, making the girls scream every time he turns around.

I suggested bobbing apples but one of the supervisors said that wasn't okay to play any more. So we've cored small apples and tied string through them and hung them in the yard. The children take turns to be blindfolded, hands behind their backs to see if they can catch an apple in their teeth. The game goes down well, and we give pre-wrapped toffee apples to the winners. Then we play a good old classic: pass the parcel. Each layer has a small bag of spooky sweets, and we play tunes from *The Addam's Family* and the *Scooby-Doo* theme tune.

'Who wants to play, Guess What It Is?' Mrs Howe asks. 'Then we'll have our absolutely disgusting Halloween tea.'

'Me,' the children all shout, trying to stretch their hands highest in the air. Mrs Howe and Mrs Cooper tell them to queue up and they escort the first child to a trolley full of big square boxes. Each has a piece of cloth covering a hole. The first child is terrified as he puts his hand in and feels around. We've stuck sandpaper on a bumpy surface, cotton wool inside toilet rolls and all sorts of strange-feeling things.

While they're playing, I help Louise, Hayley and Lauren bring the food out from the fridge onto the back tables. It feels good to be doing something together as a team although I'm under no illusion that Hayley and Lauren like me, and I'm still not certain if one or both of them are behind the poster and messages on social media. But this has to be progress.

We've really gone to town with the spooky food. A pile of mashed potatoes with chipolata fingers sticking out, drizzled in ketchup, and mummified sausage rolls, with the pastry brilliantly wrapped to look like bandages. Louise has even added two little eyes in the gap for the face. Lots of the parents have brought in cakes and biscuits, and scary crisps shaped into skeleton bones and monster faces.

When we're finished, I take the chance to check my phone. I've kept my Facebook account active, but try not to get sucked into everyone's news. I check it every few days for any vicious posts or comments. Today I have a notification that someone has sent me a message. I didn't think many people had noticed I was back on there as I've not posted anything or commented anywhere.

I don't recognise who the message is from, but I need to see it. I really shouldn't look, especially not here, but I can't help clicking it open. An image of a clown shrieks as it lurches at the screen in a jump scare. I scream and drop my phone. All the children look up at me with bemused faces. A nervous laugh escapes my lips and I tell them it's okay, just that someone sent me a scary Halloween picture. I pick my phone up, and watch the clip again. It's a clown with black menacing eyes and blood dripping from its pointed teeth, holding a chopping knife in its hand. I shiver. It's almost identical to the one in my nightmare. There's a message in red text at the bottom.

I'm coming for you. Trick or Treat?

Hayley looks at my screen over my shoulder and laughs.

Louise touches my elbow and I almost jump out of my skin.

'Sorry, I didn't mean to scare you,' Louise says. 'Are you okay?'

'Not really. Can I show you this?' I indicate for us to leave the room, away from Hayley and she follows me out to the corridor where I show her the message.

'Oh my goodness, that's terrifying.' She brings her hand to her chest and laughs.

'Why are you laughing? Didn't you see the message?'

'Come on, Ellie. It's not personal,' Hayley says, standing at the door, hands on hips. 'Whoever sent it has probably sent it to loads of people for Halloween, hoping it'll go viral.'

'She's got a point,' Louise says.

'It feels personal. Especially as I hate clowns.' An image of the man in a clown mask at the Airbnb flashes across my mind. It can't be a coincidence that I'm trying to trace whoever that was and now I've received this.

I'm hurt that Louise is agreeing with Hayley.

'Oh well, that's different I suppose, but it is Halloween. It's just someone trying to scare people.'

'Maybe, but it reminds me of those killer clowns a few years ago, chasing school children around with machetes. That was no joke.'

Hayley grins and goes back into the pre-school room, shutting the door after her.

'I remember that,' Louise says. 'My cousin was terrified. One clown jumped out on a group of kids at his school and when the parents tried to intervene, they chased them all down the road, hammer raised in their hand. The poor kids really thought they were going to die.'

'I was too frightened to go out. That was when I was on social media all the time. I was obsessed with every story that came up about it in the news. I'd try and work out how near it was to me and if they were likely to come to my town and attack me. My fear of clowns became so bad I couldn't go out for weeks. And when it came to Halloween, I had to sit indoors without the lights on, so no trick or treaters knocked on my door. I couldn't bear the thought of opening it to a clown.'

'That's quite a phobia. You knew these killer clowns were pranksters though, didn't you?'

'It wasn't a prank. Some people were seriously frightened out of their minds. I mean, having "run or die" screamed at you by a clown holding a knife, what's funny about that?'

'I don't think it's funny, but then I hate anything like that, even TV shows of people's home videos, children falling over or their cat running up a wall to escape a dog.'

'Some people love watching other people's pain and suffering. I don't understand why.' I check the sender's profile picture of a fluffy white cat. 'Do you think Rollo3456 who sent the clown clip knows me, or do you think it was random?' I click through to their friends list to see if it could be this Emma person, but it looks like a fake account because there are only a few names, all weird ones.

'It was probably random. Although anyone can hide behind a name these days. It could be someone you know who's created a new account or it could be someone you don't know who is trying to get a reaction out of as many people as possible. It might be a trick to get you to click on a link and scam you out of loads of money.'

After the note from the taxi driver and the writing in the mirror, I don't think I believe that it could be as innocent as that. I don't know who I can trust. I don't feel like going out trick or treating tonight. But I've promised Tyler, and he's so looking forward to it. I can't let him down.

35

Tyler and I are ready to go trick or treating and I'm already feeling better about the idea. I heard a few other people received similar scary Halloween messages, so it put my mind at rest that it wasn't only me being targeted. I try to see the funny side, but I can't.

I speak to Leah before we leave, telling her what happened when I went to the Islington address. Could Philippe be the one who told the taxi driver to give me that note? It can't be a coincidence that it was outside his flat. But why would he try and scare me off? What if he's lying to me about the man in the clown mask to cover up that it was him who took advantage of me? Maybe I should go back and confront him, but will I be putting myself in danger? Perhaps I should tell the police, leave it to them, but I'm not sure they'll take it seriously after all this time.

Katie texts me to say they're not ready to go out yet, so she'll meet us at the park a bit later. My mood sinks. She's probably in bed with Harry having afternoon sex, although if that were the case, I'm not sure where Joseph would be. I can't help taking it as another snub. As though Harry is deliberately trying to keep Katie away from me. Maybe I'm being childish. I shouldn't rely on her as much as I do. For her, Joseph and

Harry come first now, I understand that, I'm just not used to her being unavailable to me.

I take Tyler to every house along our street that has a pumpkin lit outside and spooky decorations. In one window is a disturbing red silhouette of a man stabbing a woman, her handprints all over the window, and the words 'Help Me' daubed in blood. It makes me shiver.

'Is Joe here yet?' Tyler asks me for what feels like the tenth time. It's gone 5 p.m. and it's completely dark now but there's still no sign of them. I check my phone. Nothing. I'm tempted to call Katie, but I'll give them a bit longer in case something's happened. I drop my phone back in my bag. It's not fair on Tyler for them not to turn up. We planned this together weeks ago. I understand that Harry is on the scene now, but it would have been nice if she'd stuck to our arrangements. She could have at least warned me if she was changing our plans. Tyler's been so looking forward to trick or treating with his best friend. And what about Joseph? Does he get a say in this? I bet he's just as disappointed as Tyler.

We arrive at the park for the local community Halloween party. The entrance is lined with cut-out pumpkins and lit up with green and purple floodlights making the usually tranquil setting feel claustrophobic and spooky. Fairy lights and spider's web floss decorate the hedges and archway. Ghostly music blasts out from large speakers and a man on stilts with a pale face, dressed as a circus ringmaster, greets us by lifting his top hat and bowing. He ushers us through the pop-up entrance made from balloons. It's already busy, filled with adults and children in fancy dress costumes of every description. Many are crowded around a jester with a painted skeleton face, who is juggling batons shaped like knives. Two men with beards stroll past hand in hand, in light blue dresses like the twins from the film, *The Shining*. I hold Tyler's hand tighter but he doesn't seem as scared as me. There are so many brilliant outfits, vampires, witches, werewolves and skeletons everywhere. I check my phone, but there's still no message from Katie. Normally I'd text her and ask where she is, but it seems intrusive now she's with Harry.

I sit on my own while Tyler plays on the red and green floodlit bouncy castle. I wave at a couple of the mums I recognise from pre-school, but they look at each other and don't wave back. They probably don't recognise me – it's hard to work out who people are under all the heavy make-up and costumes – or they're still suspicious of me after all those rumours.

We queue at the sweets stand and I buy Tyler a medium portion of black and orange candy floss that's been swirled together. Next to the stall, two jugglers are on a low stage starting a performance. There are seats set out in rows which have all been filled. I'm about to suggest Tyler sits on the grass down the front, when someone in front of us gets up and leaves with their crying baby. I gently guide Tyler to sit down before anyone else does. Fortunately, there are smaller children sitting in front of him, so he has a good view.

'I'll be standing at the back, okay?' I whisper in his ear. He's mesmerised by the flame-tipped batons the jugglers are throwing at each other, especially now it's dark, but he manages a nod so at least I know he heard me.

I position myself a little distance behind the back row, take out my phone and try to call Katie. There's no answer. As soon as I end the call it starts ringing. I press the button to answer, expecting it to be Katie, although I don't immediately recognise the number. There's a crackle on the line but no one speaks.

'Who is this?' I swivel around, trying to spot who's on the line because the same music from the park is playing in the background of the call. The line goes dead.

I cast my eyes around a second time and spot a clown holding a red helium balloon. They're making a beeline for me. I'm frozen to the spot. I've been bracing myself in case I see a clown and in a millisecond I'm back at the Airbnb, screaming at the man in a clown mask.

I want to hurry away but my feet are heavy blocks that won't budge, and I can't leave Tyler on his own. The clown is still heading towards me, then another clown holding a red balloon is staring me down with menacing black-rimmed eyes, marching in my direction. I gasp and touch my neck. My windpipe is constricted. I manage to twist round and search for a clear path to get away, but two more clowns are coming at me in different directions. I count three, four, five more clowns closing in. I'm forced to step backwards, further and further away from Tyler. He'll panic, he won't know where I am.

'Tyler!' I shout in a rasping voice over and over until my throat hurts, but he can't hear me, the music on stage is too loud. I try to reach out, but the clowns circle me, red balloons bobbing above their curly orange wigs. They laugh in deep tones, and move in closer and closer until I can smell their beer breath mixed with a spicy aroma on their bodies as they push and grab, fingers touching me, their snake-like tongues flicking in and out from their menacing black, white and red painted faces, spitting 'bitch' and 'whore' at me, so only I can hear. I hold my hands over my ears and squeeze my eyes shut.

'Help me! Please help me!' I scream.

36

I shout again, hoping someone will take me seriously and free me from this human cage.

'Ellie, is that you?' I can finally hear Katie.

Tyler's voice is nearby too, loud and scared, calling out, 'Mummy.'

'I'm over here,' I yell back, holding up my hand but I doubt if they will see me as I'm shorter than all the men surrounding me.

One by one the clowns move away in different directions as though they've done nothing wrong. I shudder. No one seems to have noticed that I was stuck in the middle, being harassed by a group of older teenage boys or young men, it's hard to say an age. Are they going round harassing women for a prank? Screams and shouts are too normal at Halloween for anyone to take seriously.

'Are you okay?' Katie runs up to me, Tyler's hand in hers, Joseph pulling her other hand.

'You've got him, thank goodness.' I could honestly cry. I reach down and give Tyler a big hug. He kisses my cheek and squeezes my hand until it hurts. I frown at him. I think he's angry with me.

'What happened? Why was Tyler on his own?' Katie asks.

'I left him sitting in the audience watching the juggler while I tried to contact you, but those clowns appeared and surrounded me. They were pushing and touching me, I couldn't breathe, they wouldn't let me out.'

'God, some people always have to go too far. Are you sure you're okay?'

'I think so.' I let out a long breath. I'm still shaky.

'I'm so sorry I didn't get here sooner. I couldn't see you; it's packed out everywhere. Everyone is dressed up so it's difficult to see who's who. When we arrived, Joseph spotted Tyler standing on his own.'

'But he was watching a show right there.' I point to the stage and the rows of chairs. 'I was standing at the back trying to phone you.' There's a different entertainer on stage now, a magician dressed as Dracula pulling live bats out of a box. How long was I trapped and separated from Tyler?

I can't help checking around us. There seems to be clowns wherever I look. One is coming closer. My stomach goes cold as he swoops towards Joseph.

'Katie, watch out!' I shout at her and pull her arm. She winces at me in pain.

'What is it, Ellie?'

'One of them has got Joseph.'

'Who?' She turns and sees what I do: a man dressed as a clown is holding onto Joseph's wrist. But Joseph doesn't look scared; he's eating the same two-coloured candy floss I bought for Tyler.

Katie laughs. 'I think he's okay, Ellie, there's no need to panic.'

She waves a hand at me. The clown lets go of Joseph who runs towards Tyler.

I frown. Is she mocking me? Doesn't she understand this could be one of the youths, who were practically grown men, who frightened me just now? Now the clown is holding Katie's hand. A scream starts bubbling up in my chest. Maybe it's me who's confused. After all, there seems to be lots of people wearing clown outfits.

It takes a long moment for it to sink in.

'Lost sight of him for a second there. He spooked me half to death,' the clown says in a West London accent. 'Sorry babe.' He lifts her hand and kisses her palm.

Katie turns to me and smiles a silly grin. 'This is Harry.'

I shut my mouth, aware it had dropped open. I don't know what I was expecting. But not this. I am at a loss. It's hard to tell if Harry was one of the clowns who frightened me, because his make-up is so thick and heavy. Chances are it wasn't him, not if he was with Katie the whole time. But he's wearing the same kind of curly orange wig as the others. In fact, they are so identical, if the police lined up every clown here, I couldn't say whether they were the ones who scared me or not.

'Nice to meet you.' I don't offer my hand and thankfully he doesn't go in for a kiss on the cheek or a hug. My green paint must be melting in the heat of my flushed face. I don't know what else to say to him. He seems nice enough.

I'm curious to find out what kept Katie so long. It's almost time for Tyler and me to head home. I'm not keeping him up late because they've only just arrived.

We stroll along to the hot chocolate stand and I tell Tyler this is his last treat because it's bedtime soon. The lady making the drinks is dressed as an elderly witch with warts on her chin and dozens of spiders painted on her neck. There's a steaming cauldron of twigs and all sorts of fake limbs sticking out of the luminous green gloop. Tyler and Joseph come away with insulated beakers of hot chocolate topped with marsh-mallows and sprinkles of chocolate spiders.

Harry insists on paying so I take the chance to speak to Katie.

'Everything okay?' I ask her.

'Yeah fine. Sorry we were so late.'

'Something happen?'

Katie blushes and I laugh.

'Oh, I see.'

She shrugs, embarrassed. I do not need details.

'Still okay for my birthday?'

She looks blank.

'Tattoo?' I remind her.

'Of course. Are you still going to have Tyler's name?'

'Yeah definitely, on the inside of my wrist. How about you, did you think of something for your nan?'

'Maybe angel wings.'

'That will be lovely.' I notice she checks where Harry is. Is that in case he's listening and he has something to say about it? I'm not sure, but she seems uneasy.

Harry is sitting on a park bench with the boys, leaning his arms on his legs, checking his phone. He looks us both up and down as we approach.

'Time this little man went to bed.' I put my hand out for Tyler to hold. He smacks it away and laughs, turning to Joseph and Harry, encouraging them to join in, which they do.

'That wasn't very nice, was it, Tyler?'

All three of them carry on laughing.

Katie and I exchange a frown and I expect Harry to calm down and set a good example, but he doesn't. Instead, he high fives them both. No wonder the kids love him, he's like a big kid himself.

'Right, that's it now, boys. You've had your fun. It's time for bed, Tyler.' It takes another few minutes of me trying to break up their fit of giggles before Tyler reluctantly stands.

Katie hugs me goodbye and I tell her I'll see her tomorrow.

'Sorry,' Harry says sheepishly as he stands up and hugs me too, even though I'd rather he didn't, because it's difficult to hug someone when I'm pissed off. His face presses against mine, as though he's about to whisper in my ear. The scent he's wearing is a mixture of tangy fruit and woody spice. Is it like one I smelt when the clowns ambushed me? I think so. It's probably a popular brand of aftershave, though; any number of men here could be wearing it. It doesn't mean he was involved.

Because if he was, it's too weird to contemplate what that would mean.

* * *

It's not until Tyler is asleep and I'm getting ready for bed, that I look at myself properly in the bathroom mirror. On top of my green witchy skin is a ghostly cast of white make-up across my cheek, transferred from

Harry's face. I lean forward and examine it closely. What was he going to say to me? I heard his breath in my ear, the sound of his lips moving together with saliva and tongue, about to say something, I'm sure of it.

While the sink fills with hot water, I scoop out a fingerful of cleansing balm and massage it onto my dry skin. The green and white face paints mix together into one. The greasiness and colour has moved into my hairline. I dunk a cloth into the hot water, squeeze it out and hold the steaming fluffy cotton square over my skin for a few seconds and take three deep breaths. The thick gunk melts away and I wipe most of it off in one sweep. I look up again at the mirror and for a second, I think I see a clown's face behind me. I jump and gasp out loud, then shake my head and look away. When I look back, whatever it was has gone. Must be my mind tricking me.

What happened is playing on my mind, those men trapping me and touching me. Perhaps I should have gone to the police, especially after the killer clown message I received earlier. But it would be my word against theirs if I could even work out who they were behind their disguises.

Who were they? Did anyone see what happened? And is it a coincidence that Harry was dressed as a clown too? Katie would hate me if I told her I thought he could be involved. I wonder if there's any way of finding out if he was one of them. Katie can't know him that well yet. He's come into her life from nowhere. She trusts him with her child, and mine.

Something about him tugs at my gut but I don't know what it is. He's not been horrible to me or Tyler. He's probably an alright bloke yet here I am thinking the worst of him. It's not his fault, it's me. Because it would take a miracle for me to trust a man again.

Once I've tied my hair up, I take my clothes off, pull back the shower curtain and scream.

'Whore' is written on the wall tiles in blood.

37

Blood is dripping all around the edge of the bath and has pooled in the centre. Someone has put the plug in.

Katie has gone too far this time. At least I assume it's her because the thought of it being anyone else is beyond me right now. I snatch up my dressing gown and wrap it around me as I storm out of the bathroom. Tyler is miraculously still asleep. I pick up my keys and march along the landing to next door, pressing hard on the bell. There's no answer at first, but then I hear laughing and giggling in the entrance hall below. I lean over the banister. Katie and Harry are staggering in, Joseph in tow holding a Frankenstein balloon and a small bucket filled to the brim with sweets.

It takes a few seconds before Katie spots me scowling at them. I must look a fright with my hair pinned up and the remnants of face paint around my forehead and ears.

'Hey, Ellie, are you okay?' she calls as they come up the stairs.

'No, I am not.' I fire each word like a bullet, then I turn on my heel and stomp back inside, leaving the door open. They follow me in sheepishly. 'Tyler's asleep,' I hiss, and press my finger to my lips, glaring at them to dare make a sound.

'What's happened?' Katie whispers, eyes wide.

I jab a finger in the direction of the bathroom. 'You might not want Joseph to see your handiwork.'

'My handiwork?' She frowns at me then at Harry and ushers Joseph into the living room as I lead the way.

Pushing the bathroom door open, I invite Katie to go in, followed by Harry who doesn't look at me or say a word. A small patch of his clown make-up has rubbed off his jawline, revealing a patch of tanned skin. His orange curly wig has shifted a centimetre showing yellowy-white roots. He must be older than I thought, maybe late forties. Katie never said. Twice her age. He clearly likes to keep in shape. His chest and stomach are ironing-board flat.

'What the hell?' Katie yells and frowns at me. 'You think I did this?'

She points at the wall. Harry is standing behind her and looks round at it.

'Yeah, yeah, very good, Katie, acting all surprised, but this is a prank too far.' I cross my arms.

'Honestly, Ellie. I did not do this.' She appeals to Harry for support. He steps towards the bath, dips his finger in the blood and licks his finger.

'Mmm, it's cherry flavoured.' He grins.

Katie's eyebrows shoot up. Her face softens and she smiles back.

'Oh yeah, so funny,' I say. 'No one else but you has my key.' I point at her.

'Look, Ellie, I'm really sorry, and I know I should have told you straight away, for security and all that, but I knew you'd be mad at me.'

'So you admit it. You did do this!'

She takes a deep breath, fixes her eyes on the floor for several seconds before looking me in the eye. 'I'm sorry, but I've lost your front door key.'

'You what? When?' I blink several times. 'You are joking?'

She shakes her head. 'I'm so sorry but I don't know when it was exactly. Maybe three, four days ago?'

'What? And you didn't think to tell me? Oh my God, anyone could have found it and let themselves in here. So you really didn't do this?'

'God no. If I lost it outside, no one would know it was for here though, would they?'

'So who did this? Where do you think you lost it?'

'I haven't a clue to be honest with you. I'm so, so sorry. I thought it was in my bag or in the kitchen. I searched everywhere and I was sure I'd find it.'

'But you haven't found it and you didn't tell me!'

'I didn't know how. I thought I'd find it before I needed to say anything. It's why we were late tonight; we were searching for it outside the nursery, the local shop, everywhere, weren't we, Harry?'

He nods, lips pursed, brow creased. I've been trying to avoid looking directly at him, but now I can't avoid glancing at his heavily painted clown face, the oversized black diamond shapes around his eyes right up to the eyebrows, the crudely drawn red mouth almost reaching each ear in an exaggerated slashed grin, like the Joker. His make-up cracks as he frowns. He must be wearing special contact lenses for his eyes to appear so black and dead-looking. I shiver involuntarily and turn back to Katie.

'I just wanted to come home, have a shower and clean myself up. I've had quite a night after you blew me out. Not to mention those clowns.' I steal a glance at Harry but he doesn't react.

I lead them back out to the hall, a nauseous sense of claustrophobia making me dizzy.

'I've told you why we were late, I'm sorry.' She glances at Harry, but he's stony-faced.

'Tyler was so looking forward to going trick or treating with Joseph. We had it all arranged, remember?'

It's so unlike Katie to let me down, especially when it comes to our kids.

'I know, and I don't know how many times I can say I'm sorry. There's always next year.'

'You say that now.' I cross my arms. 'Maybe if you'd been with me earlier, I might not have been ambushed by a bunch of clowns.'

'That's not fair.'

'How do I know your boyfriend wasn't one of them?'

'Because he was with me. Or don't you believe me about that either?'

'Of course I believe you, but these men practically assaulted me out there and I've no idea who any of them are. It's not a joke. You know how much I hate clowns.' I glance at Harry, but his face is blank except for the painted clown face that is mocking me. I shudder again.

'You're always the victim aren't you, Ellie? You can't throw accusations around like that.' Katie storms towards the front door, closely followed by Harry.

'What about all this mess?' I call down the hall, but she grabs Joseph by the arm and steams out. Harry shoots me a sorry face over his shoulder before shutting the door quietly. I'm gobsmacked. What is going on? Katie and I have never fallen out.

'What's wrong, Mummy?' Tyler is standing in his bedroom doorway, rubbing his sleepy eyes.

'It's okay, darling, you go back to bed.'

I tuck him in and clean up the mess in the bathroom before finally having a shower and going to bed myself. I lie there tossing and turning for hours, trying to work through everything that has happened today. Katie's words cut through me each time I replay our conversation. She seemed to be telling the truth, but that leaves so many questions. Who did that to my bathroom if it wasn't Katie, and who has my key? Are Tyler and I safe in our beds while we're sleeping?

38

The following morning, I get the locks changed and vow not to give anyone a spare key who I don't trust 100 per cent.

Katie and I don't speak to each other for the next two days. I keep out of her way and cry to Molly on the phone, telling her all about Halloween. She thinks I should go to the police but agrees it's going to be impossible to find out who those men dressed as clowns were and who let themselves into my home.

My thirtieth birthday is upon me and I feel washed up and old. I've been dreading this and now all I want to do is stay in bed. Katie and I had plans but that's not going to happen now we're not even talking. I wish Molly was closer; she'd want to help me celebrate.

Over breakfast, Tyler hands me a card he made at pre-school and sings happy birthday to me. It's the sweetest thing he's ever done, and I cry into his hair as I cuddle him. He's the one thing that's good in my life, that I haven't made a hash of.

Though the mystery of how he was conceived will eat at me until I find out what happened. Will I ever find out? What do I tell Tyler when he asks me who his dad is? I don't know what else I can do. If it was the man in the clown mask who was the attacker, then why was I given that message in the taxi outside Philippe's flat? What if he's lying to me and he's the one who raped me? My stomach turns cold. I trusted him. I should go to the police, but I have no proof. It's as though some hidden force is working against me to stop me finding out.

My phone pings. It's a happy birthday text from Darren. At least he hasn't forgotten me, but my mood plummets instantly remembering that Simone is expecting their baby, and in a few months they'll be married. My life in the meantime hasn't moved on one jot. I'm still a single mum working as many hours as I can.

I text back, swallowing my bitterness because I'm not a bad person. I'm glad they're happy.

How's the baby bump and the wedding plans?

All good thanks. Twenty week scan soon. How about you? Found 'the one' yet?

Yeah I have, but he's getting married and having a baby with someone else.

I press send before I can stop myself. Shit. I didn't mean it. Oh well, it's my birthday, I'm allowed to be a little bit upset. Tears drop into my mug of coffee. I wipe my eyes. I need to stop feeling sorry for myself and go and get dressed.

Hey, don't be like that. I was just thinking that now you've moved on, got yourself a good job, nice flat and quit the booze, you'll have a clean start when you find Mr Right. Learn from your mistakes, as they say.

What mistakes? What do you mean?

I take the phone into the bedroom, chuck it on the bed and start getting dressed.

You won't go getting pissed and forgetting who you're with.

Not this again.

Piss off, Darren!

Just trying to help.

Yeah right. I was NEVER unfaithful to you, I've told you that.

Maybe not, but if you weren't out of your head, you'd remember who you were with and what you did, wouldn't you?

That simple, is it?

You bloody hurt me.

What do you mean? You hurt me too.

Honestly Elle, who knows how many men you could have slept with in that state.

What?? I'm not like that, you bastard! I barely drank a thing, so why do you assume it was my fault? Couldn't possibly be some bloke getting me paralytic??

I feel like I'm standing on the roof of a skyscraper, swaying in the wind and a gust is about to blow me over the edge. Darren thinks there's one answer to everything. If women offer it about, men will lap it up like harmless puppies, so women shouldn't complain about it afterwards. We're she-devils and men have no control, poor things. Bullshit.

I stare at my phone, but Darren doesn't reply.

But it does beep. I almost drop it tapping the screen open. It's a text from Molly, wishing me happy birthday and asking if she can call me after work.

I take a deep breath and text Darren again.

Are you trying to wind me up or is there something you want to say?

When he doesn't reply, my chest and stomach ache. I shut my eyes. Everything we had together is over, there's no going back, so why does it still hurt so much? Why is he being nasty to me? He was never like this when we were together. And it feels like someone's convinced him I was sleeping around, namely Simone.

As I'm about to go out of the door, someone knocks. I open it to find Katie and Joseph standing there, her holding his nursery bag and lunch-box. Her eyes are red and puffy as if she's hardly slept.

'Happy birthday, Ellie. Could I come in for a minute?'

I stand back and she comes in, Joseph holding the bottom of her coat and peeping up at me like I'm the Grinch.

'I wanted to say sorry.' She pauses and takes a deep breath. 'For having a go at you the other day. Can you forgive me?' The expression on her face is chiselled with pain. I can't bear that she's pleading with me.

'Hey, I'm sorry for yelling too, and accusing your boyfriend.' I lean in and we hug. 'He seems really nice.' I'm ready to pull away, but she clings to me, so I let her.

'Anyway,' she sniffs, finally letting go, 'I couldn't miss your birthday, could I?' She smiles and wipes tears from her cheek.

'What's wrong? Are you okay?' I cup her elbow and try to make her look me in the eye.

'I'm fine, honestly. Glad we've made up. We're still going out today to celebrate, aren't we?'

'I'd love that, thank you.'

I'm so relieved we've made up too, and glad we're going out for my birthday, although I can't help wanting to ask her what Harry thinks about that.

'Harry's gone away for a couple of days... for work,' she says as if reading my mind. She kisses the top of Joseph's head, and he tips his chin up and stares at her.

'Oh, right.'

'Better get these little ones to school then, hadn't we? Shall I meet you back here at say 10 a.m.?'

'That would be perfect, see you then.'

After dropping Tyler off, I rush back home and get changed into a sparkly shirt and smart jeans. I switch the radio on and dance around to 'One Kiss' by Calvin Harris and Dua Lipa. It seems ages since I took the time to apply a full face of make-up. Usually, I dust on a bit of powder foundation, a coat of mascara and a nude lippy. Today I take the time to draw on black eyeliner with wings. I add a touch of moonlight eyeshadow, two layers of mascara and a red lip gloss. When the straighteners are hot, I run them through my hair, flattening all the flyaways. It's so worth it when I look in the mirror. It's been a while since I've felt this good about myself. I should make more effort to do this every day. Self-care is a new concept to me.

When I've finished my hair, standing in front of me is the woman I was before I got pregnant. The party girl. The one who knew how to have fun without worrying about the consequences, because she naively trusted everyone.

I never slept around, even when I was single. Nobody knows that I was still a virgin at nineteen years old, because it's no one's business. Why does dressing up, going out and enjoying yourself equate to being a honey pot? Darren is so wrong about me. Simone is welcome to him if he thinks that of me, or any woman.

39

By the time Katie knocks for me, I'm buzzing and ready to go. We take a short bus ride into Huntingdon and go to the Tattoo Lounge on the high street. I've been thinking about having one since Tyler was born. Maybe it's a cliché, but I'd like his name in fancy writing on the inside of my wrist.

We sit in the waiting area with a cup of coffee and flick through the albums in case something else takes our fancy. Katie wants a small pair of angel wings on her shoulder in memory of her nan.

I go first. I'm dead nervous so I concentrate on the tattoo artist's tall pile of blue woven hair. My eyes water as soon as the needle bites my skin. I try not to watch, especially when the blood trickles down my arm. Nowhere near as painful as childbirth, I tell her.

After the letter Y, I've had enough, but Katie's has begun, so I can't exactly stop and I can't give up after only two letters. She's lying face down, head on a cushion, her shirt off on one side. I can see a small curve of bruises on her forearm. I frown. I don't remember seeing them before and she's not mentioned hurting herself. I try to look closer, but I don't want to jog the needle by moving. From here they look like they could be finger marks. I'll ask her when we're done. Her tattoo is going to take longer so at least I'll have time to recover a bit before we go for lunch.

When it's finished, my skin is rosy pink all around the beautiful black writing: Tyler. I love it and hold it up for Katie to see.

'It's brilliant,' she says and puts her head down again, grimacing in pain. My tattooist wraps my wrist in film and once I've paid, I go and sit next to where Katie is still lying. I can see her arm a little more clearly now, a small blue and green row of bruises, definitely the size of finger-tips. Standing up, I pretend to be interested in the photos on the walls, but I'm checking over my shoulder, trying to get a better view of Katie's forearm. I'm sure I can see a couple of bruises on her wrist too.

'You okay?' Katie asks, catching me staring at her.

'It's looking good. You're doing really well.' I move back to the wall and one photo jumps out at me. A red and black Chinese snake tattoo on a man's upper arm and shoulder makes me catch my breath. It's just like the one on the clown's arm in the nightmare I keep having. I snap a photo of it with my phone. Could whoever attacked me have this same tattoo, or is it my brain inventing random things?

When Katie has finished, we show each other our tattoos as properly as we can, as each one is covered in the film dressing. Then we walk arm in arm to The George Hotel for lunch, elated that we actually went through with it.

'I'm paying, my treat,' Katie says as soon as we're sitting down.

'Are you sure?'

'Of course. And I want you to order whatever you like.'

I'm glad she told me before I decided what to eat because I know how tight her budget is, so I skip the starter and order chicken in white wine sauce. Katie orders the same and we have a glass of non-alcoholic prosecco each.

'My wrist is so sore. How's your shoulder?'

'Hot and painful. I don't know how people have those really big tattoos.'

The waitress brings the drinks over.

'Happy birthday, Ellie,' Katie says, raising her glass to mine.

'Thank you. I feel like a proper grown-up now I'm thirty.'

'You are. You're one of the most sensible people I know.'

'I hope that doesn't really mean boring.' We laugh. 'Here's to being brave,' I say and we clink our glasses again.

'Cheers to that.'

Katie exaggerates, wincing in pain. She always makes me laugh.

'What does Harry think about you getting a tattoo?' I take a mouthful of drink.

'He's all for it. Got loads himself.'

'Does he? Do you think you'll have any more? You talked about having one on your forearm.'

Instinctively she pulls up her sleeve. 'I wasn't sure what to go for, maybe a line from a song in a fancy script writing font – along my forearm and up to my wrist. If I can stomach the pain that is. Not sure I can now I've had a taster.'

'Same. I think that might be it for me.' I nod to the line of bruises. 'They look nasty.'

She pushes her sleeve back down. 'Oh, it's nothing.' But her face is pink.

I touch her arm gently.

'Ouch.' She pulls away, frowning at me.

'How did you get them? They look like marks from fingers pressing too hard.'

'Rough sex.' She attempts a laugh but her eyes glisten with tears. She stares down at the tablecloth for a second then looks up at me. 'Harry and I argued after we left your flat the other night. He called you my toxic friend, said you're jealous of me having a boyfriend. Said you made all that up about it being me who wrote the message in blood on the wall and in the bath just to get my attention and split us up.'

'What?' I lean towards her. 'Is he suggesting I did it myself?'

'He thinks you resent the time we spend together and are so needy you can't bear me being with him.'

'You know none of that's true, don't you?' I whip back.

Shit, my envy has been that obvious?

Katie nods. 'He was so angry with you accusing him of being one of the clowns who attacked you. Said there were so many other men around dressed like that, it could have been anyone; why else would you pick on him.'

'Christ.' I lean back in my seat. 'He doesn't even know me.'

'He was with me most of the time at Halloween, but thinking about it, he did disappear for a few minutes, came back with the candy floss for Joseph. But I don't believe he would have attacked you. He certainly didn't have time to get there and back. In any case, he wouldn't do that to you or to anyone.'

I nod, trying to take it all in. But he hurt you, I want to shout at her, but all I say is, 'Did you ever find my spare key?'

'No. We looked everywhere, stripped the house near enough. I accused him of moving it and not remembering where, so he was upset with me about that too.'

'Why would he have moved it?'

'Tidying up. He's a bit of a neat freak.'

I sip my drink, but it tastes sour, bubbles fizzing up my nose. 'Is it possible he took the key and came into my flat?' I watch Katie closely. 'Maybe thinking he needed something for you,' I add quickly because her mouth has dropped open. Have I pushed our friendship too far by asking this? It's crossed my mind a couple of times, but I've always dismissed it as me being paranoid until now. I need to know what she thinks.

'I... I don't know. Why would he?'

'To borrow something for you or to play a prank on me, maybe trying to impress you? Then it's gone horribly wrong?'

'I don't think he would do that without speaking to me first.' She holds her palm to her heart.

'The only other person who could have borrowed a key is Louise's husband, although I doubt it because one of them would have said. But I'll check.' I can't honestly see Steve or Louise borrowing my key without saying something to me first.

Katie blinks at me and tears begin to spill over. 'Harry told me to keep away from you, but I refused. I told him we were best friends, and I wasn't going to chuck that away. We help and support each other, and you would never do anything to hurt me.'

'Thank you.' I squeeze her hand. She wipes her eyes on her napkin then drains her glass.

'He yelled at me that my loyalty should be with him not you. That we were a couple now and he should always come first. He was holding my arms tightly, shaking me, and I begged him to stop.' She sobs into the napkin.

'And did he? So that's where you got the bruises?' I get up and give her a hug.

She nods, dabbing her eyes.

'I wouldn't give in and he kept on and on, shaking me, digging his fingers into my arms. Said *you women are all the same*. When I asked what he meant, he said we're all liars and prick teasers. Then he stormed out.' She holds the napkin to her face. I take her hand, and she lets me hold it. For a moment we're silent.

'I'm so sorry he did that to you, Katie. Did you report it to the police?'

'He warned me not to go to the police or there would be consequences. I don't expect to see him around again.'

I sit back down, feeling shocked. I order us both another drink and when our food comes, we both make the effort to try to enjoy it and talk about happier things, like Tyler's trip to the farm the next day. Part of me wishes I could go, but I know it will be good for Tyler's development not having me around for a change.

When we stand up to leave, I give Katie another hug. I'm glad to see the back of Harry knowing what he's really like. Hopefully that's the last we'll see of him.

40

I'm emotionally drained by the time we get back to pick the boys up from pre-school. The thought of Harry being cruel to Katie right next door, only a wall separating us, turns my blood cold. If I'd known, I could have helped her, called the police. How did I not hear anything, not even a cross word between them?

Mrs Howe is standing at the pre-school door, handing out a letter with each child. I thank her and skim over the list of last-minute reminders for the farm trip in the morning. Being on the committee means there's nothing I don't already know about. Tyler will need a packed lunch, a pair of wellies in a plastic bag, and a spare set of clothes in his rucksack. The coach will be leaving at 9 a.m. prompt and it's fitted out with seatbelts. I have everything ready at home, yet I'm still worried I'm going to forget something or wake up late. I've got an important glazing conference to go to, so I have to be on time.

Hayley and Lauren eyeball me as Tyler and I stroll back to the car. They're going to help out at the farm tomorrow because neither of them needs to go to work. Their husbands 'provide for them', is the way they put it. Maybe they think this makes them superior to the rest of us. I prefer to be self-sufficient.

I can't help wondering whether the two of them will keep a proper eye on Tyler or side-line him just to spite me? I feel bad for thinking they'd do that, but if they had to choose between looking out for their own children over mine in a difficult situation, I know which they'd choose. In the morning I'll find out which group Tyler's in, and if necessary, get him swapped to Mrs Howe's or Mrs Cooper's.

I start the car. My head is throbbing at sky-high levels of anxiety, even though I've had a good time with Katie. I can't stop thinking about Harry hurting her, being so nasty, saying those things about me and women in general.

At home, Tyler settles in front of the TV, holding a drink of squash in a beaker.

'Mummy's going to have a little nap just here on the sofa,' I tell him as I shut the living-room door. He nods and I hang a string of tiny bells on the handle, so I'm alerted if he tries to leave the room. I'm a light sleeper so I'm confident I'll hear the tinkle if he touches them. I curl up under the fleece blanket and shut my eyes for a few minutes. I might not sleep with the shouting and cheering from the TV, but sometimes shutting my eyes for a few minutes is enough to revive me.

Sure enough, fifteen minutes later I'm woken by the bells tinkling, as Tyler pulls down the door handle. He's holding himself, desperate for the loo and can't quite release the door catch with the other hand. I practically roll off the sofa, push myself up and open it for him, making sure he gets to the bathroom without having an accident.

He's hardly had any lately and it's another reason why I want him to gain a little more independence by going on the farm trip without me. I've been telling myself this for days, but it still doesn't stop me from waking up in the middle of the night worrying about him being all alone. What if he gets lost and doesn't know where any of the other children or teachers are? What if they leave the farm without him? Like the time they had a special assembly for the parents in the pre-school room and I searched and searched for Tyler's face but I couldn't see him. I thought I was going mad, that he must be hiding somewhere at the back. And everyone was listening intently to the story Mrs Howe was reading; I didn't want to interrupt. Then I stood up and asked in a panicked voice, 'Where's Tyler?' And everyone looked around in shock because they couldn't see him either. Mrs Cooper rushed outside and saw the side gate was wide open and everyone thought the worst. Then I heard him calling 'Mummy,' and I found him in the bathroom with the door ajar, sitting on the toilet. I've never got over it. The pre-school always left the side gate open, but after that they promised they would buy a lock and catch, which they did.

I'm sure they've got it all in hand. It's partly why I joined the committee, so I could find out all their plans and safety checks and have a say in them. They'll have enough parent helpers tomorrow, but even with the ratio of one adult to four children, I wonder how anyone can keep their eyes on each child every single second of the day. I struggle to keep track of one. Unless Tyler is holding my hand, he's all over the place, wandering around the shop or walking down the high street. It only takes a split second for him to stray from my sight.

I cook a pasta dinner and after I've got Tyler to bed, I call Molly on FaceTime.

'Happy birthday, Ellie,' she says with the same level of enthusiasm as she did by text this morning.

'Thank you.'

'We need to get together and celebrate. Maybe I can come and see you soon?'

'I'd love that. And thanks for the lovely presents.' I pick up a book from the pile of paperbacks she sent, stacked up on the coffee table next to me.

'I tried to tick off as many of the romance novels on your list as I could. So come on, tell me what you've been up to on your special day.'

I mention the messages from Darren this morning, saying not to sleep around when I find a new boyfriend. I'm still raging he thinks that of me. That he assumes I did that to him.

'He said I hurt him. He still believes I was unfaithful to him.'

Molly nods, frowning.

'But the way he says it is almost like he knew something because he was there. But that's not possible.'

'Unless there was a party you went to with him where you got really drunk and he found you with someone and assumed the worst?'

'I wouldn't have done that to him. But thinking about it, we did go to a house party around that time. A few of his friends had clubbed together and bought an old property. They wanted to do it up and make a bit of money. The place was in a bad state inside when they moved in, so they thought it was the perfect opportunity to have a party before they started work on it. I did drink a lot, as I always did then, but I don't remember getting together with anyone. I was with Darren, he was the love of my life, there's no way I would have done that. And you know how jealous he'd get if another man even looked my way.'

Molly nods and then exaggerates scoffing popcorn from a bowl at my soap opera life. I laugh and she bursts into laughter too.

'Come to think of it, I was chatting to the DJ that night, so Darren and I had one of our fallouts. I remember I went upstairs to the bathroom and couldn't find my way, so maybe he thinks I got up to something because I took a long time.'

'Were you talking to anyone upstairs?'

I wrack my brain. 'There was a man queuing for the loo, and we laughed about how long it was taking. But I'm sure that was it. Although now I'm thinking back, I remember he put his arm around me.'

'Could be that Darren saw this man with his arm around you. Or he saw him come downstairs and then you came down a few seconds after and he put two and two together. Maybe speak to Darren again, face to face, because if he thinks that, he should tell you.'

My mind is whirring. Does he really think I hooked up with a man right under his nose? Is this why he keeps going on about me being faithful to my next boyfriend? If it is, he makes me sick.

'So did you and Katie go out?' She picks a small marshmallow off her hot chocolate then drinks some. I wish I had made something as comforting to sip on.

'She came round this morning to say sorry for Halloween night, so we went out as planned and both had tattoos done.' I show her my wrist.

'Nice. You're braver than me, I don't think I could face the pain.'

'Wasn't that bad.' I pull a face which clearly shows a different story, because Molly laughs, then we're both laughing again.

'I'm pleased you made up. Sounds like you've had a good birthday.'

'I have, thanks. I'm glad we've made up too, although I had a strange feeling of déjà vu when I was in there. There was a photo of a Chinese snake tattoo on the wall. I had to do a double take because it looked so familiar to me, but I don't understand why, only that there's been a snake in the nightmares I keep having about the man in the mask.'

Molly frowns, her lips pursed. 'Elle, could it be something to do with when you were attacked?'

'Maybe. I don't know.' I shake my head, trying to loosen my memory. 'I've been desperately thinking where I could have seen it, but I don't remember anyone I know having a tattoo like that.'

'If it is a memory from that night, maybe it means you'll start to remember other things.'

I shudder and glance down at the rug, but the floor slides away from me. I lift my head back up to steady my vision. 'Let's not talk about that now.'

'You said you were going for a meal after your tattoo; how was it?'

I sigh deeply, trying to shake off the strange feeling enveloping me. 'It was lovely, thanks, but Katie was a bit sad. She split up with her boyfriend.'

'Oh no, why? I thought you said they were blissfully happy.'

'They were. She's been spending nearly all her time with him. Perhaps too much time. Too much too soon. When we were at the tattoo place, I noticed she had all these small bruises up her arms. I asked her about it and she told me Harry grabbed her and shook her.'

Molly's hand flies to her mouth. 'Why did he do that?'

'Apparently, they had a fight after they left my flat on Halloween night. And get this, he told her I was a toxic friend because I'd made everything up about the blood all over my bathroom. He thinks I did it to blame them for pranking me, to get her sympathy.'

'That's so screwed up.'

'Isn't it? Then Katie admitted that she lost my front door key three or four days ago. I mean why didn't she tell me? Anyone could have found it and let themselves in.'

'But let me guess, you think it could have been Harry?'

'It's possible, isn't it? What if he set me up? Did the whole blood in the bath and up the wall thing to frame me.'

'But why would he?'

'To break up me and Katie. If he's one of these controlling boyfriends, he would resent us being close.'

'Sounds like he could be behind it, deliberately hurting Katie and bad mouthing you.'

'Exactly. And before he walked out he told her all women are liars. As far as I know, she's not seen him since.'

'She's better off without him.'

'Hurt as she is, I hope she thinks the same.'

41

I'm awake earlier than usual. My eyes open about three minutes before my 6 a.m. alarm goes off. For once, I've had a good night's sleep. By the time Tyler wakes up an hour later, I am showered and dressed, a full face of make-up on.

I make his packed lunch while he eats breakfast and watches CBeebies. There's a lump of anxiety in my chest that won't shift, but I have to do this. He'll be four in six months, then he'll be starting school four months later. This is as much about me starting to let him go as it is about him learning to be happy and safe somewhere without me. Mrs Howe is a stickler for rules and regulations, so I know they'll be shepherded around the farm in complete safety. And yet I have to push away the nightmarish visions I keep having of a farmer sitting high up on his tractor, not seeing the small figure of Tyler in his rear-view mirror, or Tyler sitting with a rabbit on his lap nibbling a chunk out of one of his fingers.

In one of the pre-school meetings, I brought up the importance of counting the children onto the coach and counting them out again, so as not to leave anyone behind.

We're the first to arrive at pre-school at 8.15 a.m. We stay in the car and I go through all sorts of safety measures with Tyler, such as not speaking to strangers, staying with his group, making sure he doesn't move away from them or let them go off without him. He's memorised my mobile phone number and his full name and address. I've also written my phone number on the inside of his coat. There is literally nothing that can go wrong that I haven't prepared for. And the farm even gives the children wrist bands to wear during their stay to identify them with their school group.

In fact, if this all goes well, I might suggest to Katie that we find a babysitter and have a night out together. It's so good to have this possibility of a little freedom again.

The coach pulls up in the car park and Mrs Howe and the other staff come out of the pre-school carrying bags of provisions, such as spare clothes, bottles of water and snacks, in case anyone has forgotten anything, as well as a freshly stocked first aid kit. Even with all the prep I've done, my stomach turns over. Part of me wants to grab Tyler and take him straight home with me, to keep him safe. But I have to let him go.

I walk Tyler over to the coach with his little rucksack on his back and lunch bag in his hand. He's wearing his wellies as it rained overnight and it's still muddy everywhere. There's no point ruining a perfectly good pair of trainers.

'Morning,' I call to Mrs Howe as she steps down from the coach. The driver is walking up and down the aisle, checking all the seatbelts are working, which they hopefully are.

'Good morning, how are you?' She stops in front of me, her cheeks flush in the morning chill.

'I'm okay thanks, a bit nervous. This is the first time Tyler has gone anywhere without me.'

'He'll be fine.' She pats my arm and gives me a reassuring smile. 'We have lots of volunteers as you know, and I think there's only three in his group. Let me check for you.'

'Oh, thank you, I was going to ask you which group he's in.'

She checks on her clipboard and flicks over a page. 'Here he is, with Adam and Lucy in Hayley's group.' She looks up at me and catches my sour face.

'I was really hoping he would be in your group, Mrs Howe. He's so comfortable with you, I feel like he would be able to tell you if he needed the toilet or anything like that. He doesn't really know Hayley very well. I think he'd be too embarrassed to speak to her about something that was bothering him.'

Mrs Howe tips her head to one side. Her eyes flick over my face, but I will not budge. I will not say, 'only if it's no trouble', even though my instinct is screaming out at me not to be a nuisance. For me, there's no compromise where Tyler is concerned.

I tip my head to match hers and implore her with my eyes.

'Well, as you've asked so early, I'm willing to swap Tyler to my group.' She pencils a line through his name and adds it under hers, then moves another child to Hayley's group. 'But there are four children in my group, is that okay?'

I nod and bite my lip. I'm so grateful I could cry. Hayley seems to hate me, and I wouldn't want Tyler to be affected by that.

'Thank you, I really do appreciate it.'

'Right, let's take you in, Tyler, see if you want to go to the toilet before we set off.'

As we walk around the edge of the car park to the pre-school building, I notice several cars have started to arrive. Hayley parks up as we're passing, and I avoid looking directly at her. I wonder if she picked her group and if she'll complain that I've moved Tyler. I hope she doesn't make something of it.

At the pre-school door, I crouch down and hug Tyler. He squeezes me tight.

'You have a lovely time at the farm okay, and Mummy will see you when you get back.' My bottom lip trembles.

'Mummy has to go now,' Mrs Howe says.

A surge of panic shoots through my veins. I don't know if I can let him go. I can't bear to say goodbye. How am I going to get through the day? I'm going to be clock-watching all the time.

'Yes, Mummy's got an important conference today.' I check my watch. I need to leave soon if I'm going to get there on time. I give Tyler one last hug and Mrs Howe takes his hand. He waves to me as he walks away.

Hayley is standing behind me with her son as I turn to go back to my car.

'I hope you have a good day,' I tell her.

'Such a shame you can't come.' She gives me her false one-second smile and then goes inside.

It's a few more minutes before the children and helpers start boarding the coach. I wave to Louise who's hurrying to get on with her son. Nausea hits me as the double-decker coach slowly pulls away. I wave goodbye to my tiny boy; his legs won't even be able to touch the floor.

This is going to be a long day, but somehow I've got to get through it.

I reach work a few minutes late for the opening regional meeting. I sit at the back with the other latecomers, and doodle my way through the next hour. At the midmorning tea-break I check my phone. I don't know what I'm expecting to find but I'm tempted to text one of the mums to find out how it's going and more specifically, how Tyler is. Instead, I open the pre-school Facebook page and I'm pleased to see an update from about twenty minutes ago. There are photos showing the children sitting on low benches in one of the barns, holding and petting rabbits and guineapigs. I search for Tyler's sky-blue jacket and think I spot him in the corner of one photo. I wish I'd gone with them. This has to be the most boring conference I've ever been to, and I realise it wouldn't have mattered if I'd missed it because they're giving handouts. But I wasn't to know that.

There are two workshop sessions before lunch, designed as team-building exercises, which are more interesting, so the time seems to fly by. When the second one finishes, everyone pours into the main hall where the smell of delicious hot food is wafting out. Tables are laid with white tablecloths, the food is laid out in one corner and the serving staff are waiting on hand. I think about hanging back, eating later, but two of the workshop leaders come and talk to me and I naturally follow them into the queue for food. I sit with them and share a bottle of sparkling water. Maybe it's a good thing I came after all. One of them takes my business card and says she'll call me about a management position that's come up in the Peterborough branch. It would mean getting a childminder for Tyler's school run, but it's doable and more money.

As soon as they've moved on and are chatting to other people, I slip out to the patio. As I find my phone in my bag, it starts flashing and buzzing in my hand. I don't recognise the number and almost don't answer.

'Hello?' I ask tentatively, ready to press the end button in case it's a marketing call.

'Hello, is that Ellie? This is Mrs Cooper from the pre-school.' She pauses for a millisecond but doesn't wait for a reply. 'Mrs Howe asked me to phone you right away.'

'Is everything all right?' Adrenaline spikes through my forehead.

'I'm calling about Tyler.' From her tone, I already know it's not good news.

'What's happened?' I lean against the wall to steady myself.

She takes in a deep breath. 'He's been such a good boy and was with us all morning and sat with Mrs Howe and her group through lunch without any problems.'

'Please, just tell me what's wrong.' My stomach sinks at the possibilities flashing through my mind.

'I'm so sorry to have to tell you this, Ellie, but we don't know where Tyler is.'

42

'What do you mean?'

'He was with Mrs Howe and a moment later, he wasn't there. No one saw him leave the hall.'

'How is that possible?' I pinch my forehead, then rub the skin. She's not making any sense. None of this makes sense.

'He was with Mrs Howe, sitting right next to her but the child on her other side started having a terrible nosebleed; there was blood everywhere and I suppose in all the confusion and drama, Tyler wandered off.'

'You're saying that like it's his fault. You were supposed to be watching him.'

'We're so sorry. Mrs Howe is beside herself.'

'Sorry?' I almost laugh but I want to scream. 'Maybe he went to find the toilet to be sick. He hates the sight of blood. Have you checked all the toilets?'

'Yes, it was the first place we looked, after last time.'

'Mrs Howe was meant to keep him safe. She promised me.' My voice escalates along with my pulse, which is pounding in my ears. 'It's the first time he's been on a day trip without me.'

'I know and she's so upset for letting you down, which is why she wanted you to know straight away. We've asked all the children if they've seen him and no one has, not even the other grown-up helpers. Everyone was so taken up with Lucy's nosebleed...'

'Lucy? Wasn't she in Hayley's group?'

'Erm, I'm not sure off the top of my head.'

'Why was Mrs Howe looking after a child who was supposed to be Hayley's responsibility? It sounds like it was at the expense of my son's welfare.'

'I think Hayley had to take another child from her group to the toilet.'

'I just knew something would happen because of her.'

'What do you mean?'

'I don't know, but Hayley's had it in for me ever since that fake missing poster went up on Facebook. Mrs Howe knew how anxious I was about leaving Tyler in Hayley's care, so she moved him to her group, but Hayley has still managed to cause trouble for me and my son.'

'I'm sorry you feel that way. I'm sure it wasn't deliberate. Mrs Howe is searching for Tyler with a group of farm staff as we speak. I'm sure they'll find him.'

'He was in Mrs Howe's group because she's so experienced and because he's so comfortable with her. How can she not know where he went?' My voice is beginning to rise.

'She's busy looking for him in all the obvious places, which is why she couldn't call you herself.' Mrs Cooper's voice falters. She pauses, drawing in a breath, probably to compose herself. I can hear her slowly blowing air out of her mouth. 'Everyone is looking for him. We're all desperately concerned and anxious to find him.' Her voice catches at the end.

A stab of guilt shoot through my chest. Here I am having a go at her. It's not her fault.

'I'm sorry. I'm sure you're all doing everything you can. I'm grateful, I really am.'

Tyler is out there somewhere on his own. He'll be crying, panicking, calling for me. Has Hayley got something to do with it? It doesn't feel real. I'm frozen to the spot as though I've been hit by a stun gun. My lungs are heavy and it's hard to draw a breath. Mrs Cooper will tell me in a minute that she's been playing a sick joke on me and Tyler is right next to her, holding her hand.

But she doesn't say that. She continues huffing and puffing.

Mrs Howe had four children to look after. She's experienced. She has eyes in the back of her head, everyone says so. This cannot have happened to my boy.

'He can't have gone far, can he?'

'No, but it's a big place; there are lots of possible places to hide in the fields, barns, play centre and the main farm where the animals are kept.'

'And machinery that can't see a little boy near their massive tyres or hear him over the noise of the engines. Oh my God.'

'Try not to panic. Where we've been is a relatively small area.'

'I'm at a conference in Cambridge, but I'll leave straight away. It's a fifty-minute drive to Peterborough.'

'Okay, let's not panic. We'll see how it goes. Maybe hold off for now.'

'I should be there looking for him.'

'Try not to worry. I'm sure he's just wandered off in the wrong direction and we'll find him any minute. He could be in a tunnel in the soft play centre or hiding in the Build-A-Bear shop.'

'Okay, if you think I should wait a bit longer. But please call me as soon as you find him. In fact, as soon as you know anything.'

I end the call and crouch down, head in my hands. Am I in a nightmare? I want to call Katie or Molly or even Darren, but I can't block up the line. I text them instead.

Molly is the first to get back to me. I've told each of them not to ring because I'm waiting to hear back from the pre-school. Molly tells me to stay calm, Tyler will be okay. Something probably caught his eye, and he went to investigate. Katie offers to drive there for me and help look for him, but I say not yet, I'll wait and see if they find him in the next few minutes.

Darren asks if there's anything he can do. I'm touched that he replied straight away, considering our recent fall out.

I step back inside and grab a coffee. The next workshop starts in twenty minutes, but it's one I don't care about missing. I sit at a table on my own and stare at my phone, willing good news to light it up. One of the delegates from a different company, a guy in a dark navy suit, comes over.

'Mind if I join you?' His slicked back hair reminds me of Chandler from *Friends*.

I glance at the seat next to me as though he's talking to someone sitting there. When I look back at him, he's smiling.

'Not at all, although I'm expecting an important call any second.'

'I'll leave you to it then.' He turns to go, and without thinking I reach out and touch his arm.

'It's okay, you can sit here. I mean, I'd like you to join me.' I laugh at my awkwardness, and he laughs too. 'I just don't want you to think I'm being rude if my phone rings and I answer it, because I have to answer it. My little boy has gone missing.'

Oh God, here I go, oversharing already. I feel my face flush.

'Oh no, where's he gone missing from?'

'Nursery, a day trip. I thought they'd take better care of him, but it seems he's wandered off.'

'I'm so sorry. Can I do anything to help?'

'I don't think so, but thank you. I'm Ellie, by the way.' I offer my hand and he shakes it.

'I'm Lee. Pleased to meet you. Is it your first time at the glazing conference?'

'I've been a few times, but I'm not sure I can bear coming again. It's dead boring. There's only so much I can listen to about the labour shortages and supply chain crisis for the window and door sector and don't get me started on component suppliers. How about you?'

He laughs. 'First time. I've been to better conferences, I must admit.'

We chat about work stuff for a while and he's so easy to talk to. Though the whole time, I have one eye on my phone. When it starts ringing, he's a real gentleman and moves away so I can take the call.

'Ellie, it's Mrs Howe from pre-school. I'm so glad to be ringing you with good news. Tyler has been found.'

'Oh, thank God, where was he?' I hold my hand to my heart and my body relaxes.

'One of the dads found him in the big barn playing on a toy tractor.' She lets out a curious sound which is a cross between a laugh and a sob.

'Thank goodness. Did Tyler say why he was in there?'

'He's not said much at all, but we're not pushing him to explain just yet. It seems he wandered off by himself. We were in the big barn earlier and he really enjoyed it, so I expect he wanted to go back and play for longer. He seems perfectly happy and back playing with his friends, so I'm not concerned.'

'Thank you so much for letting me know. I'll be leaving shortly. I'll pick him up from pre-school at the usual time.'

I end the call and Lee approaches, smiling.

'By the looks of it, that was good news?'

'It was, I'm so relieved. They found him playing by himself with the toy tractors. I should have known.' I exaggerate rolling my eyes and Lee laughs. 'I'm going to have to leave in a minute, make sure I'm back in time to pick him up.'

He nods and can't seem to stop smiling at me. 'It was good chatting with you.'

'You too. Will I see you at the Christmas do?'

'I hope so.' He dips his head and when he looks up again, his cheeks are flushed. 'Actually, I was wondering if we could exchange numbers? I'd love to meet up for a drink with you sometime, soon. If you want to, of course?' His voice wavers. It's sweet that he's a bit shy, not over-confident like so many men I've known.

'I'd really like that. And thank you for the distraction.' I show him my number and he types it straight into his phone and sends me a text.

'Great, thanks. I'm glad I was able to take your mind off things briefly.' His smile lifts his eyes as he gazes into mine. 'It's been lovely getting to know you, Ellie.'

'You too. Thanks for cheering me up when I really needed it.'

He leans in and kisses me gently on the cheek. I inhale a waft of Carolina Herrera aftershave and for a second, I have trouble dragging myself away.

43

I text Molly, Katie and Darren to let them know Tyler has been found and is absolutely fine. They all text back straight away, expressing their relief.

There's hardly anyone parked outside the village hall when I get there. The coach hasn't arrived yet. I'm fifteen minutes early. I could pop home and come back but it's hardly worth it. I get out, go inside and nip down the corridor to the toilet. It's eerily quiet as I go in. A strong smell of bleach makes my nose tingle. All the toilet doors are shut, but none appear to be occupied. For some reason I feel a bit creeped out and push each door open just to make sure I am alone.

As soon as I go in and slide the lock across, the main door squeals open, then bangs shut. I can barely breathe. Whoever it is seems to be standing still, maybe by the sinks, not moving. Are they checking to see which toilet is free? Then a squeaky tap is twisted on. The water gushes out so I can't hear what they do next or whereabouts they are. The tap creaks as it's turned off and the stall door next to me is slammed and bolted.

I can't even take my trousers down let alone pee, I'm so anxious. Did someone follow me in? Can I dash out of the cubicle and back to the car park before they finish? The toilet roll is being unravelled.

I unbolt the door and run out.

Back in the car, I slide down in the seat so I can peek out of the windscreen but can't be easily seen. I must be going insane. It's probably one of the ladies from the WI who have their meetings there. And now I'm desperate for the toilet. But I need to see who it was first. I need to know if I was followed in.

The coach swings round into the car park and for a second I think it's going to take out the fence. I strain to see if Tyler is looking out of the window, but he's so tiny, I guess only the top of his head will be visible.

The door to the village hall opens and it's Hayley coming out. She's buttoning up her coat. It must have been her in the toilet. What's she doing back here already? She's supposed to be on the coach, helping out. She heads towards her car which is tucked away in the corner between two similar vehicles. I wonder when she got back. And if she was even at the farm when Tyler went missing.

Mrs Howe is the first off the coach and with Mrs Cooper's help, they shepherd all the children back round the side of the hall into the pre-school room. I hurry back into the toilets and find two or three of the WI ladies in front of the mirrors powdering their noses, making it feel a much more welcoming space.

As soon as I've dried my hands, I dash back outside and join the pre-school queue.

'How is he?' I ask Mrs Howe when I reach the front, kneeling to have a good look at Tyler before I give him a tight hug. I pull back and stroke his rosy cheeks and he beams at me, seemingly oblivious to the panic he's caused.

'Where did you get to, eh?' I say softly, smoothing down his hair and kissing his fringe. I shut my eyes for a second, smelling the scent of outdoors in his hair, grateful to have him back with me safe, and unharmed.

'Do you want to come in, Ellie, and we'll have a little chat?' Mrs Howe says quietly. I expect all the other parents have heard that my son did a disappearing act, and are thinking, *oh, what a surprise it was her son.* But I honestly don't blame Mrs Howe for wanting to keep the details quiet. Maybe that's why Hayley came home early? She might be stirring up trouble for Mrs Howe, saying she's not fit to be in charge of their children.

I nod and take Tyler's hand as she leads us into the pre-school room.

'Would you like a drink, Tyler?' Ms Lea asks him. She checks with me by giving a nod and I smile back. She then takes Tyler's hand and leads him into the play corner to fetch a small bucket of bricks. He tips them onto a table and starts stacking them.

'Do take a seat.' Mrs Howe sits at one of the small tables, her knees together, clipboard on her lap. I sit opposite. These tiny chairs make me feel like a naughty child. 'Ellie... I'm so, so sorry for what happened. After you specifically entrusted me to look after him too.'

She rests the clipboard on the table and clasps her fingers together.

I nod and sniff, trying not to cry again as I think about what could have happened, what it would be like now if he'd not been found.

'It was chaos when Lucy's nose started bleeding. And I know that's no excuse, but I was convinced I had all my group in my sights. But somehow Tyler wandered off without any of us seeing him.' She looks down at her hands. 'I will completely understand if you want to take this further and put in a complaint against me.'

'Have you found out why he went off?' I look over at where he's building a tower of bricks with Ms Lea, then back at Mrs Howe. I need some answers. This could have been catastrophic.

'He said he wanted to play on the tractor.' She opens her hands. A child's mind is a mystery to her too.

'Did he say why he didn't ask? Why couldn't he wait?'

'No. I suppose he loved it and wanted to go back, that's all I can work out.'

'Whose dad found him?'

'He didn't leave his name. He's not with our pre-school.'

'I'd like to be able to thank him. I'll contact the farm centre, see if they can help.'

'Good idea. He handed him in to the girl at reception but didn't stick around. Think he had his wife and daughter in the car. The receptionist may have taken down his number. All I know is that he said he'd gone back to the barn where they have all the play tractors out, looking for his little girl's coat, and found Tyler in there all alone.'

I gaze across at Tyler who is laughing at something Ms Lea said. He's so beautiful and perfect. Thank God he's safe. 'It was lucky he was found so quickly. And he wasn't distressed or anything?'

'Not at all; he seemed completely comfortable. The man took him straight to the main building. The receptionist said Tyler wasn't crying or asking for you.'

'That's such a relief,' I whisper, not wanting Tyler to hear me. 'I was worried he might have nightmares after this. Be scared that someone is going to take him away from me and hurt him.'

'I wouldn't worry.' Mrs Howe gently touches my arm. 'I'd be very surprised if it's affected him in a negative way.'

I tip my head to one side. 'How can you be sure about that?'

'Because he waved goodbye to the man. He knows about stranger danger, even if someone he doesn't know is being nice to him, so I thought it showed how comfortable he felt.'

'That's... sweet.' I frown.

'I think so. It was almost as if Tyler knew him.'

44

'I doubt if Tyler knew him. He does tend to be over friendly with strangers. He's not old enough to know the difference between people who are friends and ones who are just being friendly. A few weeks ago, he was chatting to a homeless man at the train station. I'm sure he was harmless, but he was a stranger nonetheless and Tyler didn't quite understand that we didn't know him.'

'I'd say he's more aware than you think. We've talked about stranger danger in pre-school a few times, and he seemed to have a good understanding. The father was being kind and friendly to him, not posing a threat, so he was just thanking him.'

'Tyler had probably seen the man earlier with his daughter, so he instinctively knew he was a good person, and probably familiar.'

Mrs Howe gives a deep sigh. 'I'm just so relieved he's okay. I couldn't have forgiven myself if anything had happened to him, especially under my care.'

'I'm not blaming you, okay?' I touch her arm with my fingertips. 'And I'm not going to put in a complaint.'

She nods, eyes fixed on the floor as though she's trying not to cry.

'By the way, I saw Hayley came back early; I hope everything is okay with her?'

'Her son became sick, so she had to bring him back, take him to the doctor.'

'Oh, I see. Who looked after her group?'

'We split the three children between the other groups. It wasn't a problem.'

I nod and smile. It doesn't explain why she was wandering around the village hall. Is her son at home on his own?

'Was she at the farm when Tyler went missing?' I try to make it sound as casual as possible.

'No, she'd already left by then.'

So that rules out Hayley having anything to do with it. Perhaps it really was just a case of him becoming curious about something and wandering off. But there must have been something other than tractors that made him walk away from Mrs Howe. I can't imagine him going off on his own like that. He's not that sort of child. Maybe it was the big train track they sometimes have out in the barn that was the draw.

Mrs Howe stands up and Mrs Cooper lets Tyler run over to me. I stand too, catching him in my arms. I hug him to my legs then kiss the top of his head, breathing in the fresh smell of outdoors, and I tell him how much I missed him today. I hold his hand tight and walk out to the car.

The car park is deserted now and the gentle breeze makes me shiver. The yellow street light flickers on and off even though there's still a fair level of daylight left, despite it being overcast, giving a strange otherworldly aura to the place. As I'm opening the back door for Tyler, I glance up briefly to see a black car skidding in through the entrance. As I strap Tyler into his seat, I'm vaguely aware of a car door slamming near me.

'I'd recognise that backside anywhere,' a familiar voice bellows behind me. I jolt and twist round, blinking in disbelief. Ian is standing there staring at me shamelessly. The shock of him turning up like this unnerves me. How did he know I'd be here, and how does he know where my son goes to school? I turn back to Tyler, my hands shaking as I fumble to plug his belt in.

'What are you doing here?' I face him, my tone like a head teacher catching a naughty pupil, but my heart is fluttering with fear.

'I was passing by and thought I'd see how my favourite girl is.'

'Seriously? You don't live anywhere near here.' My hands find my hips and I'm aware that I'm scowling. I've really had enough mayhem for one day.

'No, but I had to go to Cambridge for work and I thought, I know a special lady who lives nearby; why don't I go and catch up with her?'

My skin bristles. 'Today is really not a good time. You should have called ahead. I need to get Tyler home.' I frown.

I immediately know I should have ignored him. It's probably enough to lead him on, and he doesn't need any help. I slam Tyler's door shut then spot his shocked little face; he's probably wondering what's wrong with Mummy.

'Not so fast, you can't fob me off like that. I said I've come to see you.' In one swift step forward, he grabs my arm.

'Get off.' I half laugh trying to make light of it, but the more I pull away from him the tighter his hold becomes. I spot a sword tattoo on his right forearm and a horrifying thought comes to me. 'Do you have any others?' I ask.

'Why, do you want to see them?' He lets go and starts to undo his flies. Then he laughs and pushes his sleeve up instead.

'Everything okay here?' Mrs Howe is striding towards us, hiking her work bag over her shoulder.

'I'm just leaving, thank you.' The tension in my face and neck releases. I have a feeling she saw Ian gripping onto my arm, because she's standing there watching as I get in my car. She waits until I've started my engine. I nod at her as I pull away. Ian is left standing under the flickering yellow light, holding his pushed-up sleeve. I can just make out the bottom edge of a gold and red tattoo. It could be a Chinese snake, it's hard to say.

Within moments, Ian's black car is speeding up behind mine. I drive around the village trying to shake him off, but after five minutes, he's still following me. There's nothing I can do except go to my flat.

As I park up, I press call on my phone and ask Katie to come down and assist me.

'What's the big rush to get away from me?' Ian shouts, slamming his car door behind him. He's parked across me so I can't get out. 'I only want to speak to you.'

Katie told me the safest thing to do is to stay in my car with the windows closed and doors locked. When I don't answer Ian, he bangs on my window. Even though I know he's there, I jump in my seat, my heart beating faster. Tyler starts crying. I reach behind me sideways and hold his hand.

'What do you want?' Katie yells at him. She is standing on the pavement, arms crossed, one of her big knit cardigans wrapped around her.

'Mind your own,' he practically spits at her.

'You're the one who'd better sling their hook, before the police get here.' She taps her phone.

'You bitch,' he hisses at her then grins at me. 'I'll see you later.' He points his finger at me, thumb moving down on an imaginary trigger. Then he gets in his car and drives off.

I unlock the car and let Tyler out.

'What a nasty bit of work,' Katie says and hugs me. 'You all right, sweetheart?'

She ruffles Tyler's hair as we trudge up the stairs.

'Come in for a few minutes, I'll make us a coffee.'

I'm grateful for the offer, not wanting to go into my empty flat alone. Ian's threat of seeing me later worries me. Perhaps I should ring Molly, see if anything has been going on that I should know about since they split up. She's probably not aware that he's been contacting me. I've certainly not mentioned it. It is strange he's turned up today, after what's happened to Tyler. Is it possible he's the man who was at the farm? I wonder what he's up to.

But I don't voice any of this to Katie. Instead, I relay what happened at the farm. I go through every detail about how terrified I was Tyler wouldn't be found.

'You've had a right day of it, haven't you?' She puts the coffees down on the kitchen table and comes round to hug me.

I try not to cry and fix on the swirling milk in the coffee in front of me. The aroma is soothing, a little bit of normal. The boys are playing in the living room and we're sitting in the kitchen, so I'm hoping they can't hear us.

'Has Tyler said anything about why he wandered off?'

'Not yet. We didn't want to push him too much. I'm hoping he'll say something in his own time.'

'Was this man who found him a bit of a weirdo? Can't be too careful.'

'I've no idea. I'm wondering now if it could have been Ian. Mrs Howe said he waved goodbye to the man as if he knew him. Tyler's met Ian a couple of times when he was with Molly, so that would explain it. It's odd that he's come up here today.'

'Not odd really if you think about it.'

I frown and sip my drink.

'He's always had a thing for you and now he's not with Molly and you're single too, he's trying his luck.'

'He knows I'm not interested. We're just friends. Well, we were friends, a long time ago, although he wanted it to be more than that.'

'When did that ever stop a man? The ones I know anyway.'

'Do you think he could be the person who's been posting things about me on Facebook?'

'Seems quite likely to me.'

'I saw a tattoo on his arm, but I couldn't see if it was a snake.'

Katie takes my hand and squeezes it, knowing what I'm going to say.

'Could Ian be the man who attacked me?'

45

'My God, Ellie, you think Tyler could be his?' Katie whispers.

I nod, tears forming in my eyes. 'He's the only other person who could have known I was at the Airbnb that night because he was dating Molly. She must have told him about our plans for the trip to Jersey. Makes me feel sick just thinking about him travelling there to... to do that to me.'

'How are you going to prove it for sure?'

'I need to get him to do a DNA test, but I'm not sure how.'

'He doesn't have to know about it, just take one of his hairs or a bit of his spit.'

'Good point, like they do on detective programmes.'

She taps her phone and searches online. 'See here. It's called a discreet paternity test or secret DNA testing. Oh, hang on. It says they require consent and photo ID from all parties. It's a criminal offence otherwise.'

'Sod that. I need to know without him finding out.'

'Would you tell him if he is Tyler's dad?'

'I don't know yet. I suppose I ought to, but he doesn't deserve any contact with him.' I rub my head with the stress of it all. Is it really possible that Ian went out of his way to find me in an Airbnb? I think back to when we were friends, how much I trusted him. He was like a brother to me, so to find out he wanted more shook me. I stopped seeing him and wouldn't take his calls. The trust had gone. I couldn't look him in the eye without thinking of him looking back at me in this new way, with different feelings. Not long after, he started dating Molly. She asked me if it was okay before she said yes. And how could I object? I had no romantic feelings towards him. I'd lost him as a friend already. Could he really have been so bitter about my rejection that he planned to attack me?

Katie slips her arm around me and speaks in a low voice. 'How did the conference go?'

I'm grateful for the change of subject. 'Dead boring. I'd rather have helped out on the farm trip and stopped Tyler wandering off. Except... one good thing happened.' My face breaks into a brief smile.

'Go on.' She wriggles in her seat, beaming at me.

'I met someone really kind.'

'Oh. Tell me more.'

'His name is Lee and I think he took a shine to me too, wants to meet up.'

'Well, that's good to hear after all the shit that's been going on.'

'Yeah, I'd say so.' I smile. 'Maybe it's too good to be true.'

'Don't think like that. It's time you moved on from Darren. He certainly has.'

'I know and I intend to. Just a small matter of trust.' I squeeze my thumb and forefinger together to illustrate the zero confidence I have in men.

'You can't judge a potential new boyfriend on the sins of the old ones. I read that in a women's magazine years ago,' she says, clearly pleased with herself for remembering. We both laugh.

'I'd better go. I'm exhausted. I'm going to have a bath and an early night.'

I call Tyler and he comes running to me straight away for a change. I hug him, grateful all over again for him being found, whoever the man was.

'All right, look after yourself,' Katie says. 'Call me if that bloke comes back. Ian, wasn't it?'

'Yeah. I think I'd better call Molly.'

Back at home, I decide to cook Tyler an early tea while he watches TV. I text Molly to see if she's free for a call. A minute later, my phone is ringing.

'Hey what's up? You okay?'

I tell her about Tyler being found and Ian turning up outside pre-school, how he followed me home.

'I don't understand. Why'd he do that?'

'He made out he's working nearby, but he's been messaging me since you two split up.' I pace around the room, hand to my forehead.

'You didn't say.' Molly's tone is accusing.

I stop dead, take a gulp of breath.

'I didn't want to upset you.'

Silence. Shit. I should have told her straight away.

'I know he's always had a thing for you.'

'I'm sorry. I've never encouraged him. I was just wondering if you'd heard from him lately, if you know what this is all about.'

'I've no idea. He's not contacted me for weeks.'

'He seems to think we're going to hook up because we're both single, but I've told him I'm not interested.'

There is another silence on the line.

'You okay, Molly? I'm sorry, this must be horrible for you to hear.'

'It's not really. As I said, I knew he was still into you. Even took a swipe at me about it as he left.'

'Really? That's awful.'

'Said he only went out with me to hurt you.'

'What? He didn't mean that.'

'I think he did. Pretty nasty, isn't it? Especially after we were together over four years. I thought we were happy. I didn't realise I was his second choice. In fact, I've been wondering since how well I really knew him.'

'I can't believe he's like that.'

'Be careful, Ellie. He's got a vicious temper on him.'

I drop onto the sofa and hug a cushion closer to me. 'Do you think he could be the person who made the missing poster about Tyler and then posted the nasty messages about me?'

'Yeah, now I think about it, it could easily be him. That's the sort of thing he'd do to get back at you.'

'For the crime of not fancying him? People can't choose who they fall for. Has he always been like this, and I never realised?'

'I guess I didn't realise either. He'd always ask about what you were doing, how you were. I knew you'd been friends originally, so I tried not to let it bother me.'

'We were friends until he tried to kiss me. How did I not know he could be this spiteful?'

'Hidden it from you well. Always his best self when you were around. It's one of the reasons we split up. I couldn't bear him being nasty to me any more.'

'I can't believe it.'

'Selfish, spiteful and nasty, especially when no one was around to witness it. He couldn't stand it when you started going out with Darren. Was over the moon when he left you.'

I try to picture the Ian I used to know. The person I thought was a kind and thoughtful soul. I don't think he exists any more. I've clung on to a version of him from the past, when we were younger, when we'd laugh and mess about as friends. But unbeknown to me, he wanted to take it further, he wanted me to be his girlfriend. The idea disgusts me; he was like a brother to me, never a potential lover. Did my rejection make him come and find me and force himself upon me?

46

'Hang on a sec, Molls. Someone's at the door.' I turn and press down the catch without thinking. I cry out as the door crashes into me.

Molly is shouting, 'What's happening?' but my arm is down, by my side. I'm too taken aback by Ian, who's standing in front of me holding a bunch of flowers.

'Sorry, Elle, wasn't expecting it to open so quickly.'

'I told you to go.'

'Nah, that was your friend. Thought we could spend a bit of time together.' He kicks the door shut and thrusts a small bunch of freesias towards me, then leans in and tries to kiss the side of my face.

'I don't think that's a good idea.'

'Why not? Tell me what's wrong with me?' He opens his arms wide. When I don't answer, he lowers to his knees.

'No, please don't.' I cover my face, embarrassed for both him and me.

'I want you to go out with me, that's all. We used to be so close.'

'As friends. We were only ever friends. Then you went out with Molly.'

'Were you jealous?' He grins, showing his smoker's teeth. 'Bet you were.'

'Of course not.' I suddenly remember Molly is still on the phone. I hold it up to my ear. 'You still there?'

'That's Ian, isn't it? What's he doing there?' Molly's voice rises in pitch.

'I don't know.'

'Who's that?' He pushes himself up.

'Put me on FaceTime,' Molly says. I click the button and her face appears. 'It is you!'

'Hello Molls, nice to see you too.' Ian moves closer to see the screen, so our cheeks are touching. I pull away.

'What are you doing there?' she asks him. 'And what's with the flowers?'

'You know Elle is the only one I've ever wanted. There's always been another bloke on the scene, and now there isn't, it's my turn.' He grins at me and tries to put his arm around my waist. I step back, out of reach.

'Answer my question. Why are you there?' Molly's voice becomes screechy.

He laughs but doesn't answer.

'Were you at Sacrewell Farm today?' I ask.

He shakes his head. 'I already told you, I've been at work.'

'Did you post stuff about me and my son on Facebook, like pretending he's missing and sending nasty messages to people I know, pretending to be me or someone called Emma?'

'Woah, someone's got it in for you bad, Elle.'

'Answer her question,' Molly yells, her face reddening.

'Course not. Why would I do that? I don't go on that shit show.'

'Okay, another question for you. Do you remember the night four years ago, when Molly and I went to Jersey together? You two were dating.'

'Yeah, course I do. Your girly weekend away.'

'That's right. So did you follow us? Tell me where you were that weekend.'

'Are you having a laugh?' He pulls a disgusted face. It takes a whole second for Molly's mouth to open in response when the penny drops, and when it does so, it does from a great height because utter horror fills her face.

'I'm so sorry, Ian,' she says quietly, then turns to me. 'It can't have been him. He was away in Cumbria.'

'You seem very certain about that when you weren't before.' I look from Molly to Ian and back again, wondering if there's some joint cover up going on. She wouldn't lie for him, would she? No, she looks genuinely upset.

'There's no question, and I'm so sorry, Ian. I feel awful for not remembering straight away.'

Ian grunts at her attempt at an apology.

'So come on, why were you in Cumbria that weekend, just for the record?' I will not let it go. There'd better be a good reason.

He grumbles again before he speaks. 'I was at my mum's funeral.'

'Bloody hell, I'm sorry. I had to ask.'

'She really did, Ian.'

'I think you'd better go,' I tell him.

He scowls at me and for a second, I fear he's going to refuse to leave, but then he opens the door and marches out. I stand on the landing to make sure he goes down the stairs. I'm still holding Molly on FaceTime. 'That was awful. Sorry for dropping you in it, Molly.'

'What the hell was that all about?' She asks, looking bewildered.

'I know, right? He just barged in. He's been really creepy, following me around.'

'If he does it again, call the police.'

'I will, thanks. Why can't he accept I'm not interested?'

'What did I see in him?' She shakes her head in dismay. 'I know I should have remembered about his mother's funeral but it was early days for us, we weren't seeing each other every day. I must have blocked it out. I did offer to go with him although we'd already booked the Jersey trip. Only seemed right to offer, but he wanted to go alone to be with his family, which was fair enough.'

'Anyone order a taxi?' Ian's back, calling out as he opens the main door. 'This geezer's been waiting out here since I arrived.'

My mind is straight back in London when I was locked in that taxi, and the driver gave me that note. *Be careful what you wish for.* I still don't know what it was supposed to mean. Is it possible this is the same driver? I try to see the driver's face but can't.

'Get a photo of him, Ian,' I yell.

'Okay.' He takes his phone out of his pocket and just manages to snap a picture before the taxi drives off.

'Did you get him?' I ask, not wanting to move too far away from my open front door and leave Tyler on his own. Ian comes back up and shows me the photo he took. I hold up my phone so Molly can see too.

'Do you know who it is?' Molly and Ian ask at the same time.

It's blurred where the man has turned his head away, probably at the very moment he realised Ian had his camera aimed in his direction.

'From what I can make out, it's not the same driver from London. But there is something familiar about him.' I peer closer at the screen. 'I'm sure I've seen him before.'

I know his side profile from somewhere. Could it be Philippe? Is Jim Ball even his real name? Why use another name to advertise Leah's rooms on Airbnb without telling her? Purely to pocket the money for himself, or something more sinister? Now I know it can't have been Ian who attacked me, I'm pretty sure it was Philippe. But who is he really? He lay on that bed next to me, making out he was looking after me, but I was unconscious for hours, and now I think about it, it was after the man in the clown mask had been there, that I can't remember anything. My God, if he raped me, it means that creep is Tyler's dad.

'I took a photo of his number plate and licence number as he pulled away.' Ian swipes to the next photo.

'Bingo!' I shout. 'Well done, Ian.'

47

After Ian has gone and Molly and I have hung up, I check online and find out there's a register of taxi and private hire licences, but it looks like the council are the ones who have details about individuals and companies. Unless I want to report a taxi driver to the police, there's no way of finding out their name or who they are. I can't prove anything.

I go in the kitchen to make dinner, cooking sausages in the air fryer. While I'm waiting for the water to boil for the pasta, I pick up Tyler's rucksack. He's eaten nearly all his packed lunch and only left a banana skin and a half-eaten packet of crisps. I take his beaker out of the side mesh pocket. He's drunk most of his water, which is good considering he must have been offered other drinks at break times. His spare clothes are still folded so I take them out and put them away in his chest of drawers. The bag is empty but when I go to hang it up with his coat, something rattles at the bottom. I reach in and take out a small blue diecast sports car. It looks brand new, not a speck of dirt on it or paint worn off.

'Where did you get this from?' I ask, holding it in front of him.

He turns his head to me and shrugs, then looks back at the CBeebies programme he's watching.

'I hope you didn't borrow it from nursery.' I lean across the TV screen, so he has to look at me.

He shakes his head.

'So, come on, did someone lend it to you?'

He continues shaking his head.

'One of your friends gave it to you. To keep?'

He nods, smiling, still trying to see the screen behind me. I ought to turn it off, but I can't see where the remote control is.

'Can you tell me who that was?'

He shakes his head from side to side. A definite no then.

'Did you give them something?' It seems odd because it's not his birthday and he didn't have anything of his own to swap for it. Not that I know of anyway. But maybe he sneaked one of those small toys he gets with a takeaway into his bag, and forgot to tell me. He's done that before.

He shakes his head a few more times until he's dizzy and flops on his side.

'Not one little clue as to who it is from?'

He smiles and taps his finger on his top lip.

'You're keeping a secret?' I exaggerate by raising my eyebrows. 'You're good at keeping secrets, aren't you?'

He grins at me and nods, not giving anything away.

'Come on, just one tiny hint?' I press my palms together.

He giggles and kicks his legs up and down, banging his heels against the sofa. I start wriggling both my index fingers towards him and he knows what's coming. He throws himself backwards with a thud onto the sofa and lets out an overexcited scream as I tickle his tummy.

'Pretty please with a cherry on top,' I say in a playful voice, hoping he doesn't wet himself.

'The man, the man.' He giggles then lets out an exasperated sigh as if to say, who else would it be?

I stop dead, sitting back on my heels.

'What man?'

'The man in the car, silly.'

48

'What man was this, sweetie?' I try to keep my voice level so as not to scare him into silence, but my heart rate is shooting up and up.

Tyler shrugs.

'Darling, listen to me, are you saying you saw a man in a car, and he gave this to you?'

He shakes his head.

'Was it the same man who found you in the barn?'

He nods and sticks his tongue out of the side of his mouth.

'Did he ask you to get in his car?' Heat spikes through my chest. I can barely breathe. He was bribed with a toy. Was the intention to abduct him?

He pushes me away, leans across the sofa and buries his face in a cushion. It's been a long day. He has no patience left for me. A minute later he peeps out to look at the characters fighting on the TV screen.

'He didn't hurt you?' I stroke the top of his head.

Could he be making this up?

'No!' he shouts.

'He gave you this toy then asked you to get in his car?'

Perhaps the man took him back to meet his wife and daughter. That's what Mrs Howe said, wasn't it? But didn't he have to rush off to his family who were waiting for him? So he couldn't have taken Tyler to his car if he was in such a hurry. Unless he took him there first?

'Do you know the man's little girl?'

Tyler is no longer listening to me and if I push him, he'll probably have a tantrum and start crying. Maybe his daughter missed her pre-school coach this morning and he had to drive her to the farm. After all, Louise was late for ours and only just got there in time.

I check the time. The farm centre will still be open another hour. Are there CCTV cameras in their car park? I wonder if the father is someone I would recognise. I take my phone into the kitchen and dial the farm's number. When I get through, I ask to speak to the manager.

'I'm so sorry about what happened,' the woman says when I introduce myself. 'I can assure you we were searching for Tyler within minutes of him disappearing. Everyone was frantic, but we have a strategy in place for rare incidents such as this. We alert all corners of the farm using two-way radios, starting with the entrance, which is immediately secured and monitored for anyone trying to leave.'

'That's reassuring to know, thank you. I'm sure you did your best to find him and thankfully it wasn't too long before you did. I have to tell you I was sick with worry. I'd really like to thank the man who found him and was wondering if you could pass me his name and contact number, please?'

'I wish I could help but I'm so sorry, we don't have it. I wanted to thank him myself. Our receptionist said he rushed in with Tyler and rushed off again. Said he couldn't stop.'

'What a shame.. Do you know if he bought a ticket or had an advanced booking that might show his details?'

'Strangely, from the description we were given – he was wearing a distinctive black hoody with a Chinese cartoon image on the back – none of the staff remember seeing him around all day.'

'But he told your receptionist he had to get back to his wife and daughter, so presumably they'd spent the day at the farm?'

'I believe that's right, but like I say, we have no recollection of seeing him before then. The daughter could have been with one of the other school groups, so he didn't necessarily stay all day.'

'But you have CCTV, don't you?'

'Yes, all around the farm. In the reception area, café and outside the outbuildings and barns.'

'Could you check it please, so we can try and identify him?'

'I don't think that's necessary. I'd be happy to put a notice in our newsletter though. Perhaps the man will see it and come forward, then we can all thank him.'

'I'm sorry, I don't think I've fully explained myself.' I'm trying so hard to be polite. I swallow and pause for a second.

'I'm not sure what you mean.'

'Tyler says he got into this man's car, so I really need to know who he is.'

'What? I was not made aware of this.'

'I know. I couldn't believe it either. I mean why would a grown man, a stranger, ask my little boy to do that?'

For a moment there is silence on the line.

'Goodness, doesn't bear thinking about.'

'I don't think he touched him,' I say, letting out a sigh at the thought. 'The point is, Tyler would never make something like that up. I found a toy car I've never seen before at the bottom of his bag, and I thought perhaps he'd borrowed it from pre-school, but he told me this same man who found him in the barn gave it to him.'

'I don't know why I wasn't told this had happened.'

'I think I'm the first person he's told. This man gave him the toy to lure him into his car, I'm sure of it. And although Tyler does have a track record of borrowing toys, I believe he's telling the truth.'

The manager is silent.

'So you see, I need to know who this man is. It's possible it was a bungled attempt to take Tyler. What if he tries it again with another child?' I don't like implying this as it's unlikely anyone else is in danger, but I really need to persuade her to show me the CCTV. It's clearly Tyler and me who are being targeted. It must be the same person who was behind the poster, using it as a way of finding out where we live. And now this attempt to take Tyler away from me, it has to be his biological father, doesn't it?

'You're right. I see what you mean. Although, I wonder why he brought Tyler back?'

'Perhaps this time the man was interrupted by someone or something and felt compelled to hand the child in.'

'That is a disturbing possibility.' Silence. 'Can you get over here straight away? I'll inform the police and see if they can send someone out asap.'

'Thank you. We'll leave now.' I hang up and hold the phone to my chest. Was someone really trying to snatch my son? I was hoping for reassurances, but I've had none.

Who was this man at the farm? Is it who I fear? Images slide through my mind of Tyler being enticed into the man's car. Maybe he strapped him in. Would Tyler have shouted or screamed or was he under this man's spell, given a brand-new toy car to play with. But why did he let Tyler out again? Did the man realise the front gates would be locked within moments of Tyler being reported missing, and so he thought he'd be caught?

I need to see the CCTV with my own eyes.

49

Thirty minutes later, I pull into the farm car park. The light is beginning to fade and there are only a handful of cars there, probably belonging to staff as it's approaching closing time. A police car is parked near the entrance to the reception area.

I hold Tyler's hand tight, shuddering at the thought of him getting into a stranger's car here only a few hours ago. I may never have seen him again.

I allow Tyler to leave his headphones on because he's watching *Finding Nemo* on his tablet. In truth, I don't usually let him walk around 'plugged in', but I want to protect him from any conversations I might have with the manager and the police.

We follow the path round to the entrance. The lights are on, so we go in.

A girl with braids is on reception. She knows who we are straight away and comes round to pat my arm and ask if I'm okay. Then she shows me into an office behind her. A woman in a navy jumpsuit and flat boots stands up and strides forward to shake my hand, her other hand in her pocket.

'Come in, I'm Bethany Wood, the manager here. We spoke on the phone. This is DS Alex Chorley, who has kindly popped down to help us look into this.'

A policewoman with short silver hair sitting at the desk gets to her feet.

'Hello.' DS Chorley shakes my hand. Her gaze roves over my face as if she's trying to work something out. 'How is he?' She touches Tyler's hair lightly. He glances up at her then at me.

'He seems absolutely fine.' I put my arm around him. I give him a thumbs up and he does the same, smiling at me, looking like a giant bee in his headphones.

'Come and take a seat.' Bethany indicates three chairs.

Tyler and I sit next to the DS, while Bethany sits on the other side.

'One of my staff is going through the CCTV in the car park right now,' she continues. 'They're checking from about fifty minutes before Tyler went missing right up to the time he was handed in and a little after that, so we can hopefully capture images of the man going back to his car and driving away.'

'We've already seen a section of the CCTV footage from the car park,' says DS Chorley. 'The man in question arrives only about half an hour before Tyler goes missing.'

'Oh.' I frown. 'I thought he was already here with his daughter.'

'That's what we were led to believe. It's what he told the receptionist, but there is no sighting of a daughter with him. He parks his car and walks towards the farm alone.'

I stare at them, desperate to work out what that means. 'But the wife and daughter must be in the car when he leaves, or maybe they've already gone ahead?'

'From what we've seen, there was no wife or daughter. There is no one else in the car.'

'What?' I blink slowly, trying to make sense of it. 'Why would he lie?'

There's a pause that seems to expand time.

'We think he may have gone to the farm with the sole purpose of taking a child,' DS Chorley says. 'But we need to wait and see what the other CCTV clips show us first.'

'Of course.' I let out a breath.

'Would it be okay to have a little chat with Tyler?' DS Chorley asks.

'Yes, of course.'

I gently take the tablet from his hands and press pause. Tyler pulls a puzzled face. I lift the headphones over his head and rest them in my lap. I'm grateful he's not heard any of our conversation.

'Detective Sergeant Chorley would like to talk to you about earlier,' I say to him. 'When you got in the man's car.'

He blinks at me once and turns his head in her direction.

'Hello, Tyler, I'm Alex and I'd like to ask you a little bit about what happened today. You're not in any trouble, but I need to find out if this man is a danger to other children.'

He nods and swings his legs.

'Can you tell me why you left your group without telling Mrs Howe?'

He shrugs.

'Can you think really hard for me?'

'I don't know,' he says in a whiney voice.

'You must have an idea, darling.' I sandwich his hand between mine and rub it gently. His skin is cold and pale. 'It's not like you to go off on your own.'

He stares down at his feet as he swings them under the chair.

'Can you tell us anything about the man who gave you the toy car today?'

He shakes his head and crosses his arms too. His kicking legs go faster.

'Did he show you the toy first?'

Tyler nods, still looking down.

'Did he say he'd let you play with it if you got in the car?'

Tyler side-eyes me then nods again.

'And you didn't mind doing that?'

'No,' he shouts and kicks the chair legs with the heels of his shoes.

'Is that because he said you could keep it?'

'It's my favourite car.' He opens his fist to show it to her.

'Oh, I see. And what make is it?'

'Ferrari.' He roars like a car engine as he pushes the toy up and down his thigh.

The sergeant takes the opportunity to glance across at me, eyes wide. I dig my nails into my palm. How did this man know his favourite car? Or was it a lucky coincidence?

She asks him again what made him get up and leave Mrs Howe's side.

'He waved at me,' Tyler says.

'Oh, did he?' The DS's eyes light up.

Tyler nods.

'Did he wave at you to go over to him?'

He nods again.

'Is he someone you've seen before?'

Tyler's legs stop moving.

I daren't breathe.

He gives one decisive nod, and his legs start swinging back and forth again.

I try to take it in; Tyler knows the man who tried to abduct him.

50

'Can you tell me his name?' the DS asks Tyler gently.

He shakes his head.

'Have you been asked not to say?'

He nods with a smile as though he's saying yes to a packet of sweets.

Bethany turns to her laptop and clicks the mouse. 'The next CCTV clips are ready for us to view. Are you ready?'

She beckons to me to join her round her side of the desk. I kiss the top of Tyler's head and hand him back the tablet, then help him put on his headphones.

The first section of the footage shows the car arriving and driving straight into a parking space. A tall slim man gets out, locks the car and strides towards the farm buildings. My stomach tightens as I imagine what would have happened if he'd driven off with my son. He's wearing a hoodie, the hood up with a cap underneath, and keeps his head down so it's impossible to get a clear image of him.

'I can't pinpoint anything about him that's familiar,' I tell them, because lots of men are tall and slim. It can't be who I thought it was because Tyler's saying he's seen him before and that's not possible.

I glance up at Tyler who's innocently watching his film. Do I know this man but just can't recognise him? I wish I'd brought someone like

Katie with me now. Maybe I'm too emotional and missing something obvious.

'Shall we watch the next clip?' Bethany asks.

'Please.'

'Okay, this is slightly longer. Brace yourself. It's when the man is coming back to the car with Tyler.'

She presses play and we watch the man striding back to his car, head down, holding Tyler's hand who's trotting behind, trying to keep up. I let out a small gasp. Seeing this stranger casually walking off with my little boy turns my insides cold. Tyler doesn't appear distressed, which is shocking. Why isn't he screaming and shouting, pulling to get away from this man? How can Tyler say he knows him when I don't? The man unlocks his car and reaches in for something from the passenger seat while Tyler stands waiting. Every inch of me is telling him to run. The man comes back out with a box which appears to be wrapped in silver paper because it catches the light.

I look across at Bethany and Alex.

'My God, this was planned.' I cover my mouth with my hand.

They both nod, their faces solemn. I swallow down the scream that threatens to escape and focus back on the CCTV footage. The man has opened the back passenger door and my heart stops as I watch Tyler climbing in. The man sits in the driver's seat and hands him a can of drink, maybe Coke. It's hard to see what happens next, but the whole time the man is either twisted round facing the back, chatting to Tyler, or checking out of the windscreen and side windows as if he doesn't want to be seen. I wonder if he was spooked by one of the staff or teachers, that's why he didn't drive off with him. I reach over and stroke Tyler's hair, reminding myself that he's safe now, here with me.

Bethany pauses the clip and zooms in. 'This is about the best image we have of his face.' I peer closer but the baseball hat and hoodie obscure too many of his features. It's hard to say who he is, if I know him or not. After a few minutes, we watch him open the back passenger door and walk back to reception with Tyler, holding his hand again. Tyler's rucksack is bouncing on his back, the toy car presumably already inside.

I glance over at him – still lost in the world of Disney, thank goodness. I had no idea quite how close I came to losing him.

'Are there any other clips, of the reception area for example?' the DS asks.

'Hopefully one will come through in a few minutes,' Bethany says. She zooms in on the car's number plate and the DS calls it in.

'Whoever he is, we'll get an ID soon and hopefully the traffic police can catch him.'

'Here it is, the CCTV footage of the man taking Tyler to reception.'

We watch as he pushes the door open, head still down, ushering Tyler in front of him. He glances up slightly, talking to the girl at the desk before he even reaches her. She says something to him, and he looks up a little more. He is familiar, there's something about the angle of his jawline. I watch as the man pats Tyler's arm then spins round to leave. In that split second he glances up, clocking the CCTV camera, then looks away and a moment later he's out of the door.

'That was a clearer image of his face, I'll go back and pause it.' Bethany makes it larger on the screen then turns it to me. 'Do you recognise this man?'

I didn't want to believe it, but it's him.

51

It's Philippe. He is Tyler's father and that's why he's attempted to abduct his son. But how is it possible that Tyler recognises him? I explain to Bethany and the DS who this man is and how I know him.

'I believe he attacked me at an Airbnb while I was unconscious.' I glance at Tyler. How can something so beautiful come out of such a diabolical situation?

The DS receives a call so leaves the room. A few minutes later she's back.

'The man's car is registered to a Jim Ball from London. So far, we've been unable to locate him.'

'The owner of the Airbnb house hired him as her house-sitter while she and her husband went to America for six weeks. She wasn't aware that he used the name Philippe to rent out the rooms on Airbnb.'

'That's interesting. Presumably pocketing the money you paid him? Did he let out many rooms in her property?'

'A couple of others, I think. There was a party going on downstairs and in the big room next to mine. It's four years ago now. I believe I was attacked. I'd been given a couple of drinks and had gone to bed. A man wearing a mask came into my room in the night – I thought he broke in, but it seems the lock was already broken. I went to the house recently to try and piece together what happened, but the owner had no idea her house had been advertised on Airbnb.'

'What do you think happened to you?' the DS asks.

'When I woke up the next morning, I felt so groggy. I'd been asleep for about ten hours, but I don't remember what happened after the masked man burst in and Philippe came to my rescue. Normally I wake up in the night, have a drink of water or go to the toilet. I must have passed out. Philippe was lying next to me on the bed, fully dressed. He said I begged him to stay and protect me from the man in the mask, and he promised he would. But a few weeks later, I found out I was pregnant. I've been trying to find out what happened to me because I don't remember having sex with anyone other than my boyfriend. And I have a test that shows my son isn't his.'

The DS asks me to sit down. 'I'm so sorry, but it sounds like you could have been drugged and raped. Unfortunately, it's not that unusual.' The DS writes something in her notebook. 'We can investigate this further for you once we've picked up Jim Ball. I wonder if he was doing this elsewhere.'

'I did have this nagging worry at the back of my mind that something could have happened to me that night. Like I said, ten hours or more are completely blank. I thought I'd had too much to drink. I was too ashamed to tell my boyfriend or anyone, for fear of them judging me.'

'I'm so sorry. We'll need to take a statement from you so we can look into it, so please give us as much detail as you can remember. You might want to think about having some counselling to help you through this. I want to assure you that we're out there searching for him as I speak, and as soon as we catch him, I'll be in touch. For now, I suggest you go home, get some rest and wait for our call.'

'Thank you.'

I tap Tyler's shoulder. He looks up.

'Shall we go home?' I mouth as I pause his film and take off his headphones. He's staring straight ahead at the still of Philippe on Bethany's screen. I glance at the DS who's also watching Tyler's reaction.

'You know this man, do you?' I ask him gently.

He shrugs and stares at the floor.

'Have you been out with him before?' the DS asks.

Tyler nods.

'Did he ask Mummy's permission to take you?'

He avoids looking at me.

'Was it recently?'

He shakes his head. His legs start swinging.

'Your mummy says his name is Philippe. Is that right? Is that the name you know him as too?' Her voice rises at the end of the sentence, as though I must have got it wrong and here's his chance to put it right.

Tyler's legs stop swinging. He frowns and side-eyes me as if I don't know what I'm talking about and we're all stupid. He looks the DS in the eye, lifts his arm and points straight at the screen.

'That's Harry,' he says.

52

'What?' I cannot believe what Tyler just said. 'No, no, that can't be right.'
I stand up, my fist to my mouth.

'It is.' Tyler stamps his foot.

'I'm not saying you're lying, darling.' I kneel in front of him, holding
onto his arms. 'But you must have confused him with someone else.'

Tyler shakes his head so hard I think he's going to hurt his neck.

'This man's name is Philippe,' I say firmly and stand up. I'm not helping. But I don't know what else to say to make it clearer.

'Okay, let's all take a step back, shall we?' the DS says. 'Tyler, please
can you tell us where you first saw this man?'

He nods and we all wait for him to speak.

'Joe's house.'

I drop back in my chair.

'And who is Joe?' the DS asks.

I'm about to explain it's our neighbour, but I should let Tyler speak.

'He's next door.'

'He's my friend's son. Our neighbour.' I can't help chipping in.

'That's nice, and you met... Harry... there or somewhere else?'

'We went to the park, all together.'

'And he was with Joe's mum?'

'Her boyfriend.'

I press my fingers to my forehead as I explain about Katie's son falling off the climbing frame and how they had to go to hospital, so Harry was left looking after him. Tyler tells the DS I was mad about that afterwards and Harry thought I was being ridiculous. That's one detail I didn't know. What I want to know is why Philippe was going out with my neighbour and calling himself Harry. He never came to introduce himself to me; it can't be a coincidence. He must have known exactly what he was doing. He must have been spying on me. Getting the taxi driver outside his flat to give me that note. But why? Dating my neighbour and being friendly to Tyler to get at me or because he is his dad? What did I do to make him want to hurt us?

I must speak to Katie, warn her about Harry in case he tries to hurt her. All that time Harry was pretending to be good with children, gaining Katie's trust so she'd let him look after the boys on his own. I shudder. The thought of what he might have done to them makes me feel utterly sick.

On the way home, I go through everything that's happened in the last few hours to try to make sense of it. Why did Harry take my son into his car, then bring him back only a few minutes later? Was he really spooked and had to abort his plans to abduct him? Perhaps he was trying to get information from Tyler about me. But what? Did Leah warn him that I was going to go to the police about being attacked that night? I need to speak to him to find out what he's up to, but I don't know how to contact him except to go back to his flat. Hopefully now the police have found his car, they'll have caught up with him.

Tyler is fast asleep in the back seat when I pull into my parking space. I wait a few moments after I switch the engine off, but there are no signs of him waking up. He's had a long and eventful day. I check in the mirrors to see if I've been followed or if anyone's hanging around. Whatever it was that Harry wanted from Tyler, he knows where we live, and I don't feel safe.

Something moves near the bushes. A cat leaps out and runs past.

I tap open my phone and scroll down to Darren's number. He was my friend as well as my boyfriend for so long, I want to tell him what's happened, see what he makes of it. He cares about Tyler even if he never believed he was his father. But can I trust him? He's got Simone now, and a baby on the way. He won't want to hear about my worries.

Sod it. I press the call button and he picks up straight away. I tell him everything that's happened, viewing the CCTV footage at the farm and who the man turned out to be.

'The DS believes I was drugged that night at the Airbnb, all the signs are there. Me being knocked out for hours and having no memory of it, feeling disorientated, not remembering anything of what happened during that time, not knowing if I'd had sex or not and even if I did, I was unable to give consent... Which means I was... raped.' I fail to suppress the sob at the back of my throat.

'Christ, Elle.'

All this time, Darren has accused me of being unfaithful to him. I know what he really thinks of me. He remains silent. Probably embarrassed for me, still thinking that I got too drunk, slept with someone and can't remember. He's probably sad that I'm still making excuses for my slutty behaviour. Hot tears spill onto my cheeks and I'm glad he can't see me. All I want is for him to believe me. I should never have called him. I'm about to hang up when he speaks.

'I'm really sorry,' he says gently.

I sniff at his caring tone, giving myself away. I grab a tissue from my pocket and dab my eyes, wipe my nose. I try to speak but more tears come.

'Elle, there's something I should have told you back then...' he says quietly.

'Bit late now, isn't it?' I sniff. He pauses for a long moment.

'But I should tell you... about a video...'

'Go on then.'

'It's something I should say face to face.'

'Fine.'

'I'll phone back in the morning about meeting up.'

'Okay.' I end the call.

53

After I hang up, I slip my phone into my jacket pocket and zip it up. Whatever it is Darren has to tell me can't be that important if he's left it so long. And anyway, whatever it is he thinks he should have told me back then probably can't help me now.

I hitch the strap of my bag over my head and across my body and gently unclip Tyler from his seat. I lift him out and carefully hold him against my shoulder. I manage to lock the car without making too much noise and cautiously head towards our building. It's a slow process carrying him up the main staircase because he's getting heavier by the week. But I take it one step at a time. It's hard to believe he'll be four years old in a few months, then starting primary school. He won't be my baby any more.

I unlock the front door, carry him into his room and lay him on his bed. His hair is sweaty and sticking to his forehead. I kneel beside him and slip off his shoes and coat and lay a light blanket over him, so he doesn't get chilly later in the night. I sit on the floor watching him breathing, thankful that he's home, safe in his bed. Today could have been so much worse.

I make a round of peanut butter on toast and a mug of tea and sit in front of the television, half watching the news. There's nothing much on, so I switch it off. After a quick call to Molly to let her know we're okay, I pick up one of the new paperbacks she gave me, and go to bed.

* * *

I wake an hour later sweltering hot. Maybe I'm going down with something. I push the duvet back and glance at the digital clock next to me. It's only 10.50 p.m. There's a glass of water by my bed. I don't remember putting it there, but I'm glad I did because I'm so thirsty. I drink a couple of gulps and end up finishing it. As I lie back down, a shadow moves across the end of my bed.

'What do you want, Tyler?' I mumble, my eyelids already heavy with sleep. I try to sit up again but it's as though a heavy weight is pushing down on me.

'Tyler?' I strain to lift my head, but I can't see him and he doesn't answer. I blink, trying to keep my eyes open, staring into the darkness. Why am I so tired? I can't hold my head up any longer and flop back onto the pillow. There's a strange musty smell in the room. Something moves in front of the curtains. The silhouette of a man is standing over me. I part my lips to scream, but a rough hot hand clamps over my mouth.

54

I slowly wake up, my stomach cramping. What did I eat last night? The nightmare I had of a shadow at the end of the bed comes back to me bit by bit. The strange musty smell, and a man in my bedroom, his hand over my face. I shudder at how real it felt.

I glance at the clock. It's 10.30 a.m. I look again. It can't be. Tyler must be awake wondering what's wrong with me. I lean over the side of the bed and vomit onto the rug.

That's when I realise I'm naked. I don't remember taking my pyjamas off. I must have been boiling hot. I push back the duvet and feel the relief of the cool air. I'm covered in sweat, aching all over.

There's blood on the sheets, between my legs. A searing pain shoots through me. A weird feeling of déjà vu sweeps over me.

The door clicks and edges open. I cover myself with the duvet. I don't want Tyler to see me like this. I don't want to scare him. But it isn't Tyler standing there, it's Philippe. Harry.

My head swims. Am I seeing things? Suddenly I'm unable to speak or scream or move a muscle.

'There you are. Want some water?' He comes towards me holding a glass. He must see the confusion in my eyes because he says, 'It's okay, Tyler knows you're not well and that he's not to disturb you. He's playing on the Nintendo I bought him. Told me in the park that day he wanted one. Said you couldn't afford it, so you can thank me later.'

He clamps one hand over my mouth, muffling my alarm as he reaches under the duvet with the other hand, his arms bare in a black T-shirt. I draw in a short breath when I see the distinctive Chinese snake tattoo, bright red and gold etched on his skin, as though the creature is alive and draped across one shoulder and down his arm. All this time it's been in my nightmares, an image from when he attacked me at the Airbnb. It slithers further under the duvet, and he holds my leg. His hand is cold and strong on my naked skin. I kick and squirm but he touches me higher, more firmly, his fat tongue poking out between his teeth as he shuts his eyes, his hand rubbing up and down my groin. I jerk away, but he grabs me tighter.

'You need to keep nice and quiet, because I know you wouldn't want me to hurt Tyler.'

He takes his hands away.

'How did you get in here?' I hiss.

'You called the police, didn't you, bitch? Now they're out there hunting for me. They've snatched my car.'

'Answer my question.'

'They were all over it. Almost caught me walking back to the parking bay at the shops.'

'Why were you here, dating my next-door neighbour?'

'Why? Are you jealous?' He grins.

I cringe at his words.

'Tell me why you're here,' I shout.

'I've come to see my boy, that's all.'

'He'll never be your boy. You attacked me, didn't you.' I fight not to cry. My head's spinning, bile rising up my throat. Any drop of hope I had left that I was wrong, drains away. I can never accept this monster as Tyler's dad.

'Hey, I didn't attack you. You were up for it.' He licks his lips.

'I don't remember... anything,' I whimper and cover my face with my hands, ashamed that this has happened to me.

'That's a real bummer.'

'I remember the man in the clown mask. Who was he?'

'I don't know, some party animal who got the wrong room. You wanted me to stay and look after you, remember?'

I do remember that, but I know I didn't fancy him. I just wanted to go to sleep so I could get up early and catch the ferry to meet Molly.

'You drugged me, didn't you?' I can barely get the words out for the lump in my throat.

He grins and rubs his palms together. 'I might have given you a little dose of something in your hot chocolate to keep you calm and relaxed.' He winks.

I can't bear him looking at me, the thought of him touching me and... doing that, is sickening.

'What did you put in my drink?' My face flushes with heat.

'Don't go getting upset and yelling your head off at me.' He waves his index finger. 'I clocked the way you looked at me when I showed you to your room that day. And then the cocktails we had together on the terrace. It was very cosy. You were giving off all the signs, so don't go giving me a load of that poor-me crap you bitches always come out with.'

'What did you do to me?' I whisper and draw in a breath, unable to let it go. He... he... raped... me and he's talking about it as if it's nothing. As if he had the right to use me.

He grins and stands up. There's a bottle of water on the chest of drawers, which he grabs to refill my glass.

'You drugged and... and raped me, didn't you?' I cry.

'That's a bit harsh. You drank the hot chocolate. I didn't make you do anything. You didn't say no to anything.' He laughs.

'How could I say no? I was unconscious,' I sob.

'Keep your voice down.' Again, his voice and face change to a snarl in a split second.

'You've done it to me again, haven't you?' I cry into my hand. The smell of vomit is in my hair.

'Shut up, bitch. I could have driven away from the farm with my boy, and you'd never have seen him again, but I thought no, you'd want me to come and see you.'

'How... how did you get in here?' I can't stop shaking, my teeth chattering.

'That was too easy. Your simple little mate Katie, next door. Your spare key she couldn't find? I had that all along, but it won't work in your door any more, so I knew you'd tried to be clever and changed the locks. I thought I'd have to wake her up but she's not there this weekend, is she? But lo and behold, I still have her key and when I let myself in, what's the first thing I spot? A fluffy keyring hanging in her hallway with your shiny new key on it, waiting for me.'

He sits on the end of the bed.

'It was you who wrote on my bathroom wall and mirror.'

'That was a bit of fun. Spooked you, didn't it? Especially the clowns.' He laughs and the glass of water jiggles in his hand.

'It was you!'

'Called some of my mates, thought it'd be a crack. Seems as you've got a thing about clowns.'

The water sloshes over the edge of the glass. Maybe I can knock it over and escape. But I can't leave Tyler.

'Was it you who put the fake missing poster up on Facebook?'

'You liked that, did you? A stroke of genius, don't you think? People never bother to check it's from the police; they just forward it and forward it. I had to find out where you'd moved to.'

'But why?'

'Because you weren't going to tell me I had a son, were you? I wanted to see him, and lucky for me everyone was so obliging in the comments, telling me where you live, what pre-school Tyler goes to.'

'But how did you even know I'd had a son?' I can barely acknowledge we have a child together.

'I saw you in that Daily Mail article, about how you sobered up for the sake of your little boy. There was a photo of you with Tyler on your lap. They gave his age so I guessed he could be mine. I found photos of him on your Facebook page. I tried to message you but no, instead of answering me you came off and I couldn't find you, you ignorant bitch.'

I press my hand to my chest. I can't bear that all this is my own fault. How stupid of me. I'd been in two minds about letting them use me in that article, especially printing a photo, but the journalist insisted that seeing a young mother with her child would help others.

'You were pretending to be my friend Emma too? Why were you saying those terrible things about me offering sexual favours?'

'Because you're a whore. I mean look at the state of you. No wonder you haven't got a boyfriend. You should be grateful you've got me.'

'It wasn't you at the flat in Islington, was it?' I say, staring at his stubbly chin, the streaks of white in his dirty blond hair.

'Ha, you fell for it though, didn't you? Got a mate to stand in for me. Thought we looked enough alike for you not to notice, seeing as you hadn't set eyes on me for a long while.'

'But how did you know I was going to be there?'

'I put a tracker in your handbag when I let myself in.'

I shake my head in disbelief. Why didn't I take the signs more seriously? The TV in the wrong mode and the drawer wedged back in? I never check what's in my bag, I just take it out with me without thinking.

'Where's Tyler? I need to see him,' I whisper.

'Drink this first.'

I take the water which I'm guessing is spiked, and fill my cheeks then spit it in his face.

'You fucking bitch!' He scowls and wipes his arm over his face then grabs the bottle again and pours me another glass.

I take a gulp of breath. 'Let me see him!'

His eyes harden, glaring at me. 'You better drink it this time or you'll never see him again.' His voice is weird and tight, full of hatred.

A feeling of cold trickles into my stomach. If I disobey him again, he'll hurt Tyler or take him away. I slowly drink the water. It's like swallowing stones, knowing what it's going to do to me again.

He takes the empty glass and shoves it on to the bedside table. 'You got the message I left with the taxi driver, didn't you? *Be careful what you wish for.* What is it you wanted for Tyler? To know who his real daddy is? Well, here I am. And I'm all yours.'

He throws the duvet back and pulls me down the bed by the ankles. Everything is going blurry. My head thuds as it hits the pillow and my eyes close.

55

I come to again. I'm alone. The stale smell of vomit fills the air. Every part of my body hurts, even my eyes are sore. I wish I could bang on the wall and alert Katie, but she's not there this weekend. I could push the bed across the door so he can't come in, but what if he hurts Tyler or takes him somewhere? I'm scared I won't see him again.

Where did I leave my phone? I think back to lifting a sleeping Tyler from the car on Friday night. I slipped my phone in my coat pocket and zipped it up. Could it still be there? I think it's Sunday now. Almost midnight. If he's not moved it, my coat will be hanging in the hall behind the front door.

I force myself to sit up and shift my legs over the end of the bed. Standing up, I sway, lights darting in my eyes. I grip hold of the bedside table but my energy is low and my legs wobble. I drop back on the bed. Once again I stand up and this time I manage to steady myself on the chest of drawers in front of me. My feet are blocks of cement and it hurts to walk, but I concentrate on one step at a time.

When I reach the door, I unhook my fleece dressing gown and put it on, then slowly pull the door handle down.

The hum of the TV is coming from the living room. Tyler's bedroom door is shut. Hopefully he's asleep. I have to do everything I can to save us.

The coat rack is a few metres away at the end of the dim hall. Minimal light is coming from the darkened living room, more from the landing outside the flat which filters through the small wavy window-pane in the front door. I take each step as quietly as I can. The living-room door is barely open an inch. I daren't breathe. My head is woozy. I want to unlatch the front door and run for help but I can't leave Tyler here alone with him. I can't bear to think what he might do.

I reach my coat and feel for the phone but it's not there. A whimper escapes my lips, but I manage to cover my mouth in time. I pick up my ankle boots and peer through the crack in the living-room door.

There are a pair of feet propped up on a cushion at the end of the sofa, lit up by the flickering scenes of a late-night horror film. Philippe seems to be asleep. I need to think fast.

In the kitchen, the tiles are cold on my feet. Empty bottles of whisky and beer litter the counters. Moonlight streams in from the bottom of the blind, allowing me to search for my mobile, or the house phone or my laptop – any way of contacting someone to help me. If Darren tries to call me again, maybe he'll realise something is up. I don't know how long it'll be until he figures out something might be wrong. Molly is too far away, and Louise is on the other side of the village.

I take a deep breath and pull my boots on. I can't wait for anyone. I need to protect my son and deal with this monster myself.

As soon as the thought has sunk in, my eyes fall to the knife block tucked away on the counter. A plan begins to form in my head. I pull out one of the shorter knives, wrap the blade in a tea towel and hold it in my hand.

I freeze at the creak of a door opening and listen closely. I know the sound well. I swing round and Tyler is facing me in the hallway. He's in his pyjamas, rubbing his eyes. I hide the knife deep in my pocket and put my arms out to him. He runs towards me, and I hug him tightly.

'Are you better, Mummy?'

I put my finger to my lips and whisper in his ear that we need to be really quiet because the man he knows as Harry hurt me, and we need to leave and not wake him up. I look ahead at the front door and wonder how quickly we can reach it. It seems so far away now, yet it's a mere ten paces at most. With Tyler in tow, it may be a fraction slower. If we hurry, we can be out of here before Philippe wakes up. Opening the front door will probably disturb him.

I ask Tyler if he knows where my phone is. He shakes his head. We're on our own.

I take a deep breath, hold Tyler's hand tight and quietly stride down the hall.

'What's going on here then?' Philippe appears at the living-room door and snatches hold of Tyler around his waist. He is squinting and swaying, scratching his head with his other hand. I kick out at his shin with my boot, and he yelps and lets go of Tyler.

'Behind me,' I say, sweeping him with my arm.

'You fucking bitch!' Spit shoots from Philippe's mouth with the words.

I dig into my pocket and wrap my fingers around the handle of the knife. He straightens up and lurches towards me, his arms inches from mine as he tries to grab me. I have one small chance and I take it, plunging the blade into his stomach. There's a surprised look on his face and a beer-breath grunt from his lips.

I back away in horror as he doubles over. My heart crashes against my ribs.

'Mummy!' Tyler screams. I bend and with one arm behind me, I lift him onto my back in one scoop. For a second my knees wobble and I don't know if I have the strength. But I grit my teeth and charge towards the front door.

56

Philippe is staggering after us. With every bit of determination I have left, I reach out for the latch, but Tyler screams in my ear. Something is dragging us back. I twist round and Philippe is pulling Tyler's bare foot, crushing it in his bloodied hand.

'Come here, bitch,' Philippe snarls at me.

'Did you hurt my mum?' Tyler shouts.

'Shut it, you little urchin.' He whacks Tyler around the head and makes him cry.

'Leave him alone,' I scream and snatch up my golfing umbrella propped in the corner next to the shoe rack. 'Hold on tight,' I shout to Tyler and with both hands I swing round and jab the metal point into Philippe's wounded stomach, sending him crashing backwards against the wall in agony. I open the front door and dash outside onto the landing. With my balled-up fist, I bang on front doors, screaming for help.

'Please, call the police,' I shout, hoping someone will make the call even if they don't want to risk opening their door to me. Most people will be asleep at this time of night. 'Somebody wake up, please,' I call out as I run along the landing, thumping on each door.

At last, one opens, and Frank, a bald driving instructor, looks out. His wife Fiona, a teacher, always stops for a chat with me and Tyler at the corner shop. I'm so relieved I could drop down on my knees with exhaustion.

'What on earth has happened to you, love? Come in. You'll be safe in here.' We both look round at Philippe staggering out of my door, his arm holding his bloody stomach.

'Fiona's telephoned the police,' he says, slamming the door. 'They'll be here shortly. I don't think whoever he is will be getting far in that state.'

'Thank you. I really can't thank you enough.' I'm suddenly conscious I'm still in my dressing gown. I stink, but I must resist the urge to go and wash and scrub every trace of Philippe from my body. The police will need all the evidence they can find on me, especially his DNA.

'You poor love,' Fiona says, coming out of her kitchen. 'I'll make you a cup of sweet tea. Why don't you go and sit down, and I'll bring it through. We'll let the police know you're here when they arrive.'

I hug Tyler and kiss his hair. My teeth are chattering I'm so frozen. Frank mentions that it's started snowing. He drapes a fleece blanket around my shoulders and gives me another one for Tyler. They bring him a warm glass of milk and put my cup of tea on the coffee table. I shut my eyes and wait for the police to arrive.

57

Darren arrives at Katie's after I've come back from the police station. I've had swabs and photographs taken and I've given a statement about what happened over the last two days. My flat is still being processed as a crime scene for fingerprints and DNA, so I'm staying at Katie's. She arrived home after lunchtime and Frank and Fiona filled her in on what had happened. The first thing I did when Katie picked me up from the police station in my car was hug her.

'Darren's on his way,' she warned me as we parked at the flats. 'Turned up earlier to see if you were okay. I told him to come back tomorrow but he said he had something important to tell you and it couldn't wait. He tried calling on Saturday morning, but you weren't picking up.'

I nodded but didn't answer. Everything looked so different in the snow, as though I was arriving at a new place. All these people living in the same block, not knowing what was happening to me under the same roof. Only a wall separating us. Why didn't I scream? Maybe someone would have heard. But I couldn't risk Tyler's safety. I turn to him and stroke his hair.

'I thought you were ignoring me when you didn't pick up my

messages,' Darren says, perched on the edge of Katie's sofa, elbows on his legs, gesticulating with his hands.

'I didn't know where it was. He took it out of my pocket. I expect the police have it now.'

He nods and looks down at the carpet. 'I think he's the one who contacted me. That's what I was going to tell you on Friday.'

'When was this?'

He clears his throat. 'Four years ago.'

'What?'

'I know, I should have told you at the time.' He reaches for my hand, but I snatch it away.

'You knew who attacked me four years ago?' I sit up straight.

'Is he Tyler's dad?' He runs a hand over his eyes. I don't understand why he's crying.

I nod. 'Why didn't you tell me?'

'You have to understand.' Darren stands up and turns away, then swings back to face me. 'I thought I was sparing your feelings, your dignity.'

'What do you mean?'

'He sent me this video of you. You were lying half naked on a bed... you were out of it, I assumed you were drunk... and he was filming himself having sex with you.'

'What?' I scream.

'I'm so, so sorry, Elle.' He wipes his face with his arm.

'And let me guess, you thought it was me sleeping around?'

'I admit I was angry and thought you'd been unfaithful. I couldn't bear to talk to you about it. I deleted it straight away, pushed it out of my mind and pretended I hadn't seen it, let alone received it. But when you fell pregnant, I just knew in my gut it wasn't mine. I figured it was better to finish with you.'

'Oh, cheers for that.'

'These last few weeks brought it all back. I couldn't believe you wanted me to go through with a DNA test. When the result was negative, I thought you'd finally admit you'd cheated. But when you were still adamant you hadn't, I thought back to that video. It became harder and harder to bring it up.'

'Christ, Darren. I didn't know anything about him filming me, let alone that he'd drugged and raped me.'

'Fuck, I know, I should have taken the email to the police as soon as I received it.'

'I thought you knew I would never be unfaithful to you. It killed me that you believed that.'

'I'm so, so sorry. As far as I knew, you were on the pill, so then I wondered if you'd come off it to try and get pregnant and trap me. The trust had completely gone by then.'

'You don't know me at all, do you? Why didn't you talk to me? I was on the pill, but I forgot to take them with me to Jersey, so I missed a couple. I didn't think it would matter because I wasn't planning on having sex with anyone. Can't you see the broken trust was all in your head? How could you think I would do that to you? I thought we had something special together. But no, you finished with me and replaced me with Simone. I still believed we were right together. Why do you think I moved here?'

'I realise that now and I'm sorry.' He shakes his head. 'I'm sorry I didn't believe you.'

'So this video must still be out there?'

He nods, head down. 'He was asking me for £10,000 or he'd post it on revenge porn websites. I'm ashamed to say I didn't pay it.'

'Jesus. Because you thought the sex was consensual.'

'He made out it was. Said he was a love magnet or some such crap, could have any woman he wanted anytime because they couldn't help themselves.'

I sigh deeply at the irony and wonder what I ever saw in Darren. 'So this video is out there on who knows what websites for everyone to see?'

'I don't know what to say to you, Elle. This ugly fuck tried to scam me. I didn't have that kind of money anyway.'

'But even if you had, I'm guessing you wouldn't have paid it. Will you at least tell the police what you've told me?'

'I will. And I am really sorry.'

'I think you should go.'

Katie lets him out and I sit in a stunned silence. She comes back in and sits close to me, holding my hand in hers. I feel a tear land on my arm. I twist round and frown at her.

'He did that to me too,' Katie sniffs, 'on Halloween night after we'd been at yours and argued. He drugged me, then raped me. I was aware enough to know what was going on at first, but I couldn't move.'

'Oh no, Katie.'

She cries into my shoulder. I hug her and she hugs me back.

EPILOGUE

Katie joins me at the table on the pavement. She moves her chair out of the shade, closer to me, so we can both enjoy the hot sunshine. After the coolness of the courtroom, this is bliss. We hug, clinging to each other longer than usual, in silent acknowledgement that we're both survivors.

It took the jury forty-nine minutes to decide Jim Ball, aka Philippe, aka Harry, was guilty of eighteen counts of rape. Of me, Katie and six other women. He was given a further five years for sharing videos of the rapes on revenge porn websites. He will serve at least twenty-seven years in jail.

A DNA test confirmed he is Tyler's father. The sadness this brings me runs deep, but I wouldn't change my boy for anything.

'Are you okay?' I ask Katie.

She nods. 'Glad it's all over.'

'Me too.'

Two men on the next table look over at us and whisper to each other, then smile broadly. Katie rolls her eyes at me.

'Don't look at them,' I say.

'My therapist says it will take time for me to completely trust a man again.'

'You will. We both will.' I cover my hand over hers.

'Lee's a good man.'

I can't help smiling, remembering how we first met at the boring conference. How kind and thoughtful he was over Tyler going missing. We exchanged a few texts then waited a couple of months before I felt ready to meet up. He's been my guiding light in all this. Not asking for anything. Not demanding. Not expecting. Just there for me to talk to. And maybe at some point I'll be ready for a relationship.

We finish our coffees. I stand up first.

'This is it then, I guess.'

She presses her lips together, trying not to cry and we hug again. She and Joseph are going to stay with her mum for a while. Both our flats are empty, waiting for new tenants. Louise and Steve have been looking after me, letting Tyler and I stay until our moving date today.

'We won't be that far away. We can meet up in the holidays,' I tell her.

'We'd love that. Joe will love that.'

* * *

I drive over to pre-school to collect Tyler for the last time and take flowers to thank Mrs Howe, Mrs Cooper and all the staff. There's no one outside but the car park is full. As I hurry to the door, I check my watch, wondering if I'm late.

Mrs Howe is beaming when she opens the door and invites me in. I hand her the flowers as Tyler runs towards me. Behind him is a small gathering of parents and the other kids. They're all smiling and burst into applause.

'We heard he's been convicted,' Louise says, her face beaming. She pats my arm then continues clapping.

'This is for you and Tyler.' Mrs Howe hands me a bag of presents. 'It's from the staff and all the parents.'

'That's really kind of you, thank you,' I say to everyone. I wasn't expecting anything. I thought most of them would want to see the back of me.

'Hayley organised the collection. She's sorry she couldn't be here,' Mrs Howe says quietly.

'She found out her husband has been having an affair and they're going their separate ways,' Louise adds. 'She's moving in with her parents this afternoon.'

'I'm sorry to hear that, please send her my best wishes.' I think back to her returning from the farm trip early. I should have asked her if she was okay instead of seeing her as the enemy.

'I will, thank you,' Mrs Howe says.

* * *

I call Molly on the handsfree in the car to let her know we're on our way. Tyler is sitting in the back seat with his headphones on, bobbing his head up and down to a music programme on his tablet.

As soon as a flat came up for rent in Molly's block, she was straight on the phone to me. It made perfect sense to move near her again and get back to the life and friends I so readily abandoned.

I can finally talk about the court case now it's over, and I tell Molly everything.

'They found all sorts on his laptop and personal computer,' I say, 'links to an incel group and forum.'

'What's that?' she asks.

'Involuntary celibates. Basically, men who can't get a girlfriend, and blame women for rejecting them.'

'Sounds crazy.'

'I know. Most are genuine blokes looking online for practical advice, but some get sucked into these forums where they hear about all sorts of ways to be violent to a woman to get what they desire and as a way of revenge against all womankind. They rage against being left out of the gene pool. They believe it's deliberate that this is happening to them and don't think they're doing anything wrong. They believe it's all a conspiracy against certain types of men.'

'So was this the only way Philippe thought he could have sex with women, by drugging and raping them?'

'I think so.'

'Sick bastard.'

'I know. Well at least he's banged up now, so he can't do it to anyone else.'

It's another two and a half hours before I pull up outside Molly's block of flats. All the essentials, like duvets, kettle and a change of clothes are in the boot, and tomorrow Lee's coming to help us move our stuff out of storage.

'We're home,' I say and twist round to look at Tyler. He's beaming back at me.

ACKNOWLEDGMENTS

Behind the scenes of any published book, is a chain of people who take the time and care to make it the best it can possibly be. I'm grateful to every single person who has helped me to produce my sixth novel.

The idea for *Missing* was born out of my fear of staying in an Airbnb, compounded by a feature I read in a magazine a few years ago, about a couple of girls who woke in the night to their host standing at the bottom of their bed. I realise I'm probably in a minority with my paranoia, so I wish to apologise to Airbnb and all the kind and trustworthy people who offer their homes or spare rooms to strangers.

My other inspirations were Emily Hunt's frightening experience, documented in her book, *We Need to Talk,* and *Men Who Hate Women* by Laura Bates.

Huge thanks as always to my fantastic agent, Jo Bell. I'm lucky to have someone on my side who is so supportive and enthusiastic, especially when I come up with new novel ideas. She is the one who helps me shape them into a synopsis worthy of presenting to my editor, Emily Yau.

Having Emily as my editor is an absolute dream. She completely understands what I'm trying to convey in my novels and helps me draw out the best in them. My heartfelt thanks to her and to the whole incredible team at Boldwood Books. They go above and beyond for all their authors and it's an honour to be with such a ground-breaking publisher.

Thank you to my sharp-eyed copy editor, Candida Bradford, who promises to take all my bloopers to the grave! Huge thanks too to my thorough and thoughtful proofreader, Rachel Sargeant. I'm also indebted to the talented designer, Aaron Munday, who has captured my story perfectly in the cover of this book.

To Rose McGinty, Susan Elliot Wright and Mandy Byatt for your friendship and essential writing chats. Thank you for putting up with me on the bad days and celebrating with me on the good. Thanks too to all the readers and writers I talk to daily in the wider community, especially online. I don't get out as much as I used to, so I value all those interactions, friendships and amazing support. Thanks to Heidi Morton for taking photos of locations in Huntingdon and Alconbury which are featured in this book. She is one of many lovely mums who were welcoming and friendly at my son's pre-school. None of the characters in this book are based on anyone I knew there!

Special thanks of course to my family, for their unwavering support of me in my writing obsession, especially Mum, Dad, Richard, Charlie, Becky, Edward and Sophie.

I could not enjoy writing as much as I do without my loyal Springer spaniels by my side. Thank you, Monty and Archie.

ABOUT THE AUTHOR

Ruby Speechley is a bestselling psychological thriller writer, whose titles include *Someone Else's Baby*. Previously published by Hera, she has been a journalist and worked in PR and lives in Cheshire.

Sign up to the Ruby Speechley mailing list for news, competitions and updates on future books

Visit Ruby's website: www.rubyspeechley.com

Follow Ruby on social media:

facebook.com/Ruby-Speechley-Author-100063999185095

twitter.com/rubyspeechley

instagram.com/rubyjtspeechley

ALSO BY RUBY SPEECHLEY

Gone

Missing

THE

Murder

LIST

THE MURDER LIST IS A NEWSLETTER DEDICATED TO ALL THINGS CRIME AND THRILLER FICTION!

SIGN UP TO MAKE SURE YOU'RE ON OUR HIT LIST FOR GRIPPING PAGE-TURNERS AND HEARTSTOPPING READS.

SIGN UP TO OUR NEWSLETTER

BIT.LY/THEMURDERLISTNEWS

Boldwood

Boldwood Books is an award-winning fiction publishing company seeking out the best stories from around the world.

Find out more at www.boldwoodbooks.com

Join our reader community for brilliant books, competitions and offers!

Follow us
@BoldwoodBooks
@TheBoldBookClub

Sign up to our weekly deals newsletter

https://bit.ly/BoldwoodBNewsletter

Milton Keynes UK
Ingram Content Group UK Ltd.
UKHW041106250923
429337UK00002B/18